Border
Child

Border
Child

A Novel

MICHEL STONE

Nan A. Talese | DOUBLEDAY

NEW YORK LONDON TORONTO SYDNEY AUCKLAND

Copyright © 2017 by Michel Stone

All rights reserved. Published in the United States by Nan A. Talese/Doubleday, a division of Penguin Random House LLC, New York, and distributed in Canada by Random House of Canada, a division of Penguin Random House Limited, Toronto.

www.nanatalese.com

DOUBLEDAY is a registered trademark of Penguin Random House LLC. Nan A. Talese and the colophon are trademarks of Penguin Random House LLC.

Book design by Pei Loi Koay
Jacket design by Michael Windsor
Jacket images: (rabbit) Marco Antonio Davila Torres/EyeEm/Getty Images; and (pattern) Silvia Lavanda, (ground) givaga, and (barbed wire) yamatohd, all Shutterstock

LIBRARY OF CONGRESS CATALOGING-IN-PUBLICATION DATA
Names: Stone, Michel, [date] author.
Title: Border child : a novel / Michel Stone.
Description: First edition. | New York : Nan A. Talese/Doubleday, [2017] | Description based on print version record and CIP data provided by publisher; resource not viewed.
Identifiers: LCCN 2016020094 (print) | LCCN 2016012857 (ebook) | ISBN 9780385541640 (hardcover : alk. paper) | ISBN 9780385541657 (ebook)
Subjects: LCSH: Missing children—Fiction. | Families—Mexico—Fiction. | Mexico—Emigration and immigration—Fiction. | Mexican-American Border Region—Fiction. | Domestic—Fiction.
Classification: LCC PS3619.T6569 (print) | LCC PS3619.T6569 B67 2017 (ebook) | DDC 813/.6—dc23
LC record available at https://lccn.loc.gov/2016020094

MANUFACTURED IN THE UNITED STATES OF AMERICA

First Edition

For Eliot

The sound is gone. There's nothing left but the insomniac throbbing of crickets. Crickets in the garden, the courtyard, the back courtyard. Close, domestic, identifiable. And those out in the country. Between all of them they raise, little by little, a wall that will keep out the thing that lies waiting for the tiniest crack of silence to steal through. The thing that is feared by all those who are sleepless, those who walk through the night, those who are lonely, children. That thing. The voice of the dead.

—Rosario Castellanos, *The Book of Lamentations*

Border
Child

Prologue

Lilia thrashed and called out, uncertain if she'd given voice to her cry or just dreamed the sound. Sweat beaded between her breasts, and she lay in darkness, shaken from the same disturbing images that had jolted her from fitful slumber too many times to count. She bobbed in that brief twilight of uncertainty, between sleep and perception, unsure if she was floating away from something anonymous and terrible or sinking helplessly, rapidly toward it, pricked and paralyzed by some unidentified, poisonous barb she had not seen.

Then the gossamer veil separating unconsciousness and awareness slipped away, and she realized, as she did each time, that the one unmoored and drifting was not she but her Alejandra, though Lilia was incapable of tossing her child a lifeline, of pulling her back close. The reality cut far deeper than did the dream, for a mother unable to help a child aches far more than a mother unable to help herself.

For years now Lilia had almost seen her daughter: the small girl with a rotten front tooth, skipping down the lane dragging a tattered length of rope; the child tugging on her mother's frayed hem at the market, her hair in tight braids with lavender ribbons; the little darling in the yellow dress trailing behind her *tía* who carried a slick, silvery fish wrapped in newsprint on their way home from the pier. Each of them could have been little Alejandra. How could Lilia know?

She also saw her in shadows, just skirting the edge of her vision, but when she turned to look no one would be there. Those fleeting glimpses disturbed Lilia the most because Alejandra seemed more ghost then than flesh, and she feared her baby was dead instead of living somewhere, elsewhere, in the vast, strange world.

Chapter 1

Lilia

Lilia wished the direction of the evening breeze would shift as she diced the small octopus, dropping the chunks into the briny broth already steaming on the fire. But the wind kept its course, and the funk of her village's incinerated waste continued to waft across the courtyard. She plucked a sprig of mint from the cracked clay pot beside the kitchen door and stripped its leaves from the stem then popped them into her mouth. She chewed the herb into a slick pulp, hoping it would lessen her nausea.

Fernando sat in the dirt nearby, rolling a small truck between his bare feet. When he shrieked with laughter Lilia looked up from her work at the fire.

"What do you see, my boy?"

The child pointed at a white hen and her butter-yellow chicks pecking at the dust just beyond Fernando's new rubber ball, abandoned for now beneath the shade tree.

Lilia had not experienced any morning sickness with Fernando. Her pregnancy had gone so smoothly she'd worried something was wrong with the baby until she saw him, counted his fingers and toes, and heard him wail. His head had been bare, unlike the thickly matted scalp of Alejandra at her birth. Lilia's pregnancy with Fernando had been so different from her first that she should have suspected the child to be a boy, but no. That simple conclusion had escaped her, and instead she'd assumed the child inside her womb to be deformed, and she had not fully felt excitement or love until she'd held him and he'd suckled at her breast. Only then did her tears and prayers of gratitude emerge from somewhere unexpected and deep within her.

But this third pregnancy felt similar to her first, with daily morning vomiting, and the constant taste of bile lingering in her throat. Perhaps this baby, like Lilia's first, would be a girl child. Little Alejandra would be almost four now. Is almost four now. She is almost four, Lilia told herself. Is, not would be.

Lilia prayed daily for Alejandra's well-being and happiness. And on the days she felt her hope waning, at those dark times, she prayed to God to punish her for allowing her faith and optimism to slip. These occasional, doubtful thoughts she did not share with Héctor; she'd learned long ago she must shoulder enough strength for the both of them. Lilia ached to believe that Héctor trusted her again as fully as he ever had, that he understood the depth to which her being had been shaken with the loss of their daughter and the horrible, undeniable guilt that permeated Lilia to her marrow for her part in that loss. She longed to tell him that oftentimes as she passed the village cemetery at the top of the hill she felt it watching her closely, as if she should be there with the dead instead of walking among the living.

For months after Lilia's border crossing and the disappearance of Alejandra, Héctor sneered at the sight of his wife. He tried to hide his contempt by turning away, busying himself in some pointless activity, but she felt his scorn as sure as a slap to her cheek. Even if his countenance had not betrayed his deep disappointment in Lilia, his inability to touch her all but screamed what Lilia interpreted as disgust, perhaps even loathing. They had been the most loving, most affectionate couple in all of Mexico until that unforgettable, life-altering day at the border, when she'd arrived unexpectedly and without their child. Ah, but enough of these thoughts.

She spit the wad of mint into a gnarled hibiscus, its spent orange blossoms littering the ground around it.

Her grandmother had planted the shrub in honor of Lilia's birth, and even now, years after the old woman's passing, when Lilia looked at its large, trumpetlike flowers she thought of her grandmother Crucita, and how, at Christmastime, she would dry the blossoms to make delicious sugared candies for Lilia to suck.

"Papa!" Fernando said, waving to Héctor. "Papa home!"

Héctor, haggard and sun-darkened, brushed the boy's head with his grimy fingertips but did not scoop him up into a big hug as was his usual greeting for Fernando. He tossed a sack on the lone table in the courtyard. "Squash and onions," he said.

"José brought us an octopus this afternoon. I'm making a stew," Lilia said. "I'll roast the squash, too, if you'd like."

Héctor sat in one of the two chairs beside the weathered old table and unlaced his work boots. The breeze rattled the wind chime that hung inside the kitchen window, though Lilia didn't notice the sound until Héctor said, "Can we get rid of that thing?" He jutted his chin toward the jangling.

"You don't like it?" she said, sensing something other than the gentle clanking of the shells as the source of his irritation.

During their courtship and early marriage, prior to their time in el *norte*, Héctor wore his emotions like a banner; he'd been so easy to read. His imaginings and zest for life had drawn her to him when they were in school. Even when she'd been but fifteen years old and Héctor sixteen, they'd sit under the stars beside the bay speaking of their future, of the children they'd have, and of the life they imagined together. Lilia would have been content to live out her days in Puerto Isadore, but Héctor had held bigger aspirations and an imagination like no one else she'd ever met. He'd been silly and jovial as a schoolboy then, laughing and joking and dreaming what others might call impossible dreams. Lilia had believed in him and in his vision for their future.

"We'll go to *el norte* one day, Lilia," he'd said. "I'll go first and find work, and I'll save enough money to bring you to me."

She knew such days of innocence and pure delight would never return, yet she refused to give up on the notion of their happiness.

He lifted the other boot and began untying its laces. Without looking at her he said, "No, Lilia. I don't like the wind chime. I've never liked it."

She wiped her hands across her faded yellow apron before detaching the chime's string from the rusted hook above the open window.

She set the wind chime on the table beside the bag of squash and onions, then hoisted Fernando to her hip.

"That boy's too big to be a hip child," Héctor said, bringing a hand to his temple.

"What's wrong, Héctor?" She squeezed Fernando when he gripped her shoulder, eager to remain in his mother's arms.

Héctor slapped both hands on his thighs and sat up straight, inhaling a long, slow breath.

"Guess who I saw today, Lilia," he said, staring at her, his eyes dark, troubled.

She eased Fernando to the ground, afraid her legs would fail her under the added weight and the news coming toward her. A strange flickering played in her chest, and the ever-present bile thickened in her throat.

"Tell me."

"Emanuel," he said.

She slipped into the chair across from Héctor, her palms flat on the table between them. "Are you certain you saw him? Did you speak to him?"

Héctor brought his hands behind his head, interlocking his fingers and tilting his face toward the clouds mounding in the western sky. "I know who I saw," he said.

"Did you talk? What did he say, Héctor? Where did you see him? Oh, my God. Tell me everything."

"I don't have much to tell. No, we didn't speak. I saw him, but he didn't see me."

"Are you sure the person you saw was Emanuel? Where was he?"

"He was boarding the bus to Escondido. I know it was Emanuel. I've looked for that *pendejo* every day for years, Lilia. The man I saw was Emanuel."

"This is good news, Héctor. We'll find him!" She reached for him and took his hands in hers and brought them to her lips, tears brimming her eyes.

Héctor exhaled, and for the first time since his arrival from work, he seemed to relax, to soften, though the worry lines, long etched into his brow and temples, remained, a constant reminder to the world, to Lilia, of his grief.

"All the emotions, you know?" he said. "Just when I begin to put him and our past behind us . . ." He shook his head. "I hate him, but we need him."

Héctor stood and scooped Fernando into his arms. "Your stew smells good, Lilia."

She returned to the pot and stirred its contents with a long wooden spoon, her thoughts far away from the fire or this courtyard. She closed her eyes and inhaled sharply, her mind not on the briny scent of her cooking but lost in the memory of the lavender-scented head of her firstborn child.

Chapter 2

Héctor

Héctor lay in bed listening to the predawn awakening of his village as he imagined for the countless time what he would say if he were face-to-face with Emanuel. But as always, something in his mind would not allow the thoughts to get beyond Emanuel's eyes, and self-loathing brimmed within Héctor for his inability to conquer his foe even in his imagination.

In Héctor's envisioning of their chance meeting, he would encounter Emanuel someplace familiar, like the market or *la farmacia*. Héctor would always approach the vendor with goods in hand for purchase, mundane everyday items like matches or gum or a can of juice. The person in line in front of him would be a man in fancy clothes and spotless boots, and as the man turned, Héctor would recognize Emanuel's profile and would speak Emanuel's name. Emanuel would turn to face Héctor, less than a meter between them.

Héctor wanted to imagine punching him in the face, feeling the crunch of bone beneath his bare knuckles, and as Emanuel's blood began to flow Héctor would ask him a series of questions that would lead to Alejandra's whereabouts and her safe return home.

Héctor would think these thoughts as he worked the fields every day, as he ate his meals, as he played at the sea's edge with

Fernando. But when he lay in the dark solitude of his room each morning before work, after Lilia had risen to stoke the fire and prepare breakfast, his mind's eye would play out the imagined meeting. Héctor wanted his illusory self to cause Emanuel deep pain, the kind that scarred a body and a soul, to break him in an irreparable way as Emanuel's actions had done to Héctor and Lilia and their family. Instead, in Héctor's quiet daydreams, when Emanuel turned to him, his glare weakened Héctor, rendered him as useless as ditch water.

Héctor longed to play out the punch, the crushing blow of fist to face, but he could not. Instead, when the two would lock eyes, Emanuel's were the eyes of a god, powerful, mocking, and all knowing. He would stare at Héctor, a slow, wicked smile spreading across his face until Héctor had to look away, divert his eyes to his own shit-caked boots, and when he finally found the strength to lift his eyes, Emanuel would be gone, along with any information he held about Alejandra.

Even in his daydreams Héctor had no ability to protect his family, and that secret knowledge haunted him, vexed him like a dull thorn wedged deep beneath a toenail, its silent infection seeping into his veins.

Héctor smelled the wood smoke from the breakfast fire, and he rose from bed, resigned that he would begin every day for the rest of his life just like this until either his daughter was reunited with him and Lilia or he knew with certainty that she was dead.

A time had existed when Héctor dreamed of his potential, of the possibilities the wide, mysterious, promising world held for him, and for anyone willing to pursue his dreams, for anyone with the hope of something better, something more, even if he could not name what possibilities existed. Héctor had been that boy, that young man, but no more. In his youth he'd seen other boys, older boys, sniffing glue, their way of coping, of escape. And he'd seen the men who, after the workday, took to their bottles in the dark shadows of their village. He'd not be them. He'd never be them, he'd told himself from his earliest days.

Not many years ago, Héctor had believed that working his whole life for just a few pesos a day seemed like settling, like an admission his potential and abilities were limited. He'd dreamed of providing more for his loved ones than his family had been able to provide for him as a boy, and he'd longed to see what more he could accomplish, even if that meant leaving the place of his birth. Now his soul—at one time filled with optimism and the belief that he could do anything with hard work, hope, and determination—had hardened and become calloused by cynicism and exhaustion. How differently he now arose from his bed each day, how different his slumbering dreams had become since his return from *el norte* just over three years ago. Seeing Emanuel yesterday had ripped his wounded spirit anew.

Lilia sat outside on a blue crate, her hands wrapped around a mug of coffee. "Good morning, love. You were restless last night," she said without rising from her seat.

He bent to her and kissed her mouth. She tasted like warm cinnamon. "You weren't," he said, pouring a cup of coffee from the pot on the fire.

She shrugged. "I guess Fernando wears me out. I didn't know how active a two-year-old could be. But, oh, I do love that busy little boy," she said, smiling. "Yes, I slept hard last night."

Her comment about a two-year-old brought his mind to Alejandra, just as nearly everything did. Alejandra would have been nearly two when Fernando was born, and he wondered how she would have reacted to the arrival of a brother.

"I've been thinking about Emanuel. I'm sure you have, too. When I saw him . . ." He paused, shaking his head. "I should've felt hope, you know? Like you did when I told you I'd seen him. Instead I felt rage." He sipped his coffee and rubbed Lilia's shoulder with his free hand.

"We'll find him," he continued. "We must. And then we'll find Alejandra. Emanuel's the only person who can provide us clues to what happened to our girl."

Lilia gripped Héctor's hand on her shoulder and squeezed tight. "The past three years . . ." she began. "Maybe now God knows the timing is right. Maybe now we'll find our girl."

"I've been thinking about our time in *el norte*. In my youth everything was new, you know? I was ready to pluck the world from the vine." He laughed at his foolishness. "I wanted to feel that dew on my fingers, like when you pick the fields at sunrise? What a stupid ass I was." He shook his head. "The yearnings of an innocent boy."

Lilia smiled. "You sound like a withered old man. You're twenty-four years old, Héctor. Do you remember what you asked me the day we were sent back here from America?"

"What?"

"You asked me if I thought it was all worth it, our crossing, our time in America. You asked if it was all a mistake."

He grunted, his mind flashing to their time in America, to thoughts so knotted with memories both pleasant and horrific that unraveling the experience into a concise and sensible recollection seemed impossible. He considered the day Lilia arrived in America, but she'd arrived without Alejandra, and then, months later, the day he and Lilia found themselves in the wrong place at the wrong time and were asked by a lawman for papers they could not produce. He looked now at his wife, her gaze gentle, loving, inquisitive.

"And I said I was sure that had we never crossed, just lived out our days here," she continued, "you'd have always wondered. Always longed to cross. You would have continued to dream of America."

"I remember," he said, knowing her words to be true. Despite all they'd endured and the bone-crushing despair that tinged everything he said or did, Héctor loved Lilia with a fierceness that moved him to take her small hand in his, to press her knuckles to his dry lips and remain like that as she spoke. At times such as this, when her words proved her insight into his soul, he thanked God for her and their life together, regardless of the complexities and tribulations of that life. He knew he'd been hard on her, cruel, he supposed, after Alejandra's disappearance, but he'd come to understand she'd been even harsher on herself.

"Plenty of time yet for dreaming and for hope," she said. "Do you recall how intensely you longed to escape this village, this country?"

Héctor thought of the day he'd reached the border. *La línea* had looked nothing like he'd expected. His coyote had driven slowly along, pointing out the ill-prepared fools, many with children, sneaking through holes in the fence. A simple, rusted fence! Nothing more than that separated Héctor and his coyote from *el norte*. Héctor couldn't believe his eyes. Many at the fence carried only a single jug of water, and Héctor's smuggler's words still haunted him. *They will die,* he'd said, with no emotion, adding, *Death in the desert is the cruelest death.* He spoke of withered corpses swinging in the hot, desert wind, of men too ill from the blistering sun to proceed but too far from home to turn back. Parched, disoriented men who hanged themselves by their belts from creosote trees to end their suffering beneath the searing sky. The coyote had assured Héctor he'd not allow Héctor's bones to bleach in the desert sun, that for the fee Héctor was paying him he'd get Héctor across the border. He'd kept his promise, delivering Héctor to *el norte* in the sealed under-carriage of a truck. Lilia and Alejandra had never been far from his thoughts then. He was crossing for them, for their family's future.

Héctor looked at Lilia and nodded. "But I'll never know that intensity of hope, of possibility, again. A boy's dreams are powerful when he's inexperienced, Lilia, before he's known fierce disappointment. You and I have known these things. Our experiences have hardened us. The damage can't be undone." He studied her eyes, needing her to understand his well-earned callousness.

"I have hope yet, Héctor. Listen, do you hear that?" She turned toward the window to the room where Fernando was waking, the room long occupied by Fernando's great-grandmother Crucita. The child called softly, "Mama. Mama."

"That's the sound of my hope. Of our hope. If we fail to embrace the promise and potential of that sweet voice, then we fail God. That's what I believe, Héctor."

He pulled her close and hugged her until Fernando's call became a shout, "Mama!"

"Go get your little sound of hope, then," he said, smiling. "Your little god wants his mama."

He kissed her and watched her go inside to retrieve his son, thankful for her steadfastness, her ability to find goodness and promise always, despite all they had endured.

Chapter 3

Emanuel

Rain drummed the awning under which Emanuel sat looking out at the gray, dirty bay. Rainy season or not, the tourists flocked here in their flowery clothes, eager to shop on Acapulco's strip, to swim in the chlorinated swimming pools, and to sleep in the luxurious hotel beds. The deluge fell thick and slanting, erasing the hills and candy-colored highrise hotels across the water, and land, sea, and sky melted into one gray expanse, concealing a pair of cruise ships bobbing like miniature cities.

Emanuel sucked a long, slow drag from his cigarette, dropped it to the soft, damp earth, and crushed it beneath his boot heel. He tilted his head back and exhaled, the smoke the same lifeless color as everything around him.

"This rain," he said, shaking his head.

"What about it?" Diego said, licking the edge of the joint he'd just rolled.

"It's wet."

"Yes," Diego said.

"Funny. Rain is water, which is cleansing. But these rains wash so much pollution down from the hills, dirtying everything down here."

Diego held the joint between his lips and struck a match. "Good for the coffee crop, though, hey? And the marijuana," he

said, the burning herb pungent between them now. He passed
the joint to Emanuel. "Nothing cleansing about this downpour.
It's like the clouds are shitting. Just shitting all in the bay."
Emanuel waved off the joint. "No," he said. "Too much I have
to get done this afternoon if this goddamn rain lets up."

Diego shrugged and took another puff before pinching off
the lit end and dropping the joint into his shirt pocket. "My
father would kick both our asses if he walked up and smelled
mota. But he's gone for the day."

"You smoke that shit before you dive?" Emanuel asked. "I'd
have to do a lot more than just smoke weed before I'd dive from
the cliffs of La Quebrada."

"No, man. I smoke the marijuana after the dives. The diving
gives me a rush, you know? And the marijuana brings me back
down."

The rain began to slacken, and Diego rose. "Diving is the only
work I've known besides this," he said, jutting his chin toward
the storage building behind them. Diego's father had begun a
hotel laundry business when Diego was a boy. His grandfather
and his father before him had been in the textile industry, and
Diego's father had figured a way to capitalize on their accessi-
bility to good cotton and quality fabrics.

When he'd begun the business, all the hotels along the
strip had been doing their own linens, but Diego's father had
convinced them. On the day Emanuel came to him for a job,
Diego's father told Emanuel all about his own industriousness
and hard work, and how he valued those traits in others, and
how, eventually, the fancy hotels had been persuaded.

"Imagine," he had said, "no more linen shortages, no more
possibility of threadbare sheets, and the guarantee of luxurious
linens at your fingertips. We make it easy on these hotels, don't
you see?"

Emanuel had nodded and smiled when he thought doing

so would be advantageous, and his interview had gone well. Diego's father had hired him on the spot, and over the past two years, Emanuel had worked his way up to driving the delivery truck.

"Maybe one day I'll be too old for the cliffs," Diego said, bringing Emanuel's mind back to the present.

"How will you know when that day arrives?" Emanuel said, thinking of the crowds of disappointed tourists, cameras clenched at their breasts like strange, benign growths.

"That day will have arrived when I don't come back. When my timing is off, and I'm ground to bits beneath crashing waves on those rocks out there. Then you'll know that Diego the Magnificent's diving days have ended, eh?" He pointed at Emanuel but said nothing more, then jogged away down the palm-lined street.

Emanuel had grown up south of Acapulco, down the coast in Puerto Isadore, and he knew nothing of the cliff divers of La Quebrada in his boyhood. Diego and the other divers were part acrobat, part artist, part magician, and what they did frightened Emanuel. He often wondered, had he spent his childhood here among the divers, if the mystique of La Quebrada would be diminished for him, and that perhaps he, too, would climb the thirty-eight-meter cliff every day, utter a prayer at the small wooden altar erected above the inlet, and plunge into the sea below, all for the entertainment and pesos of tourists who perhaps half hoped a diver's timing would be off, that he'd miss the incoming wave and perish on the sharp rocks in the shallows below.

The distant hills again took shape in the haze, and at their base, just beyond the beach, the hotels stood like stalwart guardians of Mexico in all their regalia of blue, purple, coral, and green, though muted still in the lingering mist.

He glanced down the street in the direction Diego had gone, but saw only a lone pair huddled beneath an umbrella, rushing toward a taxi. He wished he had a woman, and considered stopping by the restaurant to see if Ana María was working, but he had one delivery yet to make, and besides, Ana María talked too much. The only girl he'd ever been able to tolerate for any length of time had been Lilia, and like a fool he'd let her slip away from him years ago. He thought of her sometimes, mostly on cloudless nights, not on rainy days like this. He knew he'd likely never see her again because he had no intention of heading to *el norte,* and last he'd heard that was where she was with her husband, Héctor, raising their children as *norteamericanos.*

The last time he'd seen Lilia had been the morning he'd set her and her baby up with his uncle Carlos for their border crossing. Though he knew that would likely be the final time he'd see Lilia, he could not have known then he'd not see Carlos again, either.

Emanuel had returned to their village only twice since that day. The first time had been just weeks later, to clean out Carlos's belongings after he'd been killed in a car crash. The second time had been recently, when he had to make a delivery to the airport in Escondido. The truck had broken down there, and he was waylaid for a day, waiting on a part, and so he'd caught the bus to Puerto Isadore. He'd run into a few familiar faces, but Puerto Isadore had nothing for him anymore. He'd been away too long, first in Oaxaca City with his father and now in Acapulco. That sleepy fishing village had offered little to him as a boy and even less to him now, and he doubted he would ever return.

Chapter 4

Rosa

"Sit still, child," Rosa said.

"Are you almost finished, *Abuela?*"

"You will know when I'm finished when I'm finished."

Rosa tied two tattered, red ribbons at the ends of her grand-daughter's plaits and playfully swatted the girl's bottom. "Go on, now," she said. "Go meet your *abuelo,* and help him carry home our supper."

The child ran from the yard heading toward the village pier, leaving her grandmother sitting on her favorite wooden bench beneath thin vines of purple bougainvillea. Two other children remained with Rosa, and they played with marbles, rolling them around and around the inner edge of an upside-down trash can lid. Rosa watched them a moment then checked the time on her watch.

"Your mamas will be here soon," she said to them, though the small boy barely gave her a glance, and the girl didn't look up from the marbles at all.

Rosa stood and stretched her arms above her head, yawning.

"Have they tired you today, Rosa?" Lilia said, coming through Rosa's gate, its white paint chipping and rust stained.

Even now, more than twenty years after Zarela's death, Rosa startled at how similar Lilia looked to her mother. Zarela had been Rosa's best friend, and Rosa felt Zarela's absence most when Lilia's son, Fernando, was in her care.

Rosa shrugged. "They're easy children, those two. Most children are easy if you know how to handle them."

Fernando ran to his mother's side, and Lilia bent to kiss the top of his head.

Rosa'd been keeping Fernando several days a week for Lilia since the boy had been weaned so that Lilia could sell her pottery in the market. Lilia paid her for doing so, and Rosa appreciated the small income. The girl child belonged to Rosa's neighbor Lupita, and on occasion Rosa made a few pesos providing child care for the girl, too. Besides, Fernando enjoyed having a playmate.

"How's your pottery coming along?" she asked Lilia. Lilia's interest in creating pottery had arisen through necessity. Though she'd been raised by one of the finest potters in Puerto Isadore, Lilia had shown no inclination to follow in her late grandmother's path until after she and Héctor had returned from Norteamérica and Lilia needed work.

"You tell me what you think," Lilia said, reaching into the sack draped across her shoulder and withdrawing a small clay water pitcher.

Rosa took the piece from Lilia and held it up to the sky, slowly spinning it in the sunlight, inspecting it for cracks or other imperfections. The pitcher was green glazed, with raised flowers beneath its lip. Not bad, she thought. "Marigolds?" she asked.

"Yes," Lilia said, smiling. "Keep it."

Rosa nodded her thanks. She'd known Lilia since the day of her birth, the day Lilia's mother had died. Lilia had always been kindhearted but was hardheaded and rash in her decision making, and even now, Rosa helped Lilia with Fernando more out of a sense of duty to her dead friend and for the few pesos Lilia paid her than out of respect for Lilia.

Rosa studied a small hummingbird as it darted among blossoms beside the house. She understood that Lilia appreciated her approval, but Rosa had made it clear she'd offer no false kindness to Lilia or to her husband, Héctor. She'd warned them not to go to the border, not to leave their history and their heritage behind. She loathed their lack of allegiance to Mexico, to their dead ancestors and those ancestors' struggles, and all who came before them. And though she knew little of the details of their time in America, she knew that upon their return to their village the young couple had changed, and their fresh-faced eagerness to experience the world had withered like mangos left too long on the branch. She'd shaken her head when she'd first seen them back in Oaxaca, in this village, because she knew they'd not returned of their own volition, and so she had no welcome for them, no sense of a celebratory homecoming. They'd judged their country not good enough for them. They'd been greedy for a life, for things Rosa couldn't comprehend.

And what did they know? Their beautiful child, lost somehow at the border. Lost. How could that happen? Rosa did not understand what had occurred, but her gut ached to this day when she considered little Alejandra and how sad Lilia's mother would have been had she lived to know her daughter and granddaughter and to suffer the baby's loss. Nothing in this world was more precious than a child, and though she knew that whatever had happened with Alejandra pained Lilia, had scarred her deeply, Rosa could not forgive her and Héctor for their choices.

"Do you want a drink?" Rosa asked, turning toward the house.

Fernando had returned to his game with the marbles, and so

Lilia followed Rosa inside. Rosa set the pitcher on a shelf beside a bottle of mescal and pulled down the bottle and two small cups. She poured them half full.

Lilia held the cup in her fingers as if uncertain she wanted its contents, but Rosa tossed hers back and poured herself a second.

"Héctor saw Emanuel yesterday," Lilia said, looking not at Rosa but staring into the amber liquid she held. "At least he thinks he saw him." When Rosa said nothing Lilia added, "He was getting on the bus. To Escondido, Héctor says."

Lilia could appear so childlike sometimes in her uncertainty, her vulnerability. Rosa almost felt sorry for her except that Lilia's occasional recklessness and headstrong tendencies carried too much weight and tipped the scales of Rosa's feelings toward disappointment and vexation. She took another, smaller swig from her cup.

"Maybe the man Héctor saw wasn't actually Emanuel," Lilia said. "Maybe we've hoped so long to see him that Héctor's imagination was at work."

Rosa could stand Lilia's rambling and wavering between doubt and hopefulness no longer, and she said, "The man he saw was Emanuel."

Lilia looked at her, astonishment enlivening her face. "How do you know?"

"I saw him," Rosa said. "I talked to him at the pier. He was here just a short while, but was soon to return to Escondido."

Lilia grabbed Rosa's arm. "Rosa! Why didn't you tell me this?"

Rosa looked down at Lilia's grip on her forearm, and the girl released her. "I just told you, Lilia. And I'm not sure why you care. I always said he was the better match for you, that Emanuel would make a good life for you, for a family." She could feel the heat rising in her neck. "You wanted no part of him, and so you left all you knew, the place where the bones of your grandmother and your mother lie in the ground, to go to a place you perceived more worthy than your birthplace."

"*El norte* and our village aren't the same, Rosa ..." Lilia paused, picking at a dry, brown scab on her index finger. "Life can be difficult in Puerto Isadore. Think about that. My mother died giving me life. Childbirth here can be tricky, dangerous. But that's not even the reason, really," Lilia said, struggling for whatever she wished to convey.

"When the heavy rains have come, children have drowned in the river, Rosa," she said, looking northeast where they both knew the river snaked and occasionally overflowed its littered banks, less than a kilometer from where they stood.

Rosa shrugged, recalling the bloated body of a toddler who'd been found downstream two years ago after days of downpours and flooding. She'd served as the boy's mother's midwife during his birth. "Ah, but that can happen anywhere in the world, Lilia. No man or country can control the rains or the tides."

"And the teenagers," Lilia continued, as if she hadn't heard Rosa. "The poorest ones, the ones who sniff glue in Oaxaca City, who have no hope and no chance. I'd never want my child to be like that. Teens who'd rather numb themselves, make their brains crazy on glue fumes, because they believe their future, if they're lucky, will be nothing more than stringing beads or picking vegetables to earn in a week what Héctor and I earned in a day in *el norte*. Don't you see?"

Rosa did see. She saw that Lilia had a skewed sense of things, and she shook her head in disgust. "Why do you care that Emanuel was here, girl? What difference does that make to you?"

Lilia sat down on a stool and combed her fingers through her hair. She looked wild-eyed, like a goat who'd eaten something he should have avoided.

"Oh, Rosa. You don't understand." She took a deep breath, as if preparing to make Rosa realize the importance of things. Rosa had no intention of making this easy on Lilia. She gulped the last bit in her cup and set it on the table between them. "Rosa, Emanuel is the only connection we have to Alejandra. Last we heard he was in Oaxaca City, but Héctor searched there months ago and couldn't find him."

"He's no longer there," Rosa said, imagining Héctor roaming the busy streets and lanes of the city, his efforts as fruitless as a mongrel's hopes of living in a king's palace eating scraps of juicy beefsteak. "He told me his father passed a while back and so he moved from Oaxaca City."

"Rosa!" Lilia said, with such powerful conviction in her voice and eyes that Rosa said, "Go on. I'm listening, Lilia."

"My coyote was Emanuel's uncle Carlos; he got me to the border. He forced me to hand Alejandra over to a woman he used, a coyote for babies, because Carlos told me he didn't cross with babies but this woman did. He said she was a professional."

Rosa knew all these things, had known them since Lilia called her from a telephone somewhere in Norteamérica, sick with worry just days after she'd crossed. She nodded. "Of course I know all this, Lilia."

"That horrible day plays out in my nightmares. Héctor tells me I weep in my sleep. The first time my cries woke him he said my arms were outstretched toward the ceiling, my hands clenched in fists. 'What were you seeing in your sleep?' he asked me, wiping my wet face with his thumbs. How could I tell my husband of these nightmares, of evils brought on by my own mistakes? But he demanded, 'Tell me.' And so I told him everything, the terrible scene still fresh in my head," Lilia said, looking past Rosa, recalling the horrible memories.

Rosa waited and said nothing.

"In that nightmare, and it's the same every time, I gripped

Alejandra's legs, one in each of my hands," Lilia continued, her voice softer now. "I'd just handed her over to her coyote but this woman turned into a snake as soon as I released my baby to her, swallowing Alejandra headfirst, and I told the snake woman, 'No, please! I've changed my mind! Give me back my girl. I'll go home now. I want to take her home.' But the woman's eyes had turned lifeless, like empty sockets in a living creature, and the harder I pulled Alejandra from her, the deeper my baby went down her throat. My hands were at the woman's mouth when Héctor woke me. I could feel her snake saliva on the backs of my hands and it burned, like venom. And I knew I'd never see Alejandra again."

Rosa sighed, unsure what to say.

"When I finished telling Héctor of this horrifying dream, I covered my face in my shame, but he pulled the blanket away and he held me. Really held me for the first time since we'd lost our baby girl. And that night I conceived my precious Fernando. So," Lilia said, wiping her eyes, as if suddenly uncertain how to proceed or perhaps afraid she'd revealed too much.

Lilia had not spoken to Rosa of America in years, of her and Héctor's experiences there or of their deportation. Now, with Emanuel resurfacing, Lilia's emotions and memories seemed fresh, raw, as if she had only just returned and needed to make sense of the happenings in that foreign place.

"Carlos was an evil man, Rosa. The things he did to me. You don't know what I went through, what I endured. When he got me to the banks of the big river, I swam hard, leaving him behind me on the Mexican side, and when I reached the shore of *el norte* I prayed I would never see him again. How could I know that just days later I would pray to find him, to speak to him. But God heard my first prayer, and I never saw that monster again."

"If you suffered under this man, then you should be glad he is gone," Rosa said, wondering what he had done to Lilia.

"And I waited at the border house, waited and waited for that woman to arrive with my Alejandra, though she never came. Never, Rosa! Héctor showed up to meet me at the border house, so happy and surprised by my arrival in Texas, and then so very angry, enraged that Alejandra had not arrived as I'd planned, furious that I'd entrusted that strange woman with our baby. Only what did I know, Rosa? I'd never crossed, I only did as my coyote had instructed, and what choice did I have then, after everything, after . . ." She paused and dabbed her eyes.

Rosa was hearing nothing new, and she wanted to slap the girl for dramatizing her own poor choices as if she were a victim. She would offer Lilia no comfort for this.

"And then Alejandra's coyote failed to deliver, failed to show up," Lilia said. "I thought Héctor would kill me." When she wiped her nose on the back of her hand, Rosa handed her a dishcloth.

"Go on," Rosa said, when Lilia hesitated to take the cloth.

"I begged the man running the border house to give me information on the woman who had my baby. He finally gave me a phone number, but it never worked when I called it. And then, weeks later we got word that Carlos had been killed in an accident, and with him our only known contact to the woman who'd taken my baby."

Rosa had never questioned Lilia about the events of her crossing. Without knowing all the details, empathy failed her. "Why, then, Lilia, did you not go back for her right away, back across the border?"

Lilia sighed a long, exasperated sigh. "I've asked myself that so often, Rosa. But at the time . . ." Her voice trailed off and she looked up at the passing clouds as if they might offer clarity.

"At the time, Héctor had a wonderful job with kind employers, but his work was in a place far from the border, a place called South Carolina, far from the house where the woman with Alejandra was to meet me. And we were soon to run out of money in Texas. But," she said, shaking her head as if she'd misspoken.

"But what?" Rosa said.

"But that's not why. Not exactly. Getting across the border was not easy. How could we risk going back into Mexico if our daughter had made it across? Don't you see? What if, eventually, Alejandra's coyote arrived in Texas, but Héctor and I were stuck back in Mexico? What if we'd used our one stroke of luck in our first crossing? Then what?"

"She was your blood, Lilia. I would think a mama would do everything in her power to find her child," Rosa said.

"Rosa, don't you see that I did?" she said, pulling clenched fists to her temples. "Second-guessing myself now is easy, sure, but at the time Héctor and I were sick with fear and worry. I was so young, practically a girl myself. We held out hope she would show up." Lilia shrugged. "Hope was all we had. And besides, I had no idea where to find the woman if I had gone back into Mexico."

Neither woman spoke for a full minute.

"I doubt Emanuel can offer you anything helpful, Lilia," Rosa said. He is a hardworking man, an honest man. Though Carlos was his uncle, I doubt Emanuel has any other dealings with border crossings, with coyotes. He's proud of his heritage."

"But he may know something, Rosa. Don't you understand my desperation? Wouldn't you do anything if one of your children were missing?" Lilia had begun rubbing her left palm over and over with her right thumb as if she wanted to wear a hole clear through to the thin bones beneath the skin there.

"Lilia, I'd never be in such a situation." She looked out the window. "Lupita's here for her girl."

"Rosa, do you know where Emanuel went?" Lilia pleaded. "Up the coast. Acapulco. He's been there a few years now, he said. He makes deliveries of some kind. The job provides a truck. That's all I know."

Rosa walked outside to greet Lupita and to tell the child goodbye. Lilia stayed behind in the house until Lupita and her girl were gone. Rosa imagined Lilia wiping her eyes and nose on the kitchen rag, hiding traces of her grief before resurfacing into Rosa's sunlit yard.

Later that evening as she lay in bed beside José, listening to his soft snores and the Pacific breeze blowing in through her open window, Rosa considered the possibility that Alejandra was alive and the more doubtful possibility that Emanuel could provide a link to the child's whereabouts. Allowing herself such thoughts was not her nature, but in the dark quietness of her room she pondered the likelihood. She never doubted Lilia's love and devotion to Alejandra, but, rather, often questioned Lilia's decision and her youthful folly. As she lay there considering these things, an unfamiliar heaviness settled deep in her breast. She'd always kept her babies and grandbabies near her. Why would any mother not do so? She tried to imagine how Lilia must feel every day, every moment, wondering if the child to whom she'd given life still lived, somewhere unknown, being raised by strangers. If the child were dead, well, then her spirit would be somewhere lovely where the spirits of dead children go. But, even then, where were her bones? The alternative, the idea that the child lived and walked this earth, stirred Rosa in an unexpected way. Her breath caught in her throat, and she made a small gasping sound that startled her. Only then did she realize she was weeping.

Chapter 5

Héctor

Héctor sat on the ground, seeking the little shade offered by the truck. He opened his sack with fingers that were sticky, brown-green, and nicked from his work. His nails, dirty and stained, were caked with a mucky mixture of dust and agave juice. Héctor's throat was dry and he filled his jug with water from the cooler on the back of the truck. Worse jobs existed in the world, he knew, but they were not for him. Just a few years ago he'd been a driver working his way to foreman, delivering to buyers the agave picked by the field hands, but since his return from *el norte,* such work was considered by his employer too good for him. Héctor was a deserter who'd believed himself above this work, these people, and the other workers, the ones who'd remained in this village and now shunned him.

When he'd first returned he'd begun sitting alone, and now, even though the others had warmed to him a bit, he still chose to eat in solitude, thinking about the man he'd believed he would become but never did. He envisioned the daughter his wife had lost at the border and the man who'd raped his Lilia. The others must have seen his shadowed expression, a bitterness so thick within him that he imagined he smelled of its poison, the venom oozing from his pores so that all around him understood Héctor to be toxic and someone to be avoided.

Some of the men sat under a tree in a group, a few ate with their wives, while some of the women sat apart resting in what little shade they could find up against the jungle's fringe. A young woman Héctor had not seen before this week approached the truck where Héctor reclined against the front tire. She squatted beside the back tire and Héctor felt her eyes on him.

"May I sit here? It's the only shady spot left." She spoke so softly Héctor thought the voice to be that of a child.

Without speaking he nodded and turned his attention to his lunch of tamales with dried shrimp Lilia had prepared last night for their supper.

"I'm Guadalupe," she said, biting into what looked like a bean tortilla. Héctor watched her as she took a sip of water, and he was certain he'd not seen her before.

"Héctor," he said, nodding again.

He thought she would say more, but she did not, and so after several minutes he said, "How long have you worked here? I don't recall seeing you before."

"Three days," the girl replied, her eyes large and sad.

She was beautiful in her sadness, and Héctor wondered what troubled her. Her worries could be anything, he thought, with so many wrongs in this world, so much pain and injustice. He wondered what one as young as Guadalupe would possibly know about such things. But then, as always, he thought of Alejandra and knew that injustices happened every day around the world to anyone, regardless of age or size or best intentions.

The thought of raising Fernando and the baby Lilia now carried in a world harboring these things pained Héctor, though he realized these thoughts were ridiculous. A world without pain and sorrow was not a real world.

"Where was your home before?" Héctor asked.

"Atoyac. Do you know it?" Guadalupe said.

He nodded. "Heard of it, but never been there. Beside the sea, yes? Like Puerto Isadore?"

He took a sip from his water jug, grateful for the drink though it was warm. In the fields in South Carolina he'd kept ice in the watercoolers so that even in the hottest part of the day, cold water was available to quench his thirst, to pour on his sweaty head. He knew that no one among this group of field hands could imagine such a luxury. He considered telling this young girl about the ice, and he wondered if she'd believe him, or if she'd think him a liar and reject him like all the others who now saw him as an outsider.

A hot breeze blew from the west and offered no comfort, and Héctor pondered what to say next to this girl.

He stood to refill his jug with water from the truck and asked Guadalupe, "Would you like more?"

The girl handed Héctor her cup and thanked him. It was then Héctor saw the sores on her right hand, blisters worn through, red and raw from her new job in the fields. Héctor's hands, calloused and rough, had never been as Guadalupe's were now. Perhaps boys' hands are naturally tougher. But he remembered a time when Lilia had just begun working in the fields, cutting agave, and how Héctor had wrapped them for her that first week, so long ago the memory was almost gone, like maybe someone else had experienced it and told Héctor about it.

He filled Guadalupe's cup, returned it to her, and said, "Your hand, it looks painful."

"I'm okay," Guadalupe said, and waved Héctor's concern off as if she were fanning away one of the many insects that buzzed this field. "This is nothing."

"Well, nothing or not, let me help you." He took his knife and walked to the edge of the field, where the bushes were dense and the jungle began. He cut a chunk from an aloe plant growing wild, its leaves thick with its healing salve and its yellow flowers dotted with insects and an occasional hummingbird. Héctor then cut a strip from the edge of his T-shirt. "Let me see that hand of yours," he said. He squeezed the thick aloe leaf until its juice dripped into Guadalupe's open wounds. Héctor extended the strip of cloth to the girl and said, "Wrap this around your fingers when you work. It'll cut down on the friction. You don't want those holes to wear any deeper."

Guadalupe smiled, seeming genuinely grateful for Héctor's concern and friendliness. "Thank you," she said.

"Nothing," Héctor said, waving off Guadalupe's thanks as Guadalupe had done to him.

Héctor recalled the attention he'd given Lilia's tender hands years earlier when the two of them had begun working these fields together, before he'd been promoted to driver. How bittersweet were those memories of times when their mutual attraction was still more than they could contain, when crossing the border had been nothing more than a subject of their late-night whispers before sleep.

They ate in silence a few moments before Guadalupe said, "Have you worked here a long time?"

He told her of his early days in this field, how he'd begun cutting agave when he was thirteen and how he had done so until he'd begun driving the farm truck, delivering the crop for the farmer who owned this field.

"But you no longer drive the truck?" she said, no hint of judgment in her tone.

"No." He looked toward the jungle and the men now napping, sombreros shielding their faces from the scorching sun and biting insects. He waited for her to ask him why he'd returned to this shitty, hot job when once he drove the truck, but the girl said nothing and chewed her last bite of lunch.

He glanced at her then. She looked not at him but out across the field at the endless blue-gray agave, at the spiked rows extending to the distant mountains. He studied her, took in her slender arms, her thin fingers. Her hair hung in two tight braids, their tips brushing the ground because of the way she reclined against the truck tire, her knees pulled to her chest in the posture of a child. She was a pretty girl, her figure still intact, and Héctor knew she'd never birthed a baby.

When he'd left their village for the border, Lilia's hair had been long like that, so beautiful he'd dreamed of it while they were apart, anticipating the day he'd send for her and little Alejandra, the day he could comb his fingers through his wife's thick mane and bury his face there, inhaling her scent of lavender and honey.

When Lilia arrived unexpectedly in Texas, hoping to surprise Héctor, she, like her hair, was not as he'd dreamed those many nights they'd spent apart. The coyotes had broken her spirit, had forced her to chop and dye her hair, to better match the identification card they'd provided her, and along with her spirit and hair, the Lilia he'd married had been all but lost to him.

Only recently could Héctor consider Lilia's trials, her agony during and after her crossing. He'd been so completely devastated that Lilia had somehow lost Alejandra in transit that his grief had blinded him to his wife's crippling loss, her unwavering guilt. Empathy for Lilia had escaped him for months following her arrival at the border without their child. Her plan to surprise him had taken a horrible, unfathomable, and likely irreversible turn.

"I left for a while," he said. "When I returned, my old job had been given away, as it should have been, I suppose. And so here I am in this dusty field, doing the work I did as a boy." He lifted his knife where it lay beside him on the ground and aimed the blade toward the field to emphasize his point. "My boyhood dreams were to move beyond this place, yet here I am a man. My situation remains as it was, but I no longer have such dreams."

"Have you been to the border, to *el norte*?" she asked.

Héctor thought of his job in the north, of the few months he'd actually been given his own farm truck to drive there and the freedom that truck gave him. How long ago that seemed. He'd not driven a vehicle since returning to his country. True, he'd always worried about immigration discovering him in America, but besides that, the work he did on the farm there agreed with him and he'd been grateful. And then one afternoon, when he and Lilia had stopped to check on a victim at the scene of a traffic accident, just like that, they were caught and soon on their way back home to Mexico.

"I've been there," he said. "Several years ago I crossed and worked in a beautiful place called South Carolina. Like Puerto Isadore, this place was beside the sea. You?"

"Yes. I've been there. We, my father and brother and I, crossed three summers ago. I didn't want to go, didn't want to leave my mother. But my father, he took us and we crossed with a coyote," she said, looking down at her sores.

Something in Guadalupe's past had left the girl's insides as raw and pained as the wounds on her hand. Héctor could see it in her eyes. He knew well what it was like to harbor a silent agony, one too complicated to express.

"I'm sure that was difficult," he said, pulling a pack of chewing gum from his pocket. He offered the pack to her, but she shook her head, avoiding Héctor's eyes, perhaps seeing pity in them, and began wrapping her fingers with the strip of cloth he had given her. When she had woven the strip between her fingers as he had shown her, she said, "That's good. Thank you."

Héctor stood and said, "Let me help you there," and tied the two ends of the fabric in a tight knot across the back of Guadalupe's hand.

The two spent the remainder of their break speaking of light topics, like new acquaintances do. They talked of their schooling as children in their small villages of Puerto Isadore and Atoyac. They spoke of memories of fishing and of playing basketball, an activity both had enjoyed in their youth.

Héctor had not met a new friend in months, and many who knew him had treated him so differently since his return that he often felt a stranger among old friends. Everyone in his life he had known for years and speaking of his life to one who didn't already know the details felt good. He enjoyed talking of mundane topics and of less complicated times. Héctor thought their conversation had softened the strain in Guadalupe's eyes, too. Maybe they both could benefit from this new friendship.

The remainder of the workday went as the first half had gone, as every day went, only the air seemed hotter and drier than usual.

The workers loaded themselves, weary and sticky-damp with perspiration, into the foreman's truck—a truck that should have been Héctor's, along with the job of foreman, but instead was now his old schoolmate Marcelino's—and headed back to their village.

"See you tomorrow, Héctor," Guadalupe said, as Héctor climbed down from the back of the truck in Puerto Isadore.

"Yes, sure. See you," he said. "Thanks, Marcelino," he called to the driver, who tapped the brim of his hat before continuing down the dusty road.

Héctor turned and began his short walk home to Lilia. He paid little attention to his surroundings anymore, and why should he? His village was as familiar to him as anything could be. The sounds and smells, the pigs and goats in the dirt streets.

Of course, they likely were not the exact animals he'd known in his youth, but they looked and stank and shat the same. Such things would never change here. As he turned onto the narrow lane home, he smelled onions and meat frying somewhere nearby, and his stomach rumbled with hunger. And always in everything here the salt air of the Pacific mingled with the smoky stench of burned waste, blanketing his village, seeping into its soul, uniting all Puerto Isadore's parts, both beautiful and repulsive to him.

Chapter 6

Lilia

Lilia bounced Fernando on her knee and sipped a warm mug of atole, flavored with lemon and mint. Her back ached from bending over her clay late into the previous evening, and she hoped the drink would help.

Héctor had been home from the fields only a few moments when he left again to walk down the lane to buy a few items from Armando at *la farmacia*, and when he returned Lilia would tell him what Rosa had said about Emanuel. Héctor had seemed distracted after work, and Lilia had not wanted to deliver this important news until the time felt right. She would never fully shed the guilt she wore like a heavy cloak, and no matter Héctor's disposition or what he said, she knew he would never completely unburden himself of his great disappointment in her. And so she always chose her words carefully when speaking to him about matters both light and weighty.

Héctor set the sack of goods from the market on the table and poured a drink of water from the clay pitcher.

Lilia's heart had swelled to an unparalleled capacity at Alejandra's birth, and it grew more with each passing day as the child grew. Lilia couldn't fathom that her heart's love could expand any further, yet it had with the arrival of Fernando. What a miraculous thing, the human heart, with its ability to swell and stretch beyond any boundaries. Lilia had discovered her heart had infinite capacity for both love and grief.

"Did you sell much today?" he asked.

Fernando chased a small blue lizard across the floor and out the door into the courtyard, leaving his parents alone. He was such a beautiful child with not a worry in this world except what small animal he might next spy.

"Three pieces," she said.

Héctor sipped his water and watched Fernando through the open doorway.

"How about you? A good day?" she said.

He pulled out a chair and sat beside her, finishing off the cup of water. "No different than any other. I don't imagine my days will ever vary much for a long while unless I find better work."

"What are you thinking?" she said.

"Maybe I could get a job in the hills, find work with the coffee pickers. These guys here . . . I could've never imagined the way they'd see us upon our return. Like we think we're too good for them."

She smiled a weak smile, taking his calloused hand in hers. "Well, I doubt you ever imagined you'd be back here, at least not to stay."

"No," he said.

Lilia considered how far away the coffee fields were and wondered how Héctor could possibly find work there, and if he did, what that would mean for her, for their family. The mountains were too far from Puerto Isadore for Héctor to commute every day. She kept these thoughts to herself and rubbed Héctor's forearm with slow deep circles, massaging the thick cord of muscle beneath his sun-darkened skin.

She thought of the early days of their courtship, of the late afternoons they'd spent sitting on the rocky promontory beside the bay watching the boats, the tide, the gulls, and whatever else came along as day melted into the half-light of dusk. How simple life had been then and how instantly and deeply they'd loved each other. By her sixteenth birthday, she knew she'd marry Héctor, and by her seventeenth birthday they were betrothed. Married at eighteen and a mother at nineteen, Lilia could now hardly recall the carefree nature of her youth.

"I've often wanted to tell Rosa about the soapy-smelling restrooms and the sparkling toilets in Norteamérica, you know? I've considered it, telling her about the stores larger than our entire lane, and the rows and rows of vegetables and racks of clothes in those stores. But I haven't. I haven't told anyone," she said.

"Why not?" he asked, studying her eyes, searching in an earnest way that told her he cared, that her thoughts mattered to him.

"What good would telling Rosa do? She'd either think I'd imagined such things, or she'd feel jealous or misunderstand my intentions in sharing what we'd seen. She could never comprehend the gringos' kindnesses to us or that the seabirds in South Carolina are the same kinds as here in the bay."

He closed his eyes, enjoying Lilia's touch. His obvious pleasure encouraged her. She stood, moving her hands to his upper arm and shoulder.

Lilia had never left her home state of Oaxaca before her crossing, and she could not have known then how very different Norteamérica would be from Puerto Isadore. And even in South Carolina, she could not have imagined how dirty and poverty-stricken Puerto Isadore would seem to her upon her return. She'd been ashamed of her disdain, and she'd prayed to God to forgive her, to set her thoughts as they should be, but her friends and neighbors read in her face the disgust she could not hide, and her eyes revealed her disappointment in what she saw in their ragged clothes, their dirty feet in tattered sandals, and their humble shacks.

"People are people," he said. "That's what I learned in *el norte*. Some good, some bad. Their birth country matters nothing where their hearts are concerned."

She knew he thought of the kind farmer who'd employed them in South Carolina, and of the immigration officials who'd deported them to Mexico. She, too, thought of these people daily still.

"Rosa had big news for me today," she said, working her fingers into the dense tissue of Héctor's neck.

He grunted.

"I mentioned your having maybe seen Emanuel. She said he'd been here, that she talked to him. He was here, Héctor. You did see him."

To her surprise nothing changed in his slumped, relaxed posture beneath her hands. "I know I saw him. I told you that," he said.

"But we couldn't have been sure the man you saw was actually him. But it was! Rosa said he lives in Acapulco now, that he's been there several years. He works there, Héctor."

Héctor said nothing as Lilia continued to knead his neck and shoulder muscles. She feared he was falling asleep, though she knew he'd heard her. She felt her skin would split, unable to contain her anticipation and excitement, if Héctor didn't speak, didn't tell her his plan. Héctor, the old Héctor, always had a plan, always considered his options and how to make life better.

She reached for the small jar of lavender oil beside the window and dabbed a drop in her palm. She rubbed her hands together then worked her fingers, slow and deep, into the meat of Héctor's upper back and shoulders.

Lilia wasn't sure who benefited more from her touching Héctor this way. Surely his knotted muscles softened like dough under her massaging hands, but Lilia, too, felt her stress lessen when her skin and Héctor's touched like this.

"What do you think Acapulco's like? I've always imagined it to be so fancy. I've seen the postcards, you know, the ones in Armando's shop."

He folded his arms on the table and rested his head there as if he were either relaxed or bored with the conversation. Or maybe he was just too exhausted from laboring in the hot, dusty fields.

"I went there once as a boy," he said, not lifting his head.

Lilia imagined Héctor as a small boy and wondered how much like their delightful Fernando he had been. Had Héctor's skin been as creamy soft as Fernando's? Had his downy head smelled as rosewater sweet? She waited several moments for him to say more, to tell her of the fine things he had experienced there, but when he did not, she said, "How far away is that place from here, Héctor?"

He exhaled sharply, and she could tell he considered the question. "Less than half a day by bus, I think."

Half a day! The answer to Alejandra's whereabouts may have been so close all this time.

"Then we'll go, yes? We'll go to Acapulco and find Emanuel," she said, her fingers working deeper and more rapidly into Héctor's muscles.

He moaned under her strong hands and the good pain of the massage.

"I'll go," he said. "You'll stay here. You'll never go near that bastard Emanuel again."

She rubbed his neck and shoulders until the angle of the sinking sun blinded her through the window, and even then she turned and continued to work on Héctor's forearms in silence. Héctor had made his thoughts clear concerning his journey alone to Acapulco, and this time, she would not defy her husband, not only because to do so would disrespect him but also because her trust and faith in him had become stronger than her trust and faith in herself since her crossing.

Chapter 7

Emanuel

Emanuel knew if he were to sit motionless, the air around him would be still and humid, nearly suffocating, but he sped without pedaling down the hill of the narrow, potholed street, and the temperature of the breeze as he sliced through it felt perfect against his face and bare arms. The window air-conditioning unit in his grimy apartment hadn't worked since he'd moved in, and the coolest part of his day was on his morning commute out of the hills by bicycle to work.

He passed a couple arguing, their angry voices disturbing the otherwise tranquil dawn. The woman's hands flailed about as she screamed at the man, who interrupted her, shouting back. Emanuel whizzed by them on his bike, making sure to show no interest in their dealings. Just as he passed he heard the unmistakable smack of open hand to skin, but he couldn't be sure who had slapped whom, his eyes steady on the street in front of him.

He considered how lovely some parts of his adopted town of Acapulco could be, and how frightening other sections were.

Emanuel arrived at work just as Diego arrived by bike from the other direction.

"Crazy people up at this hour," Emanuel said.

"What's that?" Diego said.

"I just saw some stupid shit," Emanuel said, shaking his head.

"Welcome to lovely Acapulco, my boy."

"Up the hill there, outside my neighborhood. Some guy and his woman shouting in the street. I think he smacked her good, too. Nobody wants to hear that before they've even had their coffee," he said, trying to make light of his irritation at the scene.

Diego unlocked the storage building. "Last summer I saw three headless women, their bodies stacked and twisted like some strange orgy. Only difference was their skin. It was almost translucent, you know? A sick gray color, like all the blood had been drained from their bodies, and you knew, even before you realized their heads were gone, that they had to be dead."

"You saw that? You serious?" Emanuel said, loading the day's neatly bundled linens into the delivery truck parked inside the small storage building. How had their conversation turned to this?

"I saw it," Diego said. "Stick around here long enough . . ." He shook his head as if words couldn't convey the rest of the images he'd seen, or, perhaps, he simply suspected Emanuel couldn't comprehend them if Diego tried to explain.

"People are crazy, man," Emanuel said, inhaling the light scent of clean linens and laundry soap as he worked to fill the truck. "I know people who do some things others may not approve of. Like my uncle was a coyote for years before he died, but that's harmless. That's nothing. Beating and killing women? Not cool."

"Hey," Diego said. "You know what a *desollado* is?"

Emanuel didn't answer Diego, instead focusing on the pleasant, breezy scent of the linens. He wondered if the man in the street had hurt the woman, and who started the argument.

"One time my neighbor's cousin had the skin peeled off his face. That's what a *desollado* is: a person who has their face peeled off by the bad guys. He'd worked for this cocaine distributor, and the boss man didn't like something my neighbor's cousin did. I never saw the guy, but I hear about this kind of shit all the time."

Emanuel had heard more than he cared to hear, though Diego seemed to enjoy the horrible details.

"I don't want to hear about that stuff," Emanuel said.

Neither spoke for several minutes, but when they'd loaded the majority of the day's deliveries Diego said, "Yeah, that's some ugly shit."

Emanuel spit and nodded. "Who the hell would do that? Why do people get into evil like that?"

"Why do you think people get caught up in shit like that?" Diego said. "I mean, you and me, we wouldn't be in that situation. We do our jobs. I take the tourists' money with my beautiful dives, and you take my father's money by kissing his ass and being the perfect delivery boy, eh?"

"I don't know, man," Emanuel said. "Something very alluring must get people involved with such bad players. It's the money, right?"

"Sure, sure," Diego said. "And maybe power and prestige, and yes, of course the money. Hey, that doesn't sound all bad! We should look into getting work as criminals, Emanuel, no?"

"And end up faceless? You're a pig turd, Diego. Stick to your diving, and I'll stick to impressing your father."

"I've had opportunities," Diego said, raising his chin and looking down his nose at Emanuel.

"Opportunities for what?"

"Running drugs or whatever else, what do you think? Opportunities to make quick money. People see my father has this delivery business and access to the fancy hotels. I've been approached, that's all I'll say. But I tell those guys, no thank you. No thank you."

Emanuel made his way toward the back shelves, collecting the final few bundles of linens. "Were you tempted?" he said.

"Of course. You see the slick guys in their snakeskin boots and thick belts. You see their expensive sombreros. You know they can get the most beautiful women. Wouldn't you be tempted?"

Emanuel considered this, especially the part about the beautiful women.

Diego continued, "But you know, then I figure the fine clothes, the ladies, they come with a price. One thing I learned from my father: Material joys and pleasures from loose and beautiful ladies are never without a price." He shrugged and slammed shut the back of the truck after Emanuel shoved in the final load. "I'll take what I got, you know? I'm happy with the skin on my face. The air in my lungs. My heartbeat."

Emanuel considered the irony of Diego's words. Half the guys in Acapulco would kill for the attention Diego got from the ladies, silly local *chavas,* yes, but also the curious Canadians, Americans, Costa Ricans, and other foreign-born tourists, intrigued and lured by Diego's athletic prowess and apparent invincibility even on frightening cliff dives.

Emanuel rolled his bike into the building where it would remain while he made the day's deliveries. "So, I'll see you later," he said to Diego.

"Later," Diego said, locking the building's door before mounting his bike to head to a morning of cliff diving.

"Thanks for your help," Emanuel said through the truck's open window, grateful for Diego's assistance each morning. "Avoid the rocks," he shouted down the street to Diego's back.

Diego threw up a hand, giving Emanuel a thumbs-up.

Emanuel made his way down the narrow side street, turning onto the main thoroughfare of Acapulco. He considered Diego's life as a famed diver and wondered if Diego's situation were different, if his father didn't own a successful business and tourists didn't flock to watch his dives, would he have considered the offers to run drugs. What would Emanuel do if someone wearing expensive boots and sporting beautiful women at his side offered him an opportunity? He pictured a gorgeous lady with smooth, creamy skin, large golden eyes, hair loose and flowing, not so much like the popular ladies in the movies but more like the women in famous paintings. He always pictured his dream lady surrounded by calla lilies, though he never told anyone this for fear he'd sound foolish. He considered the famous art he'd studied in school, paintings by Diego Rivera, José Clemente Orozco, Carlos Mérida, and Frida Kahlo. Rivera often placed his subjects among mounds of waxy, white lilies, and the blossoms enhanced the women's beauty and desirability and somehow made them seem mysterious to Emanuel.

He would like a woman who smelled of lilies, a woman worthy of having her portrait studied by Mexican schoolboys for generations beyond the painter's lifetime. But he knew, even if as a younger man the thought had intrigued him, no flicker of temptation to run with the high-stakes crowd dwelled within him. He had no stomach for such things.

Perhaps if a boy is among thugs and bandits for long enough, he adopts the mind-set that joining up in their ways is better than continuously trying to avoid them.

He pulled the truck to the delivery entrance behind Hotel Pacifico. The manager there always slipped him a sweet cup of steaming coffee, and so Emanuel made this the first stop every day. As he stepped from the truck, he heard the siren of an ambulance in the distance. He wondered if the ambulance were going to the woman he'd seen arguing in the street, but then he doubted that. Distracted in his thoughts, Emanuel didn't notice Héctor until too late, the force of Héctor's blow slamming Emanuel's shoulder against the hood of his truck.

Chapter 8

Rosa

Lilia and Rosa sat on the bench shelling peas, as Fernando chased an orange-and-black butterfly around Rosa's yard.

"What do you think this baby will be, Rosa?" Lilia said, looking toward the place where Fernando giggled, hidden behind a mass of prickly pear, its fruit red and swollen like infected thumbs.

Rosa knew the child would be a girl. She was never wrong about such things, but before speaking she turned toward Lilia and studied her belly a moment. "What do you think you're carrying?" she said, returning her attention to the basket in her lap.

"Some days I think it's a girl because I feel like I felt with Alejandra. But other times I think I'm only wishing for a girl because I miss my firstborn so much. Then I feel sinful and ashamed, as if I'm trying to replace Alejandra with a new daughter, which I could never do."

Rosa looked at her again, willing her to hush her endless chatter about matters over which only God had control. She set the basket of peas on the bench and stood, her knees popping and aching as she rose.

"Come," she said, walking inside the house.

She heard Lilia follow her.

"Just a moment," she called over her shoulder as she went to retrieve a few necessary items from the wooden box beside her bed.

When Rosa returned to Lilia she said, "Lift up your dress."

Lilia looked about her, as if to be certain no one else would see her underclothes, before she hoisted her hemline to her shoulders. Rosa put a hand on Lilia's belly, noting its pointedness. "You're not so round this time," she said.

"You think a girl, then?" Lilia said.

Rosa ignored her. She placed Lilia's face between her palms, fingering Lilia's cheeks with her fingertips. "Hmm," she said, closing her eyes and tapping the pads of her thumbs against Lilia's cheekbones.

"What?" Lilia said, sounding like a schoolgirl attempting not to laugh at something humorous. Lilia's cheeks flushed in the glow of Rosa's motherly touch, and so Rosa prolonged her examination. Fernando had come inside and stood beside his mother, eyes wide, watching Rosa.

"Come here, boy," Rosa said to him. She plucked a small pocketknife from her apron and before Fernando could protest she cut a single strand of hair from close to his scalp.

She motioned toward her bed. "Lie down," she said to Lilia, working the thin strand in a loop around a silver band she'd slipped from her own ring finger.

Lilia did as she was told. Fernando climbed in beside her as if ready for a nap with his mama. Rosa stood beside the bed and dangled the ring a few centimeters above the peak of Lilia's belly. She held her hand steady and watched as the ring at first swung from side to side before settling into a gentle, circular pattern.

Lilia smiled. "A girl?" she asked.

Rosa slid the ring back onto her finger and blew the strand of Fernando's hair from her fingertips, nodding. "Without question," she said.

"I knew so," Lilia said, smiling.

"Héctor came to see me yesterday," Rosa said. "He wanted to know everything about the day I spoke to Emanuel."

Lilia stood and followed Rosa outside again. "And what did you tell him? I know you don't care much for my husband."

"What I think of your husband doesn't matter. I understand his motives in seeking Emanuel, more so than I've understood his motives for anything else he's ever done. I didn't have much to tell him, as you know, but I told him what I could."

"And what was that?" Lilia said, looking out toward the road where a man peddling strawberries and sugarcane wheeled a wobbly cart.

"Same as I told you. I gave him all I could, which was little. I told him that Emanuel worked making deliveries to hotels, that he mentioned the name of one, Hotel Pacifico. Emanuel spoke of its loveliness, with beautiful polished stonework, vases of fresh flowers throughout, and a luxury store inside that sold jewelry and watches from Switzerland. I've never seen such a place, and I asked him to describe it to me. He said fine artwork and murals graced the walls, and the guests wore elegant, strange clothes."

"What did Héctor say, Rosa? Tell me everything. Did he think he could find Emanuel based on what you offered him? He speaks to me so little about what he's thinking."

Rosa tucked a wayward strand of her graying hair behind her ear. "After I gave him the name of this one hotel—surely one of many Emanuel services—Héctor seemed satisfied. He spoke of you, Lilia. He doesn't want to crush your hopes, but he doesn't want to build false expectations in you, either."

Lilia looked at her sandals, and Rosa couldn't be sure if she saw gratitude or embarrassment in Lilia's expression.

"Héctor's always seemed driven in ways that disrespect his heritage. But yesterday I realized his torment. His slumped shoulders, the worry lines in his young face. I saw his great pain regarding Alejandra."

Lilia nodded and shifted her weight from one foot to the other.

"He loves our children with heartbreaking abandon, Rosa," Lilia said. "Above all else, this I know about my husband."

"Héctor left, and I wished him well," Rosa said. "I'd like nothing more than for you to recover sweet Alejandra, Lilia."

"I understand this, Rosa. Héctor left for Acapulco. By bus. I packed him a sack of food, and he took what money he could. Maybe I'll see him tonight. Maybe tomorrow. I don't know how long the journey there and back will take him because I don't know how long finding Emanuel will take."

Rosa knew all this, but she nodded as if Lilia's words interested her.

"Héctor and I . . . we've fallen into a peaceful existence since our return from *el norte,* but our life together isn't what it once was," Lilia said. "Our marriage is like a shattered clay pot whose shards have been glued back in place. The thing is not what it once was, but it's been salvaged." She paused, then added, "Despite that, my love for him has never wavered."

How could Rosa explain to Lilia that such was the nature of marriage and partnerships? She lifted Fernando to her hip and kissed his dirty cheek. "You will come see your *tía* again soon, yes?" she said, touching her nose to the boy's.

The boy nodded, then squirmed free of Rosa's meaty arms.

"Everything evolves, Lilia. Do you see that shoreline there? When I was a girl it stretched much farther out at that point beyond the rocks, but the sea and the wind have changed the land during my lifetime. Though the shoreline along the bay remains sand and rock, its characteristics have changed."

Lilia studied the bay as if considering the familiar beach for the first time.

"The tide and wind over time can both erode and build a coast." Rosa paused, choosing her words with care, desiring to advise Lilia as would Lilia's mother, were she still in this world.

"I'm sure that what you're saying is true, Rosa. People change. That's natural. But what about love? Does love evolve? Can't time and experience erode love just as crashing seas and blowing storms can deteriorate a coast?"

Rosa took Lilia's hand and brought it to the crook of her neck. "Run your fingers along this bone, Lilia. Tell me what you feel."

Lilia did as she was told, gently sliding two fingers across the ridge in Rosa's flesh. "Right there. I feel a knot. What is that?" Lilia said.

"That's a place of strength that once was much weaker. When I was a girl I fell from a mango tree and snapped that bone. As the break healed, the pieces of bone meshed themselves and thickened, and their seam is now stronger than the rest of the bone. Difficult experiences do that to people's hearts and spirits just as they do to bone."

Fernando clung to Lilia's leg, his head heavy against her knee.

"We should get home," Lilia said, her fingers gently swirling through her boy's hair.

Rosa nodded. Despite whatever had happened at the border, Lilia was a good mother to Fernando. As she watched Lilia and Fernando make their way from her, she called to Lilia, "I'll pray Héctor's trip is successful."

"So will I," Lilia said.

Rosa sat on her bench and closed her eyes. Reclining against the wall of her house, she listened to the breeze rustling the bougainvillea vines, and wondered what would mean success for Héctor on his journey to find Emanuel. If he returned to say he'd discovered Alejandra was dead, then he and Lilia would have an answer and an end to the uncertainty. If he returned not knowing anything more than when he'd left, he and Lilia would remain tormented and unsure.

She decided her prayer should be that Héctor find Emanuel, that Emanuel somehow held information that directed Héctor to Alejandra's whereabouts, and that Alejandra was somewhere safe, well fed, comfortable, and healthy. Even as she offered up these prayers to God she shook her head, understanding what a far-fetched request this prayer was. The child had been separated from her mama and papa for more than three years. If she were alive but damaged in some way—oh, but Rosa couldn't let her mind go to such dark thoughts, to images of a suffering, uncared-for child.

Chapter 9

Emanuel

"Tell me what you know, *pendejo*!" Héctor said, his voice the low growl of a cornered dog.

He looked hard into Emanuel's eyes so that Emanuel felt Héctor's rage accumulating like sunlight through a lens. The intensity could spark a fire able to consume Emanuel's face. He'd never been studied with such concentrated hatred.

"What do you want to hear?" Emanuel said. "I haven't seen you in years. Last I saw Lilia she was headed to *el norte* to be with you. What do you want from me?"

Emanuel knew he wore the expression of a defenseless man encountering a dangerous strangeness, a man wary and unsure of the thing before him. Perhaps Héctor's mind had rotted on drugs, or some horrible tragedy had befallen him in Norteamérica, something that had left him sick in the head.

"My daughter. Where is she?" Héctor said, his fervor surging. He stepped so close Emanuel could smell him. His body's sweat was the sour odor of sickness, not the perspiration produced simply from hot sun or strenuous labor. Héctor smelled of worry, of aggression.

"How the hell should I know where your child is? Are you mad, man? I don't know your daughter, and I haven't seen your wife in several years. What's wrong with you?"

"You arranged a coyote for Lilia and my Alejandra. A man named Carlos, no?"

"Yeah, sure. Carlos was my uncle, but he's with God now. Why would you be angry at this?" he said in genuine bewilderment and vexation.

"Your uncle isn't with God, that I know. God would have no interest in a man like Carlos. Do you know what he did to my Lilia? Do you know that I haven't seen my Alejandra since that godforsaken day I left for the border? Do you know this, Emanuel?" Héctor was shouting at him now, jabbing a finger in Emanuel's face, his restraint not to kill Emanuel seemingly waning.

Emanuel scratched his scalp with both hands, backing up a half step as he tried to make sense of Héctor's accusations. "No," he said. "No, I don't know these things."

"You're a goddamned liar," Héctor said, again closing the distance between them.

"Tell me what you're talking about, Héctor. I haven't seen you or Lilia in years, and you've tracked me down like a crazed dog chasing his shadow. I don't know what you're after."

"You're right. I'm a man pursuing a shadow. I've been grasping at shadows a long time, and no doubt I'm mad. But I don't chase shadows from having gone mad; I am mad from having to chase shadows, shadows you created."

Emanuel stared at Héctor now, wondering if at any moment Héctor would pluck a knife from his waistband and slit him right there, gut him on the street and let the gulls pick his slick entrails for feast or entertainment.

Emanuel took a slow breath, steeling himself as if to talk a lunatic down from a ledge.

"Héctor. I don't understand what you want me to tell you. Ask me, and I'll answer."

"Where is my Alejandra?" Héctor said.

"I don't know. Explain to me why you think I'd have that information."

"The last time Lilia saw our daughter was the day Carlos forced Lilia to give Alejandra to some woman."

The insanity Héctor had been spewing began to slow and drift in the air between them. His strange, angry words were snapping together, forming a puzzle with a few mislaid pieces.

"Oh," Emanuel said. "Oh." His mind raced back to the accident that had taken his uncle's life. Authorities had said a woman had been with him, and that she, too, had perished.

"And Lilia made her way to *el norte,* only this bitch never arrived as planned. Can you understand this? Can you comprehend what I'm saying to you? We've not seen our only daughter again. Ever. She vanished. This woman who had her vanished as well. Your uncle Carlos was killed, we hear, and for that I thank God, except that Carlos held the only clue to Alejandra's whereabouts, to her coyote's whereabouts. So you, you *culo,* are all we have left. Do you understand now?"

"I didn't know, man. I don't know any of this. Yeah, my uncle died. But, oh God—why have you not come to me sooner?"

A new fury erupted in Héctor. "Come to you sooner? Do you think we haven't tried? No one knew where you were. No one in Puerto Isadore. Last we heard you were in Oaxaca City. I've been there. I have walked the streets like a madman, sat in the square for hours searching for your face among the crowds, asking people if they knew you, had seen you. No one knew where you were, and then, just like nothing, Rosa tells us she spoke to you, that you're living like a fat wealthy pig in Acapulco."

At this Emanuel laughed. "Does that look to be true, Héctor? Do I appear to be rolling in the money here in this place? You see this strip of hotels and these tourists, but do you know what lies in those hills?" He looked beyond the bay toward the smoky hills where he lived. "You can't possibly know, but I'll tell you. Crime is everywhere. I'm here to make a living off the fat tourists, that's true, but at the end of the day I go back into those hills and lock my door."

For the first time Héctor's eyes left Emanuel, and he stared down the street. A blue-and-white police truck passed by, its mounted guns at the ready. Emanuel followed Héctor's gaze.

"That truck cruises up and down this street all day so the rich *norteamericanos* feel safe. Where I live, not a kilometer away, I never see those trucks. They don't give a rat shit about the safety of the neighborhoods beyond the tourist district. What you're telling me about your daughter is news to me, Héctor. I always believed that my uncle had safely delivered Lilia and your baby across the line. I assumed when he and that lady were killed in the car wreck that she was just some loose woman he'd picked up. Carlos liked women."

"A woman was with him in the car? In the accident?" Héctor said, his eyes again locked with Emanuel's.

"Yes, yes. That much I know. I was in Oaxaca City when I was contacted that my uncle had died in an accident. A woman and her child were with him, but I assured the authorities my uncle was not married and had no children. I always assumed she was just some woman, you know?" Emanuel said, trying to shake the specter of possibility now forming in his mind. "The authorities described her as being around forty years old, twice Lilia's age, so I knew ... you know ... that the dead woman wasn't Lilia."

"Did the baby perish in the car?" Héctor said, his damp eyes glowing with intensity and a determination to see this interrogation through to a resolution that made sense to him.

Emanuel looked down at his hands and chose his words as if picking berries among thorns. "No. My uncle and the woman died, but authorities said the woman's baby lived. Because I didn't know the woman, I couldn't help them find her family or get her baby to its father. Those were not my concerns."

"This baby was a girl?" Héctor asked, his voice cracking.

"Yes," Emanuel said. The realization of what menaced Héctor now burned in Emanuel's mind with searing clarity. He understood what he'd set in motion the day he'd introduced Lilia to his uncle Carlos.

Héctor closed his eyes, his shoulders wilting as his mind and body worked various strands of information into something too heavy to bear standing upright. He leaned against a coconut palm that towered above them, and Emanuel was certain Héctor needed the tree's full support to hold him there. He wanted to reach out to Héctor, to pat him on the back and say a word of apology or encouragement.

"You . . ." he started, unsure what to say. "You could keep searching. Keep asking questions."

Héctor shook his head, his eyes still closed, his form heavy against the tree. "Where? How? That accident is long passed," he said.

"But," Emanuel said, "she has to be somewhere. I mean, doesn't she?"

Héctor clenched and relaxed his jaw then clenched it again. He nodded a slight nod. "Somewhere, yeah," he said, turning toward Emanuel.

"I'll tell you what I know about the accident, if you decide you want to go there, to the place where the wreck happened."

Héctor looked at Emanuel as if seeing him for the first time. His demeanor and expression so vastly changed that Emanuel took a step back.

"You didn't know," Héctor said. "You really didn't know about my daughter, did you?"

Emanuel shook his head. "No, man. I always believed Lilia and you were living somewhere in *el norte* with children. I wrote

Lilia off the day I last saw her. I wanted her, Héctor, but she only wanted you, and she made that clear to me."

"Do you know what your uncle did to her?"

Emanuel looked at the busy traffic now rolling along the stretch of street beyond them. How did he answer Héctor? Carlos had always been slick, arrogant. When Lilia made her decision to leave Mexico, and Emanuel could provide the way, he'd washed his hands of whatever happened after that. No, he didn't know what Carlos had done to Lilia, but he could guess. Maybe the price was worth paying if it meant Lilia arriving in *el norte* and reuniting with Héctor. Isn't that practically what she'd said to Emanuel, that she'd pay whatever she could? Emanuel should not be taken to task for helping her gain what she so desperately wanted.

"No," he said. "Lilia wanted a way to you, and I provided it. I spoke neither to her nor to my uncle after I delivered her to him and they departed."

"Can you help me get to that place?" Héctor said. "To where my daughter is last known to have been?"

"Yeah, sure. Of course. The trip will take you a few days by bus. But why not try?" Emanuel said.

"I'll need more money. For traveling that far north. For bus fare and God knows what else. My field labor in Puerto Isadore pays me centavos," Héctor said, shaking his head as if this were all too much too fast.

Emanuel thought of Diego, of the offers for quick money he'd mentioned just that morning.

"I have a friend who may be able to help you," Emanuel said. "My friend Diego the Magnificent."

"His name?" Héctor said, raising his eyebrows. "He's magnificent, is he? That's a good start."

"I'll introduce you," Emanuel said.

Chapter 10

Lilia

Lilia and Héctor sat on hard, wooden chairs across a cluttered desk from the village priest. Sitting, standing, and even lying flat was becoming increasingly burdensome, and Lilia suspected this child she carried would arrive larger than either of her others had come into this world. A metal fan, rusted and squeaking, oscillated from a high shelf, with each rotation rustling three disheveled stacks of papers, held in place on the desk by large conch shells that were bleached by sun and salt.

"What do you think could have happened to her after the accident, Father?" Héctor said.

Upon Lilia and Héctor's return to Puerto Isadore from *el norte,* Lilia had visited the village priest and asked him for his wisdom and guidance. The priest was a good man and had always provided Lilia with just the right prayer to help her negotiate the difficult situations in her life. At her grandmother's funeral, Lilia had wept with him, and he'd assured her that while the old woman had moved on to a place of deserved peace, her spirit and influence would remain a real part of Lilia forever. "Bones turn to dust," he'd said, "but love endures forever."

When she'd come to consult him after her return to Mexico, he'd been less comforting, saying only that he'd pray for Alejandra's well-being and safe return. At the time Lilia had felt great disappointment, wishing the priest had provided some helpful insight. But then, what could he have possibly said that would have changed anything?

Now, because of their locating Emanuel, Lilia and Héctor had renewed hope and curiosity about the possibilities.

The priest pulled a tattered rectangular document from his desk drawer and unfolded the paper with slow certainty. He pushed aside a couple of the stacks on his desk, and, smoothing the paper flat across his desktop, said, "Here's a map of our country. We know your Alejandra was last seen alive. We can keep faith that she's out there someplace. God heard our prayers, Lilia," the priest said, smiling weakly, his gold-brown eyes tired but comforting.

"She has to be somewhere, Father, waiting for me to come to her. I want to believe that somehow Alejandra expects her mama and papa will be with her again, the way we always returned from the fields when she was a baby and *Abuela* kept her during our workdays." Lilia looked down at a fat cockroach crawling along the cracked plaster wall beside them. "Is this foolish talk, Father?"

The priest shook his head, but before he could form an answer, Héctor said, "Just tell us the possibilities. Where might she be and how do we begin to locate her, to get her home?"

The priest took a sip of water from a pale blue clay cup on his desk. "Of course I can't answer with certainty, but you ask for possibilities. Perhaps she was hospitalized or ... who knows? I'm guessing." He studied Héctor's face a moment then looked at Lilia. "We can look into what orphanages are near where she was last seen." He took a pair of wire-rimmed glasses from his breast pocket. After slipping them onto the bridge of his nose, he dragged a stubby finger across the map.

Lilia edged forward in her chair, tracing his finger's invisible trail across Mexico.

"We were to meet in *el norte* in a place called Brownsville. For years I imagined Alejandra in that place. But now we know she never arrived there," Lilia said.

"No," Héctor said. "Emanuel said the accident was in a place called Matamoros."

The priest wrinkled his brow and tapped a finger three times on the spot that was Brownsville. "Hmm. Matamoros," he mumbled. "Yes."

Lilia looked to Héctor for guidance, uncertain whether the priest had never heard of this place or if he possessed specific information about it.

"Emanuel said Matamoros is in the state of Tamaulipas," he said.

"Yes," the priest said again. "Yes, of course. Tamaulipas is a border state. Brownsville borders Tamaulipas. And there is your city of Matamoros." He drummed the nail of his index finger on the map.

The three leaned in closer, examining the tiny word Matamoros as if the letters could reveal great secrets.

"We could contact the authorities in that area and ask what they would do with an unclaimed child."

Héctor and Lilia nodded, but neither spoke. Héctor seemed to need the priest to keep talking, to put forth scenarios that made sense and fit with what pieces of information—few as they were—that he and Lilia already knew.

"So we can make those calls. I will help you with this. The path that lies before us turns in ways that make it impossible to predict, but, nonetheless, we have a path. Do you have photos of her? If we locate her she'll have changed in looks since last you saw her. How old was your child when you lost her?" The priest leaned back in his chair, weaving his short thick fingers across his chest as if preparing to listen for a while.

"She was a baby," Héctor said.

"Yes, I had to wean her before I crossed. I would've nursed her many more months, but in preparation for her crossing I had to introduce her to a bottle. She's nearly four years old now," Lilia said, crossing her arms across her chest, recalling those painful days of throbbing breasts full of milk that no baby would suckle.

"Then now she's walking. She's talking. Your little baby is a girl now. She'll have changed in looks," the priest said. "Do you recall any birthmarks, any distinguishing markings?"

Héctor looked at Lilia to answer this for them, but all she could see when she envisioned Alejandra was a beautiful baby girl with thick black hair. Her small body had no imperfections, no marks of distinction other than she smelled of lavender and her hair stuck out at all angles since birth, but even those characteristics, scent and baby hair, would have changed.

"I'll know my baby when I see her," Lilia said, looking the priest in the eye.

"And if we find her we'll know by the circumstances," Héctor said. "We'll find her because someone will remember the parentless child of the car accident, and we'll piece together the details."

"And that woman and the evil coyote Carlos who died in the accident . . . I can describe every detail of them. He stunk of sweat and cinnamon, and she wore her nails and makeup in shades of purple. I'll never forget every detail of those horrible people. I can tell any police officer these things." Lilia sat straight in her chair, her confidence and hope finding buoyancy in this choppy sea of a situation. For once she had an answer, a factual answer, instead of guesses and unfulfilled wishes, regarding her missing child.

"And these names, Carlos and . . . Do you recall the woman's name?" the priest said. "These are real names? These are the names on these people's paperwork? On the papers they'd have had with them in the vehicle?"

"Yes. At least the man. Authorities contacted his nephew Emanuel, so his papers must have had the correct identifying information. I can't answer about the woman," Héctor said.

"My coyote called the woman Matilde. Who knows if that name was real," Lilia said.

She had not thought on the details of that most horrific day since she'd drifted into a fitful sleep, drained and weary from physical exhaustion and mental anguish in the border shack where she'd collapsed that night, anticipating Alejandra's arrival the following morning. But now, over three years later, back in her village, in the presence of the priest and Héctor, somehow the events filled her mind with such clarity she gasped, bringing both hands flat on the priest's desk before her as if to steady herself.

"Ernesto," she whispered.

The priest and Héctor stared at her.

"Ernesto," she repeated. "Ernesto! Alejandra is Ernesto. My God, I just remembered. I don't know that this will help. But that information has to help, doesn't it, Father? Ernesto!"

"Ernesto?" the priest said, looking from Lilia to Héctor and back to Lilia.

Lilia had suffered these years to erase from her mind the day she'd handed Alejandra over to Matilde. Matilde, that strange woman in the musty house with unfamiliar music drifting on sour, suffocating air. Lilia shook her head now at the memory, an instinctive reaction to ward off the painful images that had been poisonous to any budding hope since the moment she'd walked with Carlos's firm grip on her wrist from that woman's house. Only now she had to think, to reach deep and summon whatever else she could recall that might help when pieced together with forthcoming clues to Alejandra's whereabouts.

"The woman, Matilde, told me that the paper, the document she'd use at the border, would state that Alejandra was a boy. She told me not to worry, that to border patrol officers all babies look alike, and that they'd not remove Alejandra's clothing to check. She said Alejandra's name would be Ernesto during her crossing."

"Why?" Héctor said.

The question surprised Lilia. What did Héctor mean why? He must have read in her eyes her thoughts because he added, "She's a beautiful girl. Why couldn't this woman let her remain a girl? Why not give her papers with a girl's name?"

Lilia thought the answer obvious. "I suppose she had no papers for girls, but she had papers for a boy about Alejandra's age," she said. "Wouldn't you assume that?" She wished as soon as she'd spoken that her words were tiny seeds she could sweep into her mouth and swallow whole.

"I wasn't involved in your dealing with that woman or with Carlos, or with any of the decisions you made during your crossing. You chose to cross without telling me, without my blessing. Nothing is obvious to me about any of this." His rising voice in the priest's presence embarrassed Lilia, but if Héctor noticed he didn't care.

"I wasn't consulted then, though I would have assumed you'd consult me. I won't assume anything again, Lilia." His words, slow and deliberate, rolled like hot coals across her soul, burning additional, permanent, painful reminders of her bad choices. "If this Matilde was a professional coyote, one to be entrusted with our most precious possession, the assumption I'd make is that she'd have papers for both boys and girls."

The priest cleared his throat. Lilia shifted her gaze from her lap to the priest, though she felt Héctor's eyes remaining on her. "So this woman gave your child papers with the name Ernesto," the priest said. "This is helpful information. Perhaps they were forged documents or maybe they were the papers from a real child named Ernesto. If we contact orphanages and authorities near the accident scene and provide this name, perhaps that will trigger a memory that will lead you to Alejandra." Lilia nodded, grateful for his encouragement.

"Let me get to work on this," the priest said. "Give me a day or so to gather names of orphanages and the like in that area. How do you plan to proceed once you have those names?" He looked to Héctor now, and Lilia understood that even if the priest felt sympathy toward a young, expectant mother who'd lost her firstborn child, the business dealings regarding this issue would be made man to man, and Lilia would have no say in how the remainder of the process of recovering her child unfolded. This new baby was due in eight weeks, and Lilia considered how wonderful and ironic the timing if Alejandra and the little one came to her at the same time.

The cockroach emerged from behind a wooden crucifix mounted on the wall above the priest's head. As the men discussed Héctor's plan to travel north to find Alejandra, Lilia sat quietly with her hands clenched in her lap and watched the insect, his thin antennae quivering wildly as if searching for something unseen but important.

Chapter 11

The Village Priest

The village priest lit a cigarette and dropped the lighter into the top drawer of his desk. He'd been on hold with a police station in Matamoros for nearly a minute, and he considered hanging up. He sought information about the accident that had killed the coyotes Carlos and Matilde, but he feared no information awaited him on the other end of the line.

When the officer finally returned to the phone, he said, "If this child was a baby then she may have landed at Casa de Esperanza. This place is for orphaned babies, and it's not far from here." He paused. "This is all I can tell you. You must understand, we have plenty of car crashes around here, and we have even more orphans. Good luck, Padre."

"Do you have a number for this place?" the priest asked in a rush, afraid the police officer would end the call. "Perhaps a name of the priest or person in charge there?" The policeman on the other end of the line sighed like he had a thousand more important obligations than reconnecting some child from a far away village to her irresponsible parents.

The officer asked the priest to hold the line again and after another equally long wait he returned to the phone with a number. The priest wondered if the officer were a godly man and if he took satisfaction from helping others.

He thanked the officer and hung up. The priest sat smoking his cigarette, watching the shadow thrown onto his desk and floor from the large banana tree outside his open window. Somewhere a horse whinnied and a cock crowed. The priest sucked the last sweet smoke then crushed his cigarette on the concrete floor beneath his shoe.

Because his office had one of the few telephones in Puerto Isadore he was often asked to make calls or to allow others to do so. He understood and accepted this as part of his job, and he didn't mind this too much. He was certain Armando down at *la farmacia,* also in possession of a phone, greatly enjoyed listening in on patrons' phone calls, which is why many preferred to visit the priest for their telephone needs. He was such a gossip and a busybody, that Armando.

The priest stared at the pack of smokes on his desk and considered lighting another one. Instead he put the pack in his breast pocket and closed his eyes. His next call would be either the end of a long journey or the beginning of one. He supposed the journey began that day nearly four years ago when he presided over Alejandra's baptism. Soon after that he'd sat with Lilia in her home during her grandmother's wake. He recalled comforting her that evening for two passings: the old woman's passing to the afterlife, and Héctor's passing across *la línea* into *el norte.* That time, as today, seemed to be a crossroads for Héctor and Lilia's family. Looking back now, the priest realized the intersection of those two losses in Lilia's life ignited her interest in leaving Puerto Isadore, in getting to *el norte.*

He pulled the pack of cigarettes from his pocket and shook one into his palm. He reached into the drawer and withdrew a lighter. He'd known Lilia since her birth and had presided over both her *quinceañera* and her marriage to Héctor. In ways she'd been an orphan herself, having never known her father or mother, the first and only child of her unmarried parents. Ah, but Crucita, he thought, what a good and strong woman she had been, a wonderful grandmother turned mother after Lilia's mama died in childbirth.

The priest put his head in his hands and prayed before picking up the receiver to make the second call.

"Dear Father in Heaven, please guide me as I call this place in Matamoros, this place for lost children, and help me ask the correct questions, guide me to the right person who can help me reunite this lost child to her parents. If she is out there in this world somewhere, Father, help me locate her, and help me get her parents reunited with her. In the name of the Father, the Son, and the Holy Spirit. Amen."

Then, to Saint Nicholas, the wonder-worker and patron saint of children, he uttered, "Please, continue to guard this child Alejandra. Amen."

And to Nuestra Señora de Guadalupe, he prayed, "Please guide my efforts on behalf of Héctor, Lilia, and little Alejandra. Amen."

After praying he dialed the number. If the staff at this orphanage had no recollection of a child fitting Alejandra's description and story, the story of a girl named Ernesto arriving there more than three years ago, then perhaps the door on this sad situation would be closed, and his role for Héctor and Lilia would be to help them move along with their lives and their other children's lives. He could not think of another course.

On the fifth ring a woman answered the phone, and the priest cleared his throat and sat up in his chair.

"Yes, hello. Good afternoon. To whom am I speaking, please?" he said, uncertain how else to begin.

"This is Karolina. May I help you?"

"Yes, I hope you can, please, Karolina. I'm calling you from Puerto Isadore. In Oaxaca. My name is Jesús Benitez. I'm a priest in search of a child, a particular child," he said. When the woman offered no reply but "Uh-huh," he continued. "She is the child of a couple in my village, and they have reason to believe she may be there. This story is long, but the point is this: She would be almost four years old now."

"Certainly I'll try to help you, Padre, but we have many children here," she said.

"This girl was in a car accident, and the others in the car with her perished. The parents have recently discovered that their baby, her name is Alejandra, survived that accident. Only she had papers stating her name to be Ernesto."

"Ernesto?"

"Yes, it's a long story as I said. She would be nearing her fourth birthday. She is a beautiful child. I christened her," he said with pride and with emphasis to show that he had a bit of personal interest in her recovery. Perhaps that would help.

"Alejandra, but Ernesto. Okay, and when would she have arrived here? Recently?"

"Ah, no, no. The accident was in Matamoros about three, maybe three and a half, years ago. So you see she would look a bit different now than when we last saw her." He listened to silence on the other end of the line. "Hello?"

"I'm here," she said. "But you say three and a half years ago, Padre? You understand that is a long time. We have here children from newborns to four years old. We are a home for little ones only. After the age of four, or as close to four as we can estimate, since we can only guess at many of these children's ages, we send them to other places. So . . ." Her voice trailed off as if the priest were expected to follow her line of thought.

"So," the priest said, "maybe she is there among your children?"

"That's a possibility, but if she had obviously fake papers, we wouldn't know her name to be Alejandra, if she came here at all. And if she did arrive here that long ago, she may have been adopted. And if she came here but was not adopted then maybe she is still here, or maybe if she is close to the age of four she has already left us to go to one of the other orphanages or homes where we send our older ones. Understand me, we are a place especially for the babies. We don't keep them when they are school age."

Now the priest sighed, unsure how to proceed. "Many ifs," he finally managed to say.

"Of course, and surely this news doesn't surprise you. Three and a half years is a long while."

"Have you worked there many years?" he said.

"No, Padre. I'm here just six months, and the lady before me, she was here two years," Karolina said. "You're far away, down in Oaxaca. Do you know much about our orphanage and about Matamoros?"

"Only what you're telling me. I'm sorry, but I've never been that far north," he said.

"The poverty here is significant. So many people hungry and without jobs. We have more babies here than most orphanages elsewhere, I suspect. The garbage dump for many surrounding towns is located here, and it covers a vast expanse. Many children live in the dump with their mothers and usually no fathers. Many have lived in the dump their whole lives."

"This is terrible," the priest said, wondering if this could be true.

"And the people who live in the dump, they wait on the trash truck to arrive, and they fight over the trash, and a whole system, a pecking order, exists among these people. The men fight for who gets to pick through the trash first, then the prostitutes come in and service the men in order to get their cut of the food the men have picked from the trash. The children live in dirty diapers if they have diapers at all, and they are malnourished, and so are their mothers and fathers, too, if the fathers are there."

The priest prayed for these people of the trash. "My God," he said.

"So we get babies from this dump and from our streets and of course from situations as you describe involving accidents. Abandoned babies are common here. We're a busy place."

"Okay," he said, thinking. "Still, Alejandra may be there," he said more to himself than to the woman. "I suppose her parents should go there, to visit your orphanage. If they see their daughter they will know her."

"Yes, certainly they may come here. We'd need proper documentation. We'd need to know more of the circumstances of this long story you refer to, but, yes, sure. We love to reunite children with loving families, but I must tell you the chances of this girl being here . . . I just don't know."

"And one last question," he said. "When your babies there reach the age of four, where is this place you send them?"

"Oh, that's not so simple. They could go to one of many places. We have many orphanages for school-age children all over northern Mexico. Tracking her after her departure from here would prove very difficult, I suspect."

"Then her father needs to get there soon, before she's sent away with the four-year-olds. And if he gets there, and she's been sent away, then . . . then what?"

"Then if he wants to continue searching the other orphanages, he may be here for a while. Their records are not so great on children whose names we never knew."

"Alejandra's father's name is Héctor, Héctor Santos, and he will be coming to you as soon as he can get there."

The priest thanked Karolina and replaced the receiver onto the phone. He smoked the remainder of his cigarette and decided he would go home for a beer and sleep and would tell Héctor and Lilia the news tomorrow, which felt like little news at all.

On his walk home he thanked God for the beauty around him, for the goats grazing on weeds in the cemetery, for a squealing piglet and the chickens he passed in the old widower's yard, for the bountiful sea and the fruits and vegetables available to him. His people were not wealthy by any standard, but this community could eat food they grew and caught and prepared. Only the poorest among them asked for handouts, and even then, the village took care of these people. He prayed for the children of the dump, and wondered how such a thing could be.

Chapter 12

Héctor

They stood away from the swelling crowd of *norteamericanos* but close enough that Héctor could see the jagged rocks and hear the rush of water in and out of the gulch far below them. The foam sizzled, an almost melodic sound, as the waves crashed repeatedly against the dark volcanic rock. As rapidly as they'd burst forth, the waves would retreat, shrinking back into the sea with equal violence.

In certain circumstances perhaps the rhythm of ebb and flow could lull a man to sleep, but not today. Héctor watched the tourists, their skin white like the underside of fish, as if they lacked some important nutrient. Bulky cameras dangled from some of their necks, while others among them clutched shopping bags of souvenirs or held smaller cameras to their sunglassed faces, filming the jagged cliffs, the crashing white foam, and the divers who readied themselves high atop the opposite crag, beyond the gulch. The two cliffs, split by the lapping tongue of sea that separated Héctor, Emanuel, and the herd of tourists from the divers, seemed alive, like the mouth of a hungry beast, as if the world itself were licking its lips, anticipating a taste of the men about to dive into the gorge. Héctor shook his head.

"That's a long way down," he said, jutting his chin at the churning surf below.

Emanuel nodded, but because his eyes revealed no hint of concern for the divers, Héctor decided not to voice his alarm. Yet as he watched the water drop six or eight meters before it rushed in and refilled the gulch, he wondered about the timing of it all. How shallow was that strip of water when the tide dipped to its lowest? And how deep did it rise at its height?

"They know their business, you know?" Emanuel said, pointing toward three divers scaling the gray- and rust-colored rock face as if they were not men at all but rather some primitive species of monkey at play, their hands and feet making light work of what surely required greater strength and a strain of bravery mere men did not possess.

"They watch the water then they leap as the gulch fills, landing so they don't hit bottom."

Héctor had not noticed the balcony of the hotel behind them, now filling with more spectators, until Emanuel turned and said, "See them all there? They eat this shit up like sweet cake. They all, of course, secretly hope to see blood. To witness a miscalculation and a head splattered on stone, or a body crumpled in the shallows."

"Does that ever happen?" Héctor said, trying to imitate Emanuel's coolness.

"Maybe today," Emanuel said, smiling. "That's Diego there, the one in the red suit."

Way up on top of the cliff a dark-skinned man made the sign of the cross before swinging his arms wildly in wide circles as if to loosen his shoulders or to take flight with the frigate birds that drifted on currents high above them, occasionally swooping down to skim an unfortunate fish who'd risen too close to the surface.

"Diego the Magnificent?" Héctor said, studying the man's small stature, his sun-blackened skin, and his narrow waist.

Héctor's bowels turned liquid at the thought of jumping from such a height.

"Yes," Emanuel said, his smile wider still, as if he were in on a secret or a joke Héctor couldn't understand. "He's the man. He's been doing this since he was a boy."

The crowd of spectators had thickened and their excitement and impatience seemed to intensify as men checked their watches and women tinkered with their cameras and jostled restless children.

As Héctor studied the onlookers, something in their collective demeanor changed, and Héctor shifted his gaze back to the opposite cliff top where two men in matching black swimsuits raised their arms in unison.

They lowered their arms, then as they raised them a second time, they bent their knees and together sprang from the cliff, plummeting thirty-five meters like arrows shot into the foaming surf below. Queasiness rolled through Héctor's stomach, and he'd not realized he'd held his breath until he exhaled as the men popped through the water's surface. He could not believe what he'd just seen. Oh, to be so brave! He pumped his fists into the air, cheering along with the throng of sunburned strangers.

"How can they do that?" he said to Emanuel.

"Practice," Emanuel said, pointing. "Diego's next."

Diego stood between two men. He looked at each of them, nodded, then, as if commanded by the voice of God that only they could hear, the three men plunged forward in harmony. The two on the outside dove like seabirds who'd spotted the silver flash of a rising fish, but Diego somersaulted through the air between them, churning like a greased wheel before straightening and darting into the narrow inlet with the slightest splash, a whisper of an instant after the other two divers disappeared beneath the white foam.

"I've got to meet this guy," Héctor said, clapping. "He's magnificent, indeed!"

"Come, we'll get a beer and wait for him to finish." Emanuel turned and walked up the hill.

The first two divers were nearly halfway up the craggy face, climbing to the precipice, perhaps for another dive.

Not wanting to leave the show, but eager to set the process in motion for finding Alejandra, Héctor trailed behind Emanuel. He glanced back at the churning water below from where the great diver had emerged. Diego had already climbed several meters up the jagged rocks on his return to the top of the cliff. Now that Héctor had seen Diego, had witnessed his strength, his bravery, and the crowds of strangers who'd come to see this man, Héctor's hope took shape where for years only a weak shadow had flickered.

Héctor had never seen the famous wrestlers of Mexico City, but he'd read about them in comic books since he'd been a young boy. Those wrestlers had inspired Héctor in his youth; they were so strong that lesser men quivered in their presence and crowds gathered to witness their strength and bravery. Perhaps Emanuel's friend, this diver, would prove to be like those wrestlers.

This powerful man, Diego the Magnificent, would help Héctor make the money he'd need to proceed to Matamoros, enough money for bus fare, meals, and lodging if necessary. Enough money to pay for Alejandra if the orphanage forced Héctor to adopt back his own child. Enough money to line the pockets of corrupt officials if he had to do so. Héctor couldn't imagine what such profitable work would entail. Surely Diego wouldn't want Héctor to dive from the cliffs.

He and Emanuel left the cliffs and the balmy sea winds and wound their way down a hard path behind the hotel. The cooling breeze gave way to humid heat and the stench of the hotel's garbage bins. A blackbird worked a gray scrap from the trash and flapped up to the roof's edge to devour its find.

In the rooftop's sunlight, the bird's yellow eyes revealed its undeserved arrogance, and its feathers exposed a purplish and green sheen not visible in tree shade. It gobbled the scrap and squawked at the men as they passed. What a nasty bird, spending its life among bits of hot, smelly trash when the vast beautiful sea and seashore lay so nearby. If Héctor were a bird, he would be a frigate bird or a shearwater, snatching fish and small turtles from the surface of the sea for nourishment. He considered Diego the Magnificent, whom he would soon meet, and he knew that if the hand of God were to reach down and change Diego into a bird he, too, would be a great-winged bird of the sea, and nothing like the greasy blackbird with its harsh shriek and diet of discarded refuse.

The three of them sat at a metal picnic table, its paint chipped and faded a green not unlike the color of the sea foam beyond the cliffs. They sat in the sun because the shaded tables were occupied and too close together, and Emanuel seemed to feel this discussion should be held away from listening ears. Héctor and Emanuel had waited nearly forty-five minutes for Diego, their beers long gone, and sweat rolled down Héctor's neck.

Diego held a bottle of tamarind juice, its contents half consumed. He tipped it up and finished it off, and Héctor wished he had something cold and sweet to drink. "So these guys I know," Diego said, setting the empty bottle on the table, "they may have work for you if you're a good match, Héctor. They're fishermen."

Héctor wanted to ask Diego about his diving, how he mustered such courage and how long he'd been diving from these cliffs. Had he just jumped on a whim one day and liked the experience, or had he practiced on lesser cliffs somewhere up or down the coastline?

Héctor glanced at Emanuel, but Emanuel kept his eyes on Diego. Emanuel had facilitated this meeting with Diego with the slim possibility something might work out for Héctor, whatever it would be, but otherwise Emanuel seemed as uncertain about the details as did Héctor.

"I can fish," Héctor said. "I grew up on the coast." But even as he said this he doubted he understood fully what was being presented to him.

"I'm sure. Of course you can," Diego said, nodding, looking as if he could walk away from this conversation and jump from the nearest cliff or stay right here and talk about fishing or shady dealings, and none of it would elevate his pulse.

Diego wore a thin, hooded sweatshirt, unzipped with no shirt beneath it. The sleeves had been cut off, leaving tattered edges. A bead of sweat or seawater rolled down his bare chest. Somehow the outfit seemed wrong to Héctor, and he wished Diego wore something more elaborate and flashy, something to indicate to passersby that the famed cliff diver of La Quebrada was in their presence. No one would give Diego a second glance in that attire, and this disappointed Héctor. Diego was Héctor's first encounter with a famous personality, and he wished the meeting involved more fanfare.

"My little girl's been taken from me," Héctor said, unsure what details Emanuel had given Diego. "I'll do anything to get her back. If you have a job I've never done, I'll learn how to do it. I'm a quick study, and I need to make enough money to hunt for my daughter, however long the search takes." He wanted to sound brave, but even as he spoke he knew he could never dive from a cliff, knew he'd never have hordes of strangers cheering for him and snapping photos of him to take back to their homes far away. No one had ever called him "Héctor the Magnificent," and he realized how weak and despairing he must sound to this courageous and revered athlete and even to Emanuel.

"The guys I know are fishermen, like I said. I can't tell you what other endeavors they may undertake, but they have asked me about reliable, short-term help. My father's company has delivery trucks, you know? Emanuel drives one. That's an easy way to get supplies moved. These guys, on occasion, have asked to use a little space in the trucks." Diego scratched his temple like all this explaining wore him thin.

"Héctor's crossed *la línea* and come back, so he's seen some things, you know?" Emanuel said. "You can trust him. Set him up with your friends, and maybe this connection will be mutually beneficial."

Héctor had hated Emanuel for so long that hearing him speak on his behalf left Héctor uneasy, as if everything in this world stood imperceptibly off-kilter, and the sum total of the shifting left a terrifying and strange disorder.

No, if God were to craft Héctor into a bird, he'd make him a useless yellow-eyed blackbird living off man's trash. Diego would race the world's shores as a shearwater or some other great and powerful creature, but Héctor? He could never be so bold, even as a bird.

Emanuel pulled his cap down low and looked away. Héctor caught a hint of a grin as Emanuel turned, and his old distrust of Emanuel stirred.

Diego stood. "So I'll talk to these guys. I'll tell them you're interested in short-term work. No guarantees."

He raised his closed hand and bumped fists first with Emanuel then with Héctor, before turning and walking away, the back of his sweatshirt boasting in red lettering: DIEGO THE MAGNIFICENT. Héctor prayed a quick and silent prayer: *"God, let his magnificence be so."*

Chapter 13

Emanuel

Héctor's eyes shone bright, alert, and he could not stand still, like a child in need of taking a piss.

"So, Héctor," Emanuel said. "This job, I'm sure, involves fishing, but these guys Diego knows . . . I suspect the work entails more than catching snapper and baiting hooks for vacationers."

"Okay. Then what's the work? I just need to raise enough cash to get me to Matamoros and do whatever I have to do to find and retrieve my little girl," Héctor said, his willingness seeping from him like cheap cologne applied with zest.

Emanuel sat on the edge of his bed and tossed a thin blanket and pillow to Héctor. He longed for sleep and was unaccustomed to houseguests except for an occasional visit from Ana María. Diego had sent word from the fisherman that Héctor should be at the dock the following afternoon.

"I'm not going to guess what the work is, man. You'll find out soon enough. You know, Héctor, this isn't Puerto Isadore," he said, reaching for the lamp.

"What's that mean?" Héctor said.

Emanuel shifted in his bed, weary of Héctor's company. "It means, I know you lived in *el norte,* so maybe you've seen things I never have. But Acapulco is not so simple like your village. That's all I'm saying."

Héctor rustled in the darkness, settling into his makeshift

bed. Emanuel waited for more questions. When none came, he said, "Life here is fast paced. Not all people are good, you know? This isn't a backward-ass village like Puerto Isadore."

"All people aren't good anywhere you go, not just here," Héctor said.

Emanuel recalled the way Lilia had spoken of Héctor when he'd left her behind in Puerto Isadore and headed to the border, how she believed in her husband's dreams even when Emanuel had promised that he could take better care of her and that he'd never abandon her for *el norte*. For the first time, Emanuel saw a similarity between Lilia and Héctor, but the characteristics that made Lilia so desirable, aside from her physical beauty, were her trusting nature and childlike simplicity, and these traits were ill suited in a man. They made Héctor seem like a fool.

"I'm going to sleep," Emanuel said.

"Hey, thanks for hooking me up with these guys, Emanuel."

"It's nothing," Emanuel said, grateful for the darkness, the day's end, and rest.

Why Lilia had chosen Héctor over him, he could not understand.

Chapter 14

Héctor

Diego had told him the boats arrived from their charters around four or four thirty in the afternoon, and so Héctor found his way to the marina at three thirty and watched with great curiosity as boats of varying sizes eased into their moorings, their occupants windblown and colored by the sun. The boats were fancier than the skiffs he was accustomed to seeing in the bay at Puerto Isadore, and he wondered if fishermen on boats such as these were luckier than those who fished from simple skiffs. Could the fish know what type of vessel bobbed above them in the sea?

He walked the dock reading the names on the boats as they arrived. Diego had said the name of the boat was *Gabriela de la Costa,* and so this was the name he searched for among the vessels. When he saw her he was not disappointed, though he couldn't imagine any boat that would disappoint here. A larger man steered the *Gabriela* toward the dock while another leaner one prepared lines for securing her. A couple sat on the bow as if relaxing or simply staying out of the men's way.

Héctor continued his meandering about the waterfront, giving the men time to secure the mooring and settle up with their clients. Several curious seagulls flitted along the dock, eager for leftover bait tossed aside by fishermen. Héctor made his way down the marina and back at a leisurely pace, though doing so took great restraint. He watched the men as they shook hands with the couple and accepted payment from them for the day spent fishing. Héctor could not tell at that distance, of course, how much the couple paid. The day was bright with only a slight breeze, and Héctor could imagine far worse ways to make a living than drifting on the clear Pacific, rigging lines and chatting with new friends about the weather and fish and the sea.

"How's it going?" Héctor said, approaching the boat.

"Good. You?" The thinner man spoke as he sprayed blood and bits of fish from the hull. The heavier man heaved a large blue-gray fish from a white cooler and flopped it onto the dock.

Héctor extended a hand to the big man who was nearer him than the thin man and whose hands were now free but slick with fish.

"Diego sent me," Héctor said. "I'm Héctor. Diego said you might have some work for me."

"Ignacio," the large man said, shaking Héctor's hand. "Yeah, Diego mentioned you." He turned and went back to work, putting packs of little baitfish into a small red cooler of ice. "That's Santiago," he said, motioning toward his thin counterpart.

Santiago glanced up, coiling the hose he'd used to spray out the boat. "What's up, Héctor? You're pals with Diego the Magnificent, eh?"

The thought of being a friend of the famous Diego seemed strange. Could he really say yes, they were pals, after only meeting him once? "We've met," Héctor said. "He knows a guy I know from my village, Emanuel."

"He knows a guy you know," Santiago said in a voice as free of emotion as the dead fish.

"Yes, my friend works for Diego's dad in Acapulco. I grew up down the coast from here. Puerto Isadore. I've done some fishing, though never on a boat this nice. I'm a quick learner. If you can use me."

Ignacio slipped a long, thin blade from a sheath on his belt. He knelt beside the fish and turned it so its large, square head was at his knee. Héctor had never gutted such a fish and wondered about its weight and what kind it was.

"You ever caught dorado?" Ignacio said, inserting the point of the knife into the fish, just behind its large, glazed eye.

"No," Héctor admitted, wishing he could say yes. "How much does that one weigh?"

"He's a good ten kilograms, eh, Santiago?" Ignacio said, gliding the knife down the fish's side as if it were nothing but water.

Santiago shrugged. "Eight or ten, yeah," he said.

After Ignacio had cut the length of the fish just beneath its spine, he brought the blade around to its yellow belly, making a parallel cut. He lifted a long pink fillet from the carcass. "How about that?" he said, grinning. "Sweetest fish there is."

Judging by Ignacio's belly, Héctor trusted his opinion.

Ignacio flipped the fish over and repeated the cutting pattern on its other side. In a moment, two thick fillets were on ice in the large cooler. He tossed the remains of the fish overboard, and before it had drifted or sunk from sight four squawking gulls descended, pecking at and fighting over the carcass.

Santiago dug two cans of Pacifico beer from deep in the cooler beneath the fish fillets and passed one to Héctor. "So you think you're cut out to be a fisherman?" he said.

Héctor wanted to say that he was cut out to be anything he put his mind to being. "Sure," he said, accepting the cold can and wondering what Diego had told them about Alejandra and why he needed this short-term work.

"Ignacio and I run the boat, and we only need an extra hand

on occasion, you understand, when one of us can't be here," Santiago said.

"But we may have some work coming up," Ignacio said. "A job or two when we can't both be there, so we need to have someone on standby, you know. To help when needed."

Héctor sipped the icy beer. While this sounded as if, yes, Ignacio and Santiago could employ him, the offer, if this was an offer, didn't sound like the plentiful, quick money he'd been hoping to make. "Okay," he said.

Santiago took a seat on the cooler. His arms and legs were sinewy, as if he were nothing but bone, ropes of muscle, and sun-blackened skin. Both men wore sunglasses and caps.

"Some days we stay close to shore, bottom-fishing, depending what the paying customers want, you see?" Santiago said. "On those days we fish for snapper. Sometimes roosterfish. But most days, like today, we go offshore and troll for dorado, sailfish, marlin, tuna, wahoo, the bigger fish."

"The snapper are delicious and plentiful, but they're not so sexy like the big fish," Ignacio said.

Héctor nodded. He could understand that. He'd seen the fishermen from his village walking home from the pier on late afternoons and sometimes into the evenings. Some days they carried their catches, the big fish, and on those days he most admired them. A basket of snapper was pretty, would feed a family, and perhaps make the fishermen money when the café owner bought them, but a big fish—that made for an imposing sight.

"These *norteamericanos*, they like to take photos of themselves holding their big Mexican catches, you know? But sometimes they fear seasickness, and so we stay close to land and bottom-fish," Santiago said.

"So sometimes we don't know our schedule until the day

before we go out. The people book their charters with us through their hotels. Other times we know a few days ahead of time. Tomorrow we're taking two people offshore."

Héctor nodded and sipped his beer.

"Why don't you go tomorrow with Santiago?" Ignacio said. "I've got some shit I need to do, and you can get a feel for the *Gabriela.*" He looked to Santiago and added, "Hey, Santiago, we'll find out if Héctor here has sea legs."

"No puking on the *Gabriela,*" Santiago said. "Hang it overboard, man, but don't lose your breakfast on my boat."

"I'll be here," Héctor said. "And I won't puke in your boat." He'd never experienced seasickness, and he wondered if it could be controlled by sheer will. If a man could stave off the vomiting by determination and pure resolve, then he knew he'd not suffer the seasickness.

"You'll mostly work for tips and sometimes fish when the customers don't want to keep them. We'll pay you a little bit per trip, too, if this works out," Ignacio said.

Héctor wondered what kind of tips the *norteamericanos* paid. He couldn't imagine the tips would be the kind of quick money he'd hoped for, and he didn't want to spend months in Acapulco when every day Alejandra could be getting farther and farther from him.

"What kind of tips?" Héctor said. "I'll be grateful for any, you understand, but it's just that as I discussed with Diego, I've a little bit of an emergency situation. Please understand, I know we just met and of course I'll work hard . . ."

Santiago and Ignacio looked at each other.

"I need to make money, decent money, to get me toward the border as soon as possible. I lost my daughter there, and I believe she may still be there somewhere. I need to earn enough to travel there and search for her."

Santiago stood, finished his beer, then crushed the can and tossed it back into the fish cooler. He cleared his throat but said nothing, and Héctor feared he'd been too pushy with these men.

"So we'll see how everything goes tomorrow," Ignacio said. "And then we may have a little riskier work, something a little more labor intensive, and if we do, and you're up for it, we'll discuss it, and maybe that work will pay you the kind of money you need to move on in this journey of yours."

"Okay," Héctor said, unsure what else to say.

"Be here tomorrow morning by five thirty," Santiago said.

Héctor thanked them and assured the men he'd be on time. As he walked along the waterfront a yellow-bellied sea snake undulated beside the dock before slipping beneath the water's surface, diving deep. He'd seen such snakes in the waters off Puerto Isadore, and he knew their venom could be deadly. How odd nature's allure could be. If he didn't know better, he'd like to scoop up such a brilliantly colored creature and keep him in a large jar of seawater like sunshine on a cloudy day. But he did know better, and he understood that sometimes the prettiest of creatures were deceptive in their attractiveness. He hoped he'd always be able to discern the difference between benevolent and malevolent beings.

Héctor turned from the marina and began the walk into the hills toward Emanuel's apartment. He wondered if the riskier job Ignacio mentioned would take him far out to sea and if a whale could flip a boat, and what the job would pay him, and he hoped he would not vomit in the *Gabriela,* or in the great Pacific, or anywhere.

Chapter 15

Lilia

Though Lilia had been through two pregnancies already, everything about the process remained mysterious and uncertain. Perhaps such was God's plan, that no matter how many babies a woman delivered, each pregnancy would be a singular, special event with its own set of concerns and circumstances.

Héctor had been gone more than a week now, and though she did not worry as much about his safety as she had when he'd left their village for *el norte,* the uncertainty of their lives weighed on her in an unexpected way. She told herself that this separation was different from the last, that this time she'd been left with an active and curious two-year-old instead of an infant, and that last time her grandmother had been alive and of great help to her. But now Fernando gave her little rest, and her blossoming belly kept her ill and always tired.

Each morning at sunrise and again before settling into bed at night, Lilia held her rosary and uttered prayers to Jesus Christ, to the Virgin of Guadalupe, and to San Cristóbal, the patron saint of travelers, asking for Héctor's safety. Then she would light incense, just as her grandmother Crucita had always done, as an offering to the local gods to appease them and ask that they protect Héctor and allow him safe passage through unfamiliar territory. These worries, along with her weary body, left little room for other concerns.

Yet most days she made her way to Rosa's without complaint to leave Fernando, and then on to the market where she would set up her pottery in hopes of making a few pesos. Rosa, who'd birthed five children of her own and had helped birth many other babies, including both of Lilia's, would likely have little patience with Lilia's complaints of weariness and the increasing achiness in her lower back. With only one child at home to tend to, how could Lilia grumble? And so wearing her most cheerful face she delivered Fernando to Rosa's house, where the boy giggled upon seeing Rosa and toddled off to play without hesitation.

When she reached the market, several sellers had already arrived and were setting up their wares. From wire racks a blind old woman and her grandson sold handmade dresses for little girls. Another table offered whistles, dolls, maracas, and other such trinkets, and a third vendor sold brightly colored hammocks piled high in red, blue, yellow, and orange.

The morning sun throbbed as Lilia stood at her table beneath a small, tattered umbrella made of faded yellow fabric that did little to alleviate the oppressive heat. She pulled her white plastic chair beneath a nearby guanacaste tree and sat, waiting for someone to wander by and show an interest in her wares. She knew her behavior was lazy, of course, and she should remain at the table where it stood street-side. There she could catch the eye of anyone strolling by, and she could entice them to her goods with a gentle smile and a "*Buenos días.*" But the heat would prove nearly intolerable before day's end, and so she would take to the tree's shade when she could do so.

Her remote village was nothing like celebrated Acapulco, where Héctor now worked, yet its coast and waters were beautiful, and so the more adventurous explorers would travel down to Puerto Isadore to dive and sun on its coppery beaches.

Before Lilia and Héctor had experienced *el norte*, she'd felt proud, even honored, when travelers passing through her village asked to photograph her or sometimes even her modest house with its broom-swept yard on the rare occasion they wandered up her lane. Now she felt something very different at those rare times. After living in *el norte* Lilia understood the tourists photographed her not because of her exquisite beauty, the loveliness of her shade tree where iguanas often sunned, or even the tidiness of her courtyard. They snapped their pictures because the poverty of her village interested them. The children playing in the dust, rolling their marbles on lids of barrels, the rooster scratching in the pile of corn husks behind a mud shack, a family's clothes drying on the barbed wire strung across their side yard, all these images intrigued the *norteamericanos* because such sights seemed dirty and foreign to them. She imagined them returning to their large, clean houses that smelled of chemicals and cleaning supplies and showing their neighbors the photos. She felt no ill will toward the Americans; they had been kind to her. Her disdain was aimed inward, at her country, her village, and even herself. Had she never gone to America her eyes would still be blind to the extreme differences. She'd only ever known washing her clothes outside on the washboard, using the toilet outside, and bathing in cool water, unless she heated it on the fire. Now that veil had been lifted, and nothing she could do would lower it.

When tourists chose to spend a few pesos on Lilia's pottery she felt as near to her departed Crucita as one could feel to an ancestor. And at those times Lilia's gratitude swelled for her grandmother's artisan skills and ability to pass them on to Lilia. No one would ever make pottery as beautiful as old

Crucita's, but Crucita's hand was evident in all Lilia made, and she knew her grandmother's spirit persevered despite the decay of her bones. And when she thought of Crucita, of her tremendous Mexican pride, Lilia's shame over the poverty in Puerto Isadore lessened, and she knew she had much in her heritage of which to be proud.

At midmorning the first potential customers approached her table. Lilia suspected they were *norteamericanos* by the paleness of their eyes and hair. The sun-pinked couple wore swimsuits, though the woman wore a thin cotton dress over hers, and they carried small sacks with flippers poking from each. Like most of the foreign visitors to Puerto Isadore, these people were divers. Ever since she'd left South Carolina, Lilia wanted to ask traveling strangers if they knew her employers on the tree farm where she and Héctor had worked. But as quickly as the urge to ask struck her, the realization followed that America was a country of tremendous size, and perhaps these people, if they were even from America, had never been to South Carolina.

The woman picked up a small, brightly colored iguana Lilia had recently created. Most of her pieces she'd fashioned on her potter's wheel, but a few animal pieces and some crucifixes she'd lately begun making by hand. Today, in addition to her cups, vases, and pots, she'd brought along the iguana, a lizard, a pair of butterflies, a rooster, and two crucifixes. She'd not sold any of those yet, and she tried not to seem too eager when the lady fingered the smooth blue-glazed iguana.

The woman's eyes, the bluest eyes Lilia had ever seen, glistened when she looked at the man, and Lilia wondered if perhaps the iguana appealed to the woman because it nearly matched her eyes. The woman said something to her partner in a language that was neither Spanish nor English. The man spoke to her softly, smiling, and Lilia wondered if they were newly wedded. The couple's obvious mutual adoration filled her with a sudden and unexpected longing for Héctor's companionship, his presence, his touch. Lilia's love for her husband had never wavered, and at times she missed him with an intensity beyond measure. The man turned to Lilia, and in Spanish said, *"¿Cuánto cuesta?"*

"Tres pesos," Lilia said, at once holding her breath, afraid the man would walk away.

Instead he fished into his bag and retrieved a small billfold from which he pulled the money and paid her.

"Gracias," she said, then added, "You are American?"

The couple understood the word American, but shook their heads. *"No, no. Somos alemánes."*

They smiled then walked away hand in hand, the woman carrying the iguana as if she'd found a treasure. Lilia had never met anyone from Germany, and she admired how tall and strong they looked. Somehow they reminded her of her employers in America, which was silly really, since those farmers were much older and had nothing at all to do with Germany as far as she knew. Maybe the kindness in their eyes brought to mind her former employers.

By the afternoon Lilia had sold two more pieces, but her back pain had become insufferable. Likely the other vendors would remain a couple more hours, but Lilia could bear neither the heat nor the discomfort of her muscles any longer. With as much care as she could muster, she wrapped her wares in pieces of burlap and loaded them into a sack.

When she'd finished she realized how parched she'd become. She sat again in her chair beneath the guanacaste tree and wiped her brow.

"Are you well, lady?" The young boy who'd been selling dresses with his blind grandmother shouted to her from his table. He held a can of guava juice, which reminded Lilia she had a few sips of water yet in her lunch sack.

"Yes, yes, I'm okay," she said, waving his concern away and hoping he'd turn his attention back to his old *abuela* and their racks of dresses.

She found her bottle of water and sucked down the remaining drops, then stood to begin her slow walk to Rosa's where she would retrieve Fernando before going home. Of late her days often ended with Fernando curled beside her in bed, where everything about him soothed Lilia and eased the strains of her long, hot days: his soft, rhythmic breathing; the gentleness of his little finger looped around her finger as he slept; the scent of his hair; and the utter stillness of her boy when he'd settled into deep, peaceful slumber.

The small sip of water only intensified Lilia's thirst, and as she walked she daydreamed of chugging a liter of water and of diving into a cool early-morning sea.

When she was a girl, Lilia's favorite time to swim had been just after sunrise, when the water lay like blue-gray oil as far as her eye could take her. Where the sea and sky met would be indeterminate because the heavens, too, at that early-morning hour stretched infinitely in the same steely expanse that somehow represented both nothingness and everything at once. The coolness of water and air at that hour appealed to Lilia, but perhaps what was most enchanting about an early-morning swim in the Pacific was the sense that both earth and sea lay fresh, undisturbed, and full of potential.

She suspected that Héctor had held such a vision of an ever-budding world from the time he was old enough to form thoughts. His desire to work every bit of pulp from the ripe fruit that was his existence filled him with an unparalleled curiosity and energy that had drawn Lilia to him years ago in their youth. She wondered if that lost zest for being would return to him, to them, if, when, they got their Alejandra back.

She tried to hold on to the tranquil image of the sea as she made her way to Rosa's house, but her body defied her mind, and so her thoughts shifted to the shooting pain that at times came so sharply she had to stop, set down her sack of pottery, and rest. She cupped her hands beneath her belly. A foot or knee or perhaps a tiny elbow momentarily protruded there as if the baby inside her understood Lilia had placed a hand near her womb.

"I feel you," she whispered to her child.

An old man driving two oxen pulled a wooden cart of bricks past Lilia where she sat beside the road. His sombrero shielded his eyes from the harsh sun and from Lilia, but he nodded at her as he passed. The oxen kicked up a cloud of dust, and Lilia stood to avoid breathing it and to continue on her way.

From where Lilia stood she could see down the hill to the bay and skiffs, some bobbing there and others pulled high up onto the sand. A man sat beneath a thatched roof working on his fishing nets while a small child hopped among the nets stretched out before the man. A brown-and-white dog rested beside the man's chair, and beyond the waves breaking onshore, the choppy water glistened like shattered glass in the sunlight. Of course, that scene might be soothing to some, perhaps to the German tourists, but the image of a more tranquil morning sea had settled in Lilia's mind, and she decided that some day soon she would wake Fernando early and swim with him at sunrise, the time when the world's sharp edges dulled and softened.

By the time she arrived at Rosa's the pain in her lower back was such that every step nearly buckled her knees and sweat slicked her forehead.

"Something's wrong with me," she said, leaning against Rosa's doorway.

"Are you in labor?" Rosa said, pouring Lilia a cup of water.

"I can't be in labor. I have weeks left yet."

Rosa handed her the water, snorting. "You can't be, eh? Tell that to the thousands of babies who've surprised their mamas by coming early. Only God and a baby know when the time is nigh. Drink."

Lilia drained the cup and passed it back to Rosa. "I was so thirsty. Thank you."

Rosa refilled the cup. "If you're thirsty you are beyond dehydrated. By the time your body asks to be quenched, you're long past due for a drink. If you're not careful you sure enough will have Fernando a baby girl to torment sooner than you've bargained for, Lilia."

Tears filled Lilia's eyes and spilled down her cheeks. She inhaled a deep slow breath in an effort to stop them, but they flowed unstanched. "I hurt, Rosa. I don't think I can walk home."

"Come, lie down."

Rosa helped her to a cot behind the house where the breeze came in from the bay. She placed the cup beside Lilia along with a full pitcher of water. "Stay right there, and don't get up until the water is gone from that jug. Drink it dry."

Lilia nodded. "Where's Fernando?"

"Ah, your boy is having a grand day. Don't you worry about him. José took him down to *la farmacia* for a candy and then to watch the boats come in. José didn't fish today, and so I told him to go get me a fish for my stew. He and Fernando will be along soon."

Lilia drank the water and closed her eyes and thought of Héctor. The sea breeze and a chirping flock of birds eating berries from a nearby tree lulled her to sleep, and when she awoke Rosa stood beside her braiding her granddaughter's hair.

"I have some things for you, Lilia," she said, then swatted Rosita on the backside. "Go on, now," she said to the girl, though not in an unkind way. The girl smiled at Lilia, then went inside the house.

Lilia sat up. "I'm feeling better, but I need to pee."

"Of course you do. You drank a horse's share of water. Go, relieve yourself, and when you come back drink this, and then you can walk home if you feel like going." Rosa placed a little cup of mescal on the table.

Lilia looked at the honey-colored contents and shook her head. "I don't think I have the stomach for that, Rosa."

"Let me tell you something, child," Rosa said. "You want that baby to stay inside you a while longer yet, don't you?"

Lilia nodded. "Yes, Rosa."

Rosa picked up a broom and began sweeping. "One way to help ensure a baby stays inside the womb is by her mama relaxing. I have delivered half the babies born in this village. The mothers who are worriers, who stay nervous all the time, or who work too hard and put stress on their bodies without the proper nutrition and rest, they're the mothers of babies who arrive early. A little bit of mescal each evening will help you relax and will keep that baby growing inside you until the proper time."

Lilia was already making her way toward the latrine behind Rosa's house. The pain in her back had subsided, but a twinge lingered still.

"I'll drink your drink, Rosa. I'll do what you say," Lilia said, feeling that Rosa was the only one she had left to guide her, and vowing that she'd do all she could to protect her unborn daughter. She had failed her firstborn by making reckless decisions, and she'd not lose another child because of her foolishness.

Chapter 16

Héctor

"See, there," Santiago shouted over the boat's engine. He pushed the throttle down as the men headed in after a full day of fishing offshore.

Héctor followed his gaze toward a rocky promontory to their left and nodded.

"Remember that spot. Make note of where it is, and tomorrow I want to see if you can find it again on your own," Santiago said.

"Sure," Héctor said, wondering about the significance of that place. Perhaps the fishing along that coastline would prove fruitful. Santiago had been a good boss and teacher, less chatty than Ignacio but more instructive. Maybe his pointing out the fertile fishing territory to Héctor meant more money would soon come Héctor's direction.

Two businessmen from Mexico City sat on the boat's bow. Even if they had not talked about money and banking transactions, Héctor would have been able to tell they were men of privilege because of their soft hands and expensive-looking sunglasses and watches. They'd caught five dorado and a tuna, and they seemed pleased with the day, like they were used to such success in all they attempted and anything less would have been a problem. The businessmen had been working their way through the cooler of beers since midmorning. Santiago and Ignacio always supplied a packed cooler, but these guys were indulging in the beers more than most. Héctor had already filleted their fish and packed the meat on ice. He'd cleaned the bow and put away the lines and packed up the ballyhoo they used for bait. The work suited him, and he'd decided after his first day that he could be comfortable fishing for a living. Santiago and Ignacio seemed pleased, too, offering him a beer or two to take home after each day's work. They always took the tips from the clients and then doled a few pesos out to Héctor, but Héctor hoped, before too much longer, the tips and his pay would increase. He'd need to make more money if he were to leave Acapulco by the deadline he'd set for himself.

When Ignacio brought the *Gabriela* into the dock, Héctor tied the bowlines and helped the drunken businessmen off the boat. While one of the men went to Santiago to settle up for the day, the other slipped Héctor a wad of bills and slurred a thank-you for a great day out on the water. Héctor shook the man's hand while stuffing the money into his pocket. He knew Santiago had not seen the man hand him the tip, and he watched as the other man paid Santiago. Today's excursion had been Héctor's third on the *Gabriela,* and always the customers had given their tips to Ignacio or Santiago. Somehow—perhaps Ignacio and Santiago had indicated to them—the customers understood that Héctor was not the boss and that his tips would be filtered down through the boat owners. But he also knew Ignacio and Santiago expected him to hand over any tips he received directly, that they would divvy them as they chose.

Héctor hoisted the small but heavy Styrofoam cooler the clients had brought along, now filled with fish fillets on ice. He passed it to the more sober-seeming man of the pair.

"Good day today," Santiago said, as the businessmen stumbled away with their catch. "Those guys were loaded. In more ways than one." He laughed in a lazy, tired sort of way and peeled off a few pesos for Héctor.

Héctor took the money, and, though he'd considered keeping the bills he'd crammed in his pocket, withdrew the tip and handed the wad to Santiago.

"What's this?" Santiago said, studying the crumpled pesos in Héctor's palm.

"The other guy, the really drunk one, gave it to me," Héctor said.

A smile conveying Santiago's great satisfaction spread across his face. "I told Ignacio. I told him," he said, nodding, accepting the bills Héctor proffered.

"Told him what?" Héctor said, grabbing the trash sack from the boat, as Santiago smoothed the bills and counted them, not answering Héctor's question. At least two dozen empty beer cans rattled when Héctor disposed of the sack in the large trash bin on the dock.

"I told him we'd not have to take a knife to your throat, that's all," Santiago said, his eyes sparkling at what he must have deemed a funny joke.

When Héctor began spraying out the hull of the boat, Santiago said, "What do you think, Héctor? You like fishing on the *Gabriela*?" He was eyeing Héctor in the way he always did when some mysterious subtext seemed to exist beneath their conversation.

Héctor weighed his words but spoke breezily. "I've always enjoyed fishing and working outdoors. This work suits me, but . . ." He hesitated.

"But what?" Santiago said, putting away the bait and riggings.

"But I should be getting on to Matamoros soon, and I'd hoped to earn a bit more money before I head that way."

Santiago cracked open the last can of beer remaining in the boat and took a long swig, studying Héctor. "Those fat dogs from Mexico City seemed to enjoy their day with us," he said.

Héctor nodded and continued scrubbing the bow where fish blood had baked into a brick-red stain.

"Fair enough, Héctor. I hear you," Santiago said, as if he'd just made up his mind about something. "Do you recall that spot along the rocks, north of here, that I pointed out to you?"

Héctor had been anticipating this conversation about the craggy promontory. Santiago had worn an unusual and serious expression when he'd pointed out the spot.

"Of course," he said. "I know the spot."

"Good," Santiago said, nodding in approval. "I'm going to send you there for me later this week. Could be tomorrow. Could be in three days."

"Okay," Héctor said, ceasing to scrub the blood, waiting for Santiago to elaborate.

Santiago peeled most of the money off the stack then passed the remainder to Héctor. "You'll make a pickup. It'll be quick. You'll pull up to those rocks, and you'll find a wooden ladder fashioned up the southern end of that cliff. It's not easy to see until you're within a couple of meters of the rock face. Get to the top, meet a guy who'll be expecting you. He'll have a big cooler for you. Get the cooler back here to me as fast as you can. That's it." Santiago shrugged as if to emphasize the simplicity of this whole process, but he watched Héctor at an odd angle, as if he were sizing him up anew.

"And the money for this?" he said without meeting Santiago's stare.

Santiago sipped his beer and seemed to mull the question. "If the outing goes well and you get the cooler here with no problems, I'll pay you three times what you make on a fishing trip."

With each of the three fishing charters he'd taken, Héctor had earned more than the previous outing.

Santiago must have mistaken as doubt Héctor's reticence while calculating his earnings. Santiago added, "How about eight hundred pesos? If all goes well."

"Just tell me when I go," Héctor said, wondering, among his many unspoken questions, what could be in that cooler.

Chapter 17

Lilia

Lilia heaped a mound of gray clay onto the wide, flat stone where women in her family had worked clay for more than a century. The clay felt cool between her palms and the working of the damp earth soothed her, as if she were stepping onto a pendulum somehow, falling into an ever-present rhythm begun in some primordial time by all the women who'd come before her. Today she would make small decorative jugs, something her grandmother would never have considered doing. Nor would Crucita have experimented with colors. Crucita's pottery had been beautiful, yes, but always pieces with designated function and purpose, like water jugs and comals for making tortillas or toasting chili peppers. After being in America, Lilia developed an interest in artful, almost whimsical pieces, something her grandmother would never have understood or valued. Lilia began kneading the clay, working in cattail fluff as the clay softened in her hands. The downy cattail, stripped from plants growing beside the river, improved the workability of the clay. The finished pieces would shrink less and would be less likely to crack in the kiln because Lilia, like her grandmother, incorporated cattail.

An old man named Jaime had traveled through Puerto Isadore every couple of weeks for years, hauling clay in sacks across the back of a donkey. On rare occasions, Crucita had purchased from him, but she swore the quality of her finished pieces to be inferior when she used Jaime's clay. She had preferred to mine her own material. Lilia's earliest memories centered around clay and pottery and always Crucita. As a small girl Lilia would go with Crucita to dig clay at their secret spot. They'd travel to the banks of a river that flowed just beyond their village, and together they would pick cattails and dig all the clay they could carry home in Crucita's wobbly-wheeled goat cart. The clay was dense and heavy and in need of a two-week soak before her grandmother would use it. No less than two weeks, the old woman had insisted, and to this day, Lilia heeded her grandmother's wisdom and refused to work her clay until she'd soaked it two full weeks in the shaded barrel behind her house.

Now, with her rounded belly and troubling back pain along with the demands of little Fernando and Héctor's absence, Lilia had resorted to buying clay from Jaime. This last batch she'd purchased a few days before Héctor's departure for Acapulco. She'd stirred it each day in its water bath, slowing encouraging the clay to release bits of stone and twig and other debris, urging those unwanted parts to sink to the bottom of the barrel. The process had paid off, and the mound she now worked felt pure and smooth to her fingers.

She pounded the lump over and over against the surface of the stone, as if the clay were a misshapen ball refusing to bounce for her. As the lump rounded, Lilia's hands found a rhythm: Slap, slap, slap-slap. Slap, slap, slap-slap. The top portion narrowed and the bottom spread until the clay took on the shape of a cone. She hummed a nameless tune as she worked, losing herself in the time-honored tradition of her mother's people, a mother she'd never known by sight or sound but to whom she felt a connection as palpable as the earth caking her hands.

She lifted the cone of clay with her left hand and with her right fist began tapping the center of its thick bottom, harder and harder until her rhythmic, dull punch punch punch rounded and hollowed the shape into a bell with her fist inside. She slowly twirled the bell of clay on her fist by slapping the outside with her open left hand until its surface had thinned and smoothed, its walls building.

Lilia stood and stretched, unable to lean over her work for any extended amount of time. A streak-backed oriole landed on the barbed-wire clothesline above her, and Lilia, watching him hop between one of Fernando's shirts and a pair of her socks, admired his bright yellow plumage. When he flew away to a nearby treetop, Lilia resumed her seat.

She placed a shallow plate on top of an overturned bowl and set her upturned bell of clay atop the plate, then she began spinning the plate. This Zapotec wheel was simple but efficient, and, according to Crucita, had been used in their village and throughout Oaxaca since ancient times. Lilia valued her grandmother's teaching and knowledge more now since Crucita had passed to the spirit world. Crucita had seemed judgmental, even cruel, in her old-fashioned ways and opinions of Lilia's generation. Now Lilia understood that her grandmother's sentiments stemmed from a fear that her way of living would be lost, replaced with techniques and objects and beliefs so at odds with what she'd always known that they would be unrecognizable to her, and what a frightening possibility for an old lady to consider.

But some old practices weren't without problems. Lilia thought of her mother, dead from delivering Lilia, and how when Fernando was born, Lilia had had to go to the fancy clinic in Oaxaca after Rosa had detected the boy was large and wrong-side-down for delivery. Lilia had assumed that hard, rounded lump in her pelvis to be the unborn baby's head, ready to dive into the light of the world. But no, Rosa had said, "That's the baby's bottom, wedged tight where it should not be, and delivering him could cause you both great troubles."

Thinking about Fernando's birth, Lilia instinctively brought her hand to her lower abdomen where a thick scar from her caesarean section snaked beneath her swollen belly just below the elastic of her underpants. The scar, pink, angry, and jagged, reminded Lilia that she'd likely still have her own mother if Crucita had known or even had the ability to get her to a hospital. How many times had she considered that alternative to history? Perhaps she, too, would have passed to the spirit world had Rosa not insisted that Fernando was breech and made Héctor get Lilia to Oaxaca City on the bus.

The surgery and Fernando's delivery in the clinic had taken all of Héctor and Lilia's savings, including the U.S. currency they'd received from their American employers the day before Héctor and Lilia had been deported. Oh, how kind the American farmers had been to them! Even now, years later, an occasional letter would arrive, postmarked from America, often at Christmastime or on Héctor's or Lilia's birthday, containing a twenty- or a fifty- and once or twice a hundred-dollar bill. But more often than not, the envelope would arrive with a kind letter making reference to the farm or the weather or fishing or money enclosed, but the envelope would have been tampered with, and the money would be gone. Héctor didn't have the heart to tell the gringos that their monetary gifts sometimes never made their way to his and Lilia's hands.

By late afternoon Lilia had completed four pieces. She polished them to a shine with an ancient lump of quartz that had belonged to Crucita and to Crucita's mother before her.

If Lilia could make at least that many pieces tomorrow and

again the day after that, she would load them all into the pit behind her house, then seal the opening of the cavity with moss, whole cattails, mud, and broken shards of old pots. She'd fire them there below the ground where heat and smoke would transform the pieces into pottery, black as coal chunks, both beautiful and useful.

The shadows had grown long when Lilia heard Rosa's and Fernando's voices from inside her house. Fernando emerged from the house first, rushing into his mama's open arms.

"Easy, boy," Rosa called to him, just a few steps behind. "You'll knock your mama off her stool."

Lilia kissed Fernando's head, inhaling the scent of her son, a unique mixture of sweat and sugar and fish. Fernando's unabashed greetings were the best part of any day, and Lilia squeezed him in her tired, swollen hands. "My boy," she said, looking into his bright, smiling eyes.

"You made good work today?" Rosa said, pulling up a plastic chair that had been leaning against the house. She sat and took a pipe from her pocket and lit it with a match.

"I did, thanks to your entertaining this fellow." Fernando had climbed onto Lilia's knee, nestling into her arms and sucking his dirty thumb. He began to twirl a lock of his hair around and around his left index finger, a sure sign that sleep would soon find him.

Rosa puffed her pipe, looking up at the bright oriole that had returned, now sitting in Lilia's mango tree. "That boy's good company. My grandchildren enjoy him, too. The important thing is that you don't do too much in the coming weeks. Sitting here making pots in the shade is probably a good way to pass the time. You feel okay today?"

Lilia never felt very good anymore. Her back always hurt, though some days the pain bothered her more than others.

Walking aggravated her body, and even standing for any length of time brought shooting pains across her back and down her legs. But sitting here, shaping her pottery from lumps of gray clay, she could do that. And so she said to Rosa, "I'll be glad when this baby arrives, but I'm okay."

"Don't rush her or God," Rosa said, tapping the pipe against her chair, emptying its contents onto the ground, before placing it back into her pocket. "I should get home. Do you need anything before I go?"

Lilia eased Fernando from her knee and took her time working her way up from the chair to a standing position. Sticky from sweat, her bottom and legs stuck to her skirt, and she suddenly felt bone tired and in need of bathing and her bed. She turned toward the house where Fernando had already begun walking, as if he, too, craved the bed that awaited them there.

"Lilia!" Rosa gasped.

Lilia turned to her friend. "What?"

Rosa pointed at Lilia. "Your skirt, Lilia."

Lilia looked down, grabbing the back of her skirt, lifting and twisting the fabric so she could see what Rosa saw, though, by the expression on Rosa's face, Lilia already knew what she'd find and what trouble the crimson stain portended.

"Let's get you inside," Rosa said, grabbing Lilia by the elbow.

Chapter 18

Ana María

A fat American family had just been seated in Ana María's section. The husband and wife looked alike the way husbands and wives often resemble each other after many years together. She hoped if she ever got married she'd marry a handsome man, lean, with full lips and smooth skin. That is how she'd like herself and her husband to appear in their later years, the beautiful envy of everyone who saw them.

She greeted them with "Hello. How are you?" Four of the approximately fifty English words she knew. Like many American tourists, they replied *"Hola"* and commenced to chat her up in indecipherable Spanish mixed with English that she could barely understand.

These Americans chose this restaurant, Señor Juan's Texas Rib Shack, in Mexico and spoke bad Spanish to a waitress who tried to greet them in their native tongue, English. Ana María would never understand people. Why not eat Mexican food when in Mexico? They could eat Texas ribs back home. Americans intrigued her. Still, she longed to visit America, to see American rock-and-roll bands and American football players like the Dallas Cowboys and to visit huge stores like Macy's that held a parade with giant floats in November, which always showed on the televisions in Acapulco. One day she would get there, and so she worked every shift she could grab at Señor Juan's Texas Rib Shack to save her pesos.

"*Un* rib platter *con Tejas* toast, *por favor, y una cerveza fría,*" the fat man said, grinning at Ana María with pride at his use of Spanish.

His wife ordered the green salad with fried chicken strips, "And *una cerveza* for *moi,* too," she said.

Ana María didn't think *moi* was an American word, and her suspicion that the woman had butchered her Spanish was confirmed when the husband laughed and the wife turned red in the cheeks but giggled, too.

The couple's two fat sons ordered Cokes, barbecue sandwiches, and french fries. The bigger of the two boys said, "Are they called Mexican fries here?" And his mother said, "No. french fries are french fries all over the world, sweetheart. Even in Meh-hee-co." She smiled at Ana María, and Ana María smiled back then left to prepare their drinks. That's when she saw Emanuel enter and sit at the bar. He winked at her before she slipped into the kitchen to turn in the food order. She'd not heard from him in several days, and she wondered if that guy from Puerto Isadore was still sleeping on his floor.

The American family reminded Ana María of flan, soft and gelatinous. After she delivered their plates of food and refilled the boys' soda glasses and brought the parents each another beer, she joined Emanuel at the bar. They were her last table, and for now they seemed content, so she would visit a few minutes with Emanuel.

"They are like custard, those people. If you cut them I bet they would bleed thick cream."

"Maybe they're big tippers, you know? Keep their drinks filled and food in their mouths, and you'll have your beer money for the night. You can buy my drinks," he said, running a finger down her forearm. His touch tickled.

"You still have your friend sleeping at your place?"

He sipped his beer, and she wondered if he were thinking of a way to get his houseguest gone so he could take her home with him when she got off work. "He's still there. But not much longer and he'll be gone from here."

"Why's that? You going to kill him?" She teased him. Ana María had sensed Emanuel's irritation with the guy a while back, like they weren't good friends but Emanuel seemed to owe him a favor.

"No, no killing. He's got plans to move on, that's all."

"You never told me why he's here. He's your cousin or something? Family?"

"No, no relation. But his wife's an old friend of mine, and, you know . . ." He paused and studied the beer can in his hand like he'd never seen a beer can before. "I'm helping out a friend of a friend."

Something about his expression, the way he hesitated when she asked about his connection, told her Emanuel had a history with his houseguest's wife.

"His wife, you dated her?" Ana María shouldn't care, but she wanted to know. Life is all a matter of figuring out angles, of uncovering slight particulars that can make big differences in the way a person goes about her dealings. So if Emanuel and his guest's wife used to have something between them, she needed to know. Ana María wasn't sure of Emanuel's intentions with her, but she wasn't sure of her intentions with him, either. Some days his interest in her, desire for her, shone as clear as air, but then he'd become scarce, and she'd not see him for days. She liked having her own space, and as long as he treated her with respect and smiled in her company, she enjoyed the gaps when he'd not come around Señor Juan's for a few days or, occasionally, weeks.

He looked at her like he was holding back a smile. "Don't

you worry about that, beautiful." He ran his finger down her arm again, but this time his touch didn't tickle. His finger felt like a cat's tongue, rough and annoying, as if by flirting with her he could soften her edges.

"I'm not a worrier," she said, taking the rag from her hip where she'd tucked it into her shorts. She wiped the bar in front of them where Emanuel's beer can had made a wet ring.

"So this guy and his wife are going through a tough situation," Emanuel continued. "Héctor is a straight-up gentleman, but he needs money quick, and I'm not even going to go into that whole story with you right now. But I've hooked him up with some fellows."

Smugness hung about Emanuel this evening. He'd come into Señor Juan's Texas Rib Shack like he was Señor Juan himself, though Ana María often wondered if Señor Juan even existed. The man who owned the restaurant was named Charlie, and he was an American who came down six months out of the year. Emanuel looked good. He always looked good, with his strong arms and quick smile, but a bigheaded man had no place in Ana María's life. She'd had enough bigheaded men to last her three lifetimes.

"Is that right? Who do you know who can hook a person up with quick money? Some bad people out there, Emanuel."

"You're telling me about bad people?" he said, shaking his head and looking up at the multicolored bottles on the wall above the bar. "You wouldn't believe shit I've seen, girl." He took another sip of his beer, and Ana María walked over to the Americans' table. All their plates were empty except for one of the boy's. He continued to eat french fries.

"Do you have a dessert menu?" the other boy asked.

"Oh, let's not do dessert here," the mother said.

Ana María began clearing the dishes.

"Let's go for ice cream down the street. I saw a cute place . . ." the mother was saying, but Ana María retreated with their dirty plates before the woman finished telling the family her plans for a sweet finish to their evening.

She returned to their table with their bill and had turned to walk away when the father said, "Wait, *por favor,* señorita. I'll have some *dinero* right here in *uno momento.*" He fished a credit card from his wallet and passed it to Ana María with a wink.

When she'd run the card and delivered it to the man, she returned to the bar where she noticed Emanuel had switched to red wine. He was the only man she knew who enjoyed wine as much as or more than beer or tequila. She wondered how much he'd already had before he arrived. She suspected that swagger he wore like a cloak tonight came from plentiful alcohol flowing through his body.

"So who'd you connect Héctor with? You don't seem like you'd know the seedy types."

"Who's seedy?" he said, tapping his fingers on the bar to the beat of the music the bartender turned up as the last table of diners, the fat Americans, cleared out. "I didn't say anything about seedy people."

"You said you were trying to help him make quick money." Ana María knew about quick money. She'd had a brother killed working for a cartel up in Hermosillo. Nothing good came from quick money.

"Diego the Magnificent knew some guys. Some fishermen. Far as I know they are just catching fish. I didn't ask." He shrugged like this made sense, and maybe his words did fit together in a way that meant something decent and acceptable, but Ana María didn't think so.

"Who are the guys? I know all the guys around here," she said.

He looked at her sideways and tilted his chin. "You do, eh? Maybe you should get to know this guy right here a bit better." He tapped his shirt over his heart.

"You think so?" she said, unable to suppress a grin, even if Emanuel was too sure of himself like the cock that crowed each sunrise outside her window. She'd awoken every day for years with her first thought being of killing that rooster.

He leaned close to her, his mouth at her ear, and placed two fingers under her chin. "Yes, that is what I think," he whispered. His breath warmed her ear, and his lips brushed her earlobe.

"So he's still at your place?" she said, lowering her voice. Maybe Emanuel was drunk, but he smelled citrusy, like fresh limes, and she suspected he didn't come to Señor Juan's Texas Rib Shack just to sit and drink alone. He'd come to see her.

He took a big sip of wine. "He'll be here until Santiago and Ignacio finish with him."

"I know those guys. That's who he's working for? Santiago and Ignacio?"

Emanuel nodded, bobbing his head to the beat of the drums playing over the restaurant's stereo.

"A bad bunch," she said. "No telling what those guys are into. But don't say I said that, because what do I know? But I hear things. If your houseguest is working for them, you'd be best getting him out of your space tonight. My sister used to run with Santiago and his bunch."

"You got a sister?" He raised his eyebrows. "She looks as good as you?"

Ana María knew he wanted a reaction. She'd not give him what he prodded her to get. "I had a sister," she said.

Emanuel studied her face. She expected him to say "Had a sister?" and then question her about Isabella, and she'd be ready with her response, with tales of Isabella's fondness for dangerous friends and drinking, a fondness Isabella shared with their brother, Marcus. Instead, Emanuel nodded, as if he understood everything without her explaining anything. He ran a finger around the lip of his wineglass, and suddenly Ana María felt more compelled to tell him about Isabella than if he'd asked her to do so.

"She was two years older than me, and our brother, Marcus, was a few years older than her." She paused. "Was," she said again. "No more, neither of them. And that Santiago is bad business."

Emanuel sat up and took a gulp of wine, finishing off the glass, at once seeming sober and serious. "I don't know Santiago or Ignacio. But Héctor needed money, and Diego said he knew these guys. I hooked up a friend with what he needed, and now I'm out of the deal."

She studied him. Ana María wanted Emanuel to be one of the good guys. "But he's still staying at your place?"

"He is, but just a while longer," he said.

"Then you're not out of the deal at all, are you?" she said.

"I owe the guy that much," Emanuel said.

"Why? Why do you owe him anything?" She stood, needing to get back to work refilling sauce bottles and wiping down her station.

He looked at her as if he weren't sure whether to answer, order another drink, or leave. She gazed into his eyes, hoping to learn more about him from something she'd see there.

"Just one of those debts, you know? I'm tired of talking, Ana María, and I've got to get up early."

"Okay," she said. "I'll see you around, then."

"Yes, sure you will, beautiful," he said, kissing her on the cheek, his expression dull, subdued. Then he slipped out the door.

Ana María watched him go, detecting a slight unsteadiness in his gait. She wondered what she'd said to darken his mood.

Chapter 19

Héctor

Héctor perched on the handlebars like some wild, hard-clawed bird weathering a storm, his grip curled tight with knuckles white, as Emanuel roared down the hill toward the setting sun and the bay. Héctor considered that his head could split like a ripe melon if a weary mongrel stepped out in front of them or if Emanuel's tire hit a pothole. He tried to focus on the beauty of the Pacific as the sun melted into the sea at the horizon, but his mind jerked back and forth between the uncertainty of the job he'd soon do for Santiago and the very real possibility that he'd fly from Emanuel's bike, his skin sloughing behind him along the pavement.

When they reached the boat dock, Héctor hopped off, his legs wobbly.

"So whatever you're up to, don't get yourself killed," Emanuel said, a slight grin on his lips.

Emanuel was always funny like that, saying what he meant, but disguising his concerns with playfulness. In a flash, and not for the first time, Héctor imagined the moment Emanuel talked Lilia into accepting his offer to arrange her crossing. Naïve Lilia, only recently did Héctor feel empathy for her and the struggle she'd endured when he'd left her behind with Alejandra during his trek to *el norte*. The past couple of weeks with Emanuel, a man he'd hated more than anyone he'd ever known, had exposed Héctor to Emanuel's personality and habit of skirting the fringe of things. Héctor couldn't quite shape in his mind a coherent description of Emanuel's ways, but he understood him to be wily, knowledgeable, and connected, but maybe shadowy in his dealings. Or not. After all, he hooked up trusting Lilia with Carlos and got her across the border, though with the highest price imaginable, and within two days of Héctor's arrival in Acapulco he'd introduced him to the famous Diego the Magnificent who had set him up with Santiago and Ignacio. All the while Emanuel remained in the background, not really involved in any of these arrangements other than introductions.

Héctor's hatred of Emanuel had thawed since he'd helped Héctor find work for quick money, and he'd allowed Héctor to sleep on his floor the past couple of weeks, but his distrust of Emanuel lingered.

"I plan to keep living a while longer yet after tonight, but thanks for the positive thoughts," Héctor said, looking down the dock at a couple of young boys fishing.

"So what're you doing tonight exactly?" Emanuel said. He was staring at the *Gabriela,* securely tied in her berth, with no sign of Ignacio or Santiago on the boat or around the dock.

Héctor had only told Emanuel that he had to go out on the *Gabriela* this evening for work, but nothing more. Emanuel knew enough to know the fishing charter trips departed in early morning, never at sunset.

When Héctor didn't answer, Emanuel said, "What are you catching in the dark? Sharks?" He cocked his head sideways and grinned broadly now.

"No sharks," Héctor said. "I'm supposed to be meeting someone out there." He nodded toward the open water.

"Meeting someone?" A shadow crossed Emanuel's face. "Where? Out on the ocean?"

"On the rocky shore, a cliff actually, a ways from here," Héctor said, his voice sounding oddly childlike.

Emanuel planted his feet on either side of the bike, like he'd not be leaving Héctor just yet, not until he had a few more questions answered.

"Who?"

"I don't know. But when I get there, I'll know who when I see him," Héctor said.

"Is this where your quick money comes into play? What are you doing out there?"

"I'm meeting a guy, okay? He's handing me a cooler. I'm bringing it back here where I'll deliver it to Santiago. That's it. That's what I'm doing."

Emanuel stared at him as if he were trying to make up his mind about something.

"I'll see you back at your place later," Héctor said over his shoulder. He could feel Emanuel watching him go, and somehow that sent a shiver through him, as if this moment mattered more than the moments leading up to it. Héctor wondered what thoughts Emanuel had as he watched him. Did Emanuel think he'd never see Héctor again? Maybe no one Héctor knew would ever see him again. How could he know? Upon what kind of crazy journey was he embarking?

"Well, what's in the cooler, Héctor?" Emanuel said.

Héctor turned back toward him and took a few steps in Emanuel's direction so he wouldn't have to speak too loudly. "I don't know what's in the cooler, man." Admitting as much aloud made him feel even more like an innocent little boy. "I think I prefer not knowing."

"So you won't take a look inside once you're alone with it?" Emanuel asked.

Héctor shrugged. "Probably not. Anyway, Santiago told me not to discuss this with anyone."

Emanuel's hands flew wide. "Then why the hell are you telling me?"

"You asked," Héctor said, turning back toward the boat. "Besides," he said, "you're the one who introduced me to Diego, and he hooked me up with this job."

"You've got to be careful, smart. You know?"

Héctor gave him a thumbs-up without looking back.

"Don't let the sharks eat you!" Emanuel hollered as he pedaled away.

Héctor hoped Emanuel would go drinking at the rib shack where that pretty girl he fancied worked. If Héctor were lucky, this evening would go by without a glitch, he'd be back asleep at Emanuel's place before Emanuel got home from his night of carousing, and tomorrow he'd have eight hundred pesos in his pocket.

That knowledge and the very real possibility of earning eight hundred pesos for a night's work bolstered him, and he untied the *Gabriela*'s bowline. The engine cranked on his first try, and Héctor took this to be an indication that the rest of this excursion would go as easily. He took one last look around the dock to be certain no one watched him, though even as he did so he wondered why that mattered. Plenty of people took sunset or moonlight boat rides. Nothing should seem odd to anyone strolling this area as Héctor puttered away from his mooring. The only people within sight were the young boys at the far end of the dock, and they busied themselves with a small, flopping fish one of them had just landed.

Héctor had been their age . . . what? . . . maybe ten years ago? The old-timers always spoke of the quick passing of time, but Héctor had dismissed their musings as the meaningless babble of old men. Now he saw the truth in their words, and an unexpected yearning for days long gone filled him with melancholy like he'd never known.

The ride to the rocky promontory, Héctor's destination, would take about twenty-five minutes or so. The seas were calm, and the sky, though cloudy, portended no impending storms. He'd seen the spot from the boat in the daylight, but he'd not attempted to locate the place in the dark. He wondered why whatever he was now doing had to be done at nighttime. He wondered many things. Whom would he meet? Had Ignacio and Santiago met this person on other moonless nights, or was this the first time such a meeting had been arranged? The biggest, most pressing mystery of all centered on the cooler Héctor was to obtain. This question had been burning in Héctor's curiosity since he'd agreed to make this run for Santiago: What was in the cooler? Why couldn't Santiago just get it himself? Why the secrecy? Why the mantle of darkness? Héctor tried to concentrate on a single star low in the east where the sky was darkest. The job he would perform tonight hung as mysteriously as did that pinhole of light so far in the distance he could only guess its shape.

He wondered what Lilia was doing, was thinking, this evening. What did she see this very moment as Héctor rushed toward the calm expanse of sea before him? The realization struck him then that Lilia would never have attempted a crossing had Héctor not gone before her. An obvious fact, but a truth he'd sidestepped in his anger and grief.

Once Héctor cleared the bay he gunned the *Gabriela*'s engine, the shoreline shrinking behind him. A few minutes later, about fifty meters ahead of him, a mother whale and her baby breached, and Héctor slowed to watch their silhouettes rise twice more before resuming his steady course. He wondered how long young whales stayed with their mothers before setting out on their own. No other boat disturbed the water's surface this evening, and for this he was grateful. He prayed he'd have no one to whom he must explain his actions as night settled over the coastal waters of Acapulco.

By the time he neared his destination everything about him lay hidden in darkness, and the lights of the land had faded to nothingness to the southeast. He shifted the engine to neutral and coasted toward the bluff until the tide slowed him, pushing him in the opposite direction, and he began to paddle the short stretch toward the rock face where he believed the wooden ladder lay against the cliff like some strange, leafless plant, snaking its way toward the top. He'd brought along a flashlight in his pocket, but he'd hoped not to use it. He listened, wondering who may be waiting in the darkness just a few meters above him, but he could hear only wind and the lapping of the water against the boat and the rocks.

When the bow bumped against the scarp he felt with his hands the slick wet stone for a place to wedge his anchor. He poled along with his paddle, running his fingers across the crag. The boat banged against the rocks as Héctor pushed along the wall, squinting into the darkness for the boards Santiago had promised ran up the cliff, but Héctor couldn't find them, and he began to doubt himself. Maybe he'd pulled ashore too early, or perhaps he'd run too far to the north and passed the spot altogether.

The wind began to kick up and with it Héctor's unease. His shirtfront felt damp from either sea splash or sweat, and as he fingered the rock surface, groping for the wooden slats of the promised ladder, he wondered what creature took its nightly refuge among these crannies. The *Gabriela* knocked against rock hidden just beneath the water's surface, jarring Héctor, and he steadied himself with the paddle. He imagined that sunken boulder, once a part of the rock face looming above him, splitting from where it'd been for thousands of years and crashing down into the water below. He wondered how long ago that had happened and if another jagged fragment might sheer from the cliff and crush him here. Who would find him? Maybe he'd lie pinned to the stony bottom forever, entombed in seawater, destined to be the food of crabs and sea snakes and the small sharks that darted about these gravelly shallows.

His hand clumsily struck a weathered board, and he grabbed it, pulling the boat with nearly imperceptible headway against the lapping water. Everything about him seemed electric, holding more potential for danger than he'd known in daylight on these waters. He wedged his anchor among some rocks and tied his bowline around the lowest wooden slat fastened there. He wondered who had secured this makeshift ladder and how sturdy these steps could be. He fingered the wood for nails. Someone had gone to great trouble in drilling these nails into the cliff side to secure the steps, each about a third of a meter long, and perhaps that someone waited above for him now.

Héctor craned his neck, studying skyward, but the ladder and the rocks were veiled in velvety darkness. He inhaled a deep breath and hoisted himself from the boat, careful not to slip on the slick, wet rocks, and mouthed a silent prayer before ascending. He noticed—or thought he noticed—two quick pricks of light maybe fifteen or twenty meters above his head where he believed the cliff's edge to be, but then the seamless darkness returned, and he doubted he'd seen any light at all.

Chapter 20

Karolina

The small child showed all the signs of malnourishment. His hair, discolored and dry, looked dull as straw, and his soft belly protruded with no muscle strength to hold his abdomen tight. Karolina knew, without a doubt, he had worms. They always had worms.

"Any idea of his age?" she asked the police officer, though she kept her eyes on the listless child, his arms thin as sticks.

"Not really. I received him from an old man who drives the trash truck. The driver, his name is Francisco, found the little fellow sitting in the mud beside his dead mother, a prostitute the trash man recognized from his years working the dump."

The child wore only a dingy T-shirt, a size too small, and nothing more. His feet, legs, and bottom were caked in dried mud, and several of his many sores and scrapes appeared infected. He rubbed his eyes with dirty fists, and Karolina suspected him to be at least two and a half years old, though he looked much younger.

Perhaps one day such sights would breeze by Karolina without affecting her, but she could not imagine that day. She reached for the child, and the officer passed him to her. A patch of hair was missing from behind his right ear, and the hair that remained was sparse and brittle.

"The old trash man said he'd seen the child's mama around the dump for the past few years. He suspected she was about seventeen. He thought she had at least one other child, but he couldn't be sure he wasn't confusing her with another whore out there," the officer said.

The child weighed about what a healthy one-year-old should weigh. Though Karolina was just twenty-six, she felt she'd seen more than a lifetime's share of abandonment, starvation, homelessness, and extreme poverty among helpless children.

"He can't walk," the officer said. "Nothing visibly wrong with his legs, but he isn't capable of walking."

Karolina shook her head and brushed the child's hair from his eyes. "He's likely lame from lack of maternal nutrition during the pregnancy. And, of course, this little guy's own poor nutrition his whole miserable life." She stared into the child's dark eyes as she held him, his eyelids heavy and rimmed in dust. She gently swayed, losing herself in her imaginings of his difficult, almost impossible existence.

"Well," she said. "I need to put down a name. What did you say was the driver's name who discovered him?"

"Francisco," he said. "But I don't know his last name."

"That doesn't matter. Francisco is what I'll put down for this child's name. You are little Francisco, no?" she said, tickling the child's exposed and swollen belly. He did not respond with a giggle or even a grin, but stared at her blankly, perhaps wondering where his mama had gone.

The officer turned to go.

"Hey, let me ask you something," Karolina said. "Any chance you remember a car accident a few years ago involving a baby girl?"

He scratched his chin. "You have any more information than that? I've been around a lot of crashes, you know? And unfortunately plenty with children involved."

Yes, of course he had, Karolina thought. "This crash involved a couple, both killed, and the baby, the little girl who was the lone survivor, had false papers. The papers claimed her name was Ernesto. Maybe you remember something about that?" Karolina said, gently rubbing the listless boy's back as she spoke.

"No," the officer said, shaking his head as he turned again to go. "I don't recall anything like that. I can't help you. Wish I could."

Karolina nodded and mumbled a thank-you, then took Francisco to the nurse to clean him, feed him, and perform a physical exam.

When she'd left him there, she washed her hands and fixed herself a cup of coffee before completing paperwork on the boy. She thought about the phone call she'd received from the village priest down in Oaxaca; she'd been so busy she'd not had time to investigate the possibility that the child he sought resided here. How could she even begin to find an answer for him? So many children had passed through the doors here, and the majority of them with little or no documentation accompanying them upon their arrival. She could pore over files, looking for a story that matched the one the priest had relayed to her, or she could study files dated in the time frame the priest thought the child had arrived, or she could ask the staff who'd been here that long if anyone recalled admitting the infant girl child who'd arrived with fake papers bearing a boy's name.

She looked up when the buzzer at the front door sounded, and through the glass she saw a thin, bleary-eyed young woman holding two matching babies. Twins. Karolina's efforts on behalf of the priest in Oaxaca would have to wait. She went to the door, praying the small, tired woman at the threshold had come simply asking directions to another place, but even as Karolina's fingers gripped the worn knob she knew better. At this rate she'd soon be turning babies away.

Chapter 21

Lilia

Lilia lay flat on her back with a thick, hard pillow under her hips, as if elevating her bottom would keep the baby inside. Rosa had helped her change her skirt and underwear and fetched her a glass of water. Rosa's solution to most of life's troubles involved water: drinking it, bathing in it, listening to it, swimming in it, soaking a rag in it infused with mint and lavender leaves and draping it across one's neck or brow, or across one's wrists.

"You're fortunate to live in modern times, Lilia," Rosa said, laying a soft blanket across Lilia's legs. Lilia knew Rosa intended her words to comfort and soothe her like the blanket, to envelop her in a feeling of well-being and relief, but the sweat beading along the dark hairs above Rosa's lips betrayed her, and Lilia sensed Rosa's concern.

"When I was a girl," Rosa continued, "my older sister labored in childbirth for four days. The ancient medicine woman in our village had birthed hundreds of babies, I'm sure. She'd helped deliver my mama, my siblings, and me, but she couldn't help my sister. Caesarean deliveries existed far away in big-city hospitals, but here in Puerto Isadore such possibilities were unknown. You think this surgery is rare now? In the days of my youth no one knew these procedures existed."

"She died in childbirth?" Lilia said, taking a small sip of lukewarm water and thinking of her own dead mother.

"Oh, no, though sometimes I know she wished she had," Rosa said, her brow creased in memory of a distant and hard time. A half-grown chicken strutting through Lilia's house flapped up onto the table beside the bed, and Rosa swatted it away with the back of her hand.

"The baby arrived stillborn. We had no way to get to a clinic as you were able to do in Oaxaca City when Fernando decided to enter this world upside down." Rosa smiled a weary smile, no doubt recalling a private sense of pride for diagnosing Fernando's breech position, which probably saved Lilia's life.

"In those days the village medicine woman was all a young mother had, you see," Rosa said. "Not so different from today, but today we can get to a bus route. Today we can travel to a clinic if we must."

Lilia nodded, gently rubbing her belly with the pads of her fingers, as if willing this child to live and not do as Rosa's sister's child had done.

"My sister labored too long. I remember hearing her cries and feeling afraid. Our mother made me stay outside where I slept on a mat with my younger brother. Even so, we heard our sister's wailing day and night, day and night, and day again, and yet, the baby would not come.

"This would have been my first niece or nephew, my first close experience with human birth. I'd witnessed the births of goats, dogs, piglets, calves, but my sister seemed to be struggling far more and far longer than any animal I'd ever seen give life, and I knew then I'd never have a baby." Rosa smiled and shrugged. "Ah, but we see how that vow worked out."

Lilia thought of Rosa's five children who, as far as Lilia knew, had entered the world with no great difficulty.

"Her head—the baby was a girl—was wedged hard against my sister's pelvis, cutting off the blood supply that eventually killed the baby but also the tissue there. My sister's birth canal and urinary tract were destroyed. Everything down there," Rosa said, shaking her head. "She lost her dignity that day along with her first and only child."

Lilia studied her friend's face, but Rosa's mind had drifted far from this moment, far from Lilia, and she no longer gave the pretense of nonchalance at Lilia's predicament with her own unborn baby.

"Even after the bleeding stopped and the normal time for healing had passed, my poor sister could never control her water."

As if reading Lilia's mind, Rosa turned to her. "And I don't mean the way you sneeze and lightly wet your underpants, Lilia. All mothers know that experience. No. My sister's bladder and rectum were worn through and incapable of maintaining their functions.

"No one could stand the smell of my sister, though of course we loved her and did our best. She bathed in rose and lavender water each night and each morning for the rest of her life, and she carried chips of fragrant soap in her pockets in an effort to mask the stench of urine and feces she could not contain. My mother stitched little pouches into the waistbands of her skirts where she'd tuck orange peels, flower blossoms, anything to hide the odor of her incontinence."

"That would be a miserable existence," Lilia said softly, hoping she'd not face a similar fate.

"Yes, miserable." Rosa nodded. "She was never the same gentle person she'd always been. Of course, she was bitter from losing her first child, and in such a physically difficult way, but then her husband left her. The seed of bitterness swelled and ripened into the nastiest of fruits. She grew ashamed, though, of course, what could she do? I don't recall my sister ever smiling again, such trauma to her body and spirit. She lived out her days an outcast."

If Rosa's story was meant to cheer Lilia about her good fortune of living in such modern times, the effort fell short. Her sister's sad tale tapped into a vein of hot tears that flowed from some place deep and unexpected in Lilia.

She anticipated Rosa scolding her for crying and telling her she would not suffer a similar fate as had Rosa's sister, but instead Rosa said, "Don't get up. I'll be back shortly," then she headed out the door.

Lilia grew heavy eyed and floated to sleep listening to the gentle cooing of a dove somewhere beyond her window. She awoke to Rosa standing over her with a basket in her arms.

"Are you bleeding much?" she asked.

"I don't think so. I did as you said. I haven't gotten up."

"Are you in pain? Feeling any cramps?" Rosa asked, setting the basket on the floor beside Lilia.

"No. I feel tired but otherwise not bad," Lilia said.

"This is good, Lilia. In order to keep this baby inside you must do as I say. No cocoa for you, no chocolate. Nothing that will stimulate you or the baby. We will keep your water pitcher filled, and you must drink all day and during the night. You should feel you are going to float away on the sea of water you're drinking."

"Yes, okay," Lilia said, noting the change in Rosa. No longer reminiscing about the past, Rosa's demeanor was businesslike and authoritative.

"You'll have three small cups of mescal a day, one in the morning, one with lunch, and one before bed. The alcohol will prevent contractions and relax your uterus. We must keep you from going into labor, keep your cervix from dilating. Each day we prevent these things, that baby will stay inside and grow. Her lungs will strengthen, and she'll have a better chance of thriving when she decides to enter this world."

These instructions did not surprise Lilia; alcohol and water were staples of Rosa's treatments.

"Here, drink this," Rosa said, passing Lilia a cup of some peculiar-smelling elixir.

Lilia brought the cup to her nose. "What's in this?"

"You'd rather not know," Rosa said, pouring herself a hefty cup of mescal and leaning back in the chair she'd pulled beside Lilia's bed.

"It smells horrible, like a dead fish," Lilia said, taking the tiniest sip.

Rosa nodded and licked her lips. "Yes," she said, "I suppose it does." She tipped back the cup of mescal until she'd drained it, then placed the cup beside the bottle on the table.

"Dear Mother Mary of Jesus," Lilia said, trying to swallow the cup's contents in one big gulp. "I can't do this."

Rosa laughed, poured herself another cup of mescal, and looked into Lilia's cup. "Halfway there, girl," she said, sitting back in her chair.

Lilia eyed her, resigning herself to the reality that Rosa always won. She finished off the fishy liquid in a final, desperate gulp, then brought the back of her hand to her mouth to suppress the vomit she felt surfacing.

"Keep it down," Rosa barked, all softness gone from her voice.

Lilia squeezed her eyes shut tight and willed the nauseating liquid to settle into her stomach.

After a full minute, Rosa said, "That's it. Good. Very good."

"Well?" Lilia said, when she could speak, her gut churning.

"Well, what?"

"What was that?" Lilia said.

"Fish oil, wild yam root, and orange juice," Rosa said, her eyes sparkling.

"I need some mint," Lilia said, closing her eyes and reclining onto her pillow. "That was the foulest concoction."

"That foul drink will save your baby. The fish and the yam offer something magical, medicinal, that lowers inflammation and will keep contractions at bay, and the citrus juice is packed with important vitamins that help with swelling and general well-being.

"I'm not finished with you yet, girl. Pull up your skirt," Rosa said, reaching down for something beside the bed, which Lilia couldn't see. When the hem of her skirt was just beneath her swollen breasts, Rosa laid a warm, damp cloth across Lilia's lower belly.

"How's that?" Rosa asked, though Lilia knew Rosa cared nothing for an answer.

The warmth did feel comforting, calming, and Lilia again closed her eyes, trying to concentrate on the pleasure instead of the fish slime lingering in the back of her throat.

"I soaked the cloth in a tincture made of herbs, roots, and berries from my garden. They relieve cramps, though you say you're having none yet, and that is a good sign. The solution will relax your muscles and calm your female parts. How do you feel?"

Aside from the horrible but slowly fading taste in her mouth, Lilia had begun to loosen up, and the tension she hadn't realized she was carrying had subsided. "Relaxed," she said.

Fernando toddled into the room holding the rascally hen that had been pecking through the house. "Look!" he squealed. "I got it. I got the chicken, Mama!"

"Come here, my boy," Lilia said, reaching for Fernando's unavailable hand that gripped the squirming, fluttering hen a bit too tightly. "Let that silly chicken go, and give your fat mama a kiss."

The boy would not release the pullet, but leaned into Lilia and gave her a wet kiss on the cheek.

"So," Rosa said, standing with a soft grunt that hinted at her aging bones and joints. "Every day, you know what you must do. If you're not hardheaded as is your tendency, and you do as I instruct, this baby will stay put and grow as she must grow. Come, Fernando."

The sweet child, still clutching the agitated hen, kissed Lilia's cheek once more then gingerly extended the fowl to Lilia's face. "Chicken kiss you, too, Mama."

"Ah, yes. Thank you, señorita," Lilia said to the chicken, then added, "Run along, now, with Tía Rosa, Fernando."

Rosa left the room, and Lilia listened to her and Fernando talking beyond the window in the yard behind the house, though she could not make out their words.

She thought of Héctor. If he called her on the priest's phone, Lilia would likely not be able to take the call, now that Rosa had forced her to bed. Perhaps Héctor and Alejandra would return home soon, and perhaps this baby would remain in Lilia's womb long enough to survive and live a normal life, and Lilia and Héctor would live out their days with their three children and maybe more, despite the problems with this pregnancy.

Those thoughts comforted her and gave her buoyancy when she felt herself sinking in her despair. When bad thoughts entered her mind, she willed them away through prayer and by conjuring pleasant images like snapshots from the happier, more carefree past.

Yet for every hopeful thought she could muster, a dark possibility would creep into her head. Then she'd consider the very real likelihood that Alejandra had long been dead, her thin, white bones resting someplace Lilia would never see; and that Héctor could die in Acapulco or other parts north in his efforts to find Alejandra, and Lilia would never see Héctor again; and that this baby growing inside her would arrive too early, with a brain not fully formed and the bones of a cripple so that Lilia would live out her own days tending a sick, malformed invalid whom she'd have to carry everywhere and feed mashed mango and melon long after the child's teeth had grown in.

She imagined spiders crawling across the arms and legs of her frail offspring, who, because of deficiencies, could not scrape the toxic, biting bugs from its own limbs. Lilia would try to brush them off the feeble child, but the spiders would advance and creep across Lilia's face as well, and she could do nothing to stop them.

Lilia hadn't realized she'd almost fallen asleep, that her wakeful musings had drifted toward nightmarish imaginings, that Fernando stood beside her bed and tickled her cheek with a fresh, green sprig and whispered, "Here, Mama. You sleeping, Mama? Rosa said for me to bring you mint."

Chapter 22

Ana María

Emanuel and Diego the Magnificent sat on stools looking more drunk than sober, though sometimes gauging those two proved difficult, especially Diego. Ana María had been working the back of the restaurant, not the bar where the men sat, but she'd seen them drinking beer and a couple of times throwing back shots of some liquor, though she couldn't tell what kind. A rerun from yesterday's World Cup match between Mexico and France played on the small television above the bar, but the sound was off. Everyone knew Mexico had won, 2–0, but still, no one could get enough of *futbol,* especially during the World Cup.

"Ana María," Diego shouted, when she stepped behind the bar to wash her hands and remove her apron. The earlier crowd had thinned to a lone couple who'd paid but lingered over drinks in the back.

"You two up to no good as always?" she said, popping the top from a bottle of Carta Blanca for herself.

"Look at you, drinking on the job, beautiful lady," Emanuel said, shaking his head in mock disapproval, and she knew by that lazy smile and his tired eyes he was drunk.

"No, no, that's okay, Emanuel," Diego said, winking at her. "When the waitress is as lovely as Ana María here, they're allowed to do as they wish."

"You two are as drunk as sewer rats," she said, scowling with hand on hip, suppressing a grin, though both men's eyes had returned to the television behind her.

"Sewer rats? Us?" Emanuel raised his eyebrows and looked Diego up and down. "Yes, you're probably right about this guy. But me, I'm nothing of that sort."

"Listen, gorgeous. The workweek is done, at least for the common sort like my boy Emanuel here, and so we're celebrating his day off from my father's whip cracking. And we're celebrating this win playing out up there on that screen. Plus, I'm diving tomorrow, and so I won't drink past midnight, but until then . . ." He raised his bottle of beer to Ana María and to Emanuel and then toward the television. They clinked bottles before they all took swigs.

The old cook stepped out from the kitchen in back, his apron dirty and an ever-present scowl on his brow, mumbling something about effeminate French *futbol* players, until he saw Diego. "Look who's in my café! Hey Diego, what can I fix you to eat? Anything you want."

"Surprise me, friend!" Diego shouted to the cook, slapping hands with him.

The cook raised a finger. "I got for you just the thing," he said. "What's the score here?" He jutted his gray-stubbled chin toward the television.

"Up by one," Diego said. "Great goal by Javier Hernández."

"I hate the French," the cook said. "After that tie with those South Africans we need this win, eh Diego?"

"We'll win," Diego said, like some great soothsayer, as if the world didn't already know Mexico had won this game a full day earlier. He half raised his beer to the cook, who turned and stepped back into the kitchen.

"What's that guy's name?" Diego said, with no hint of embarrassment that he couldn't recall the cook's name.

"That's Abejundio," Ana María said. "You're so famous and popular, you can't remember all your fans' names, eh Señor Magnificent?"

Diego shrugged. "I don't know that I've ever met that guy, Ana María," he said, lowering his voice as if at once defending and acknowledging his arrogance.

"Hey, where's your friend Héctor?" Ana María said, looking at Emanuel. Héctor had been here a couple weeks now, but rarely did Ana María see Emanuel and Héctor out together. She often thought of Héctor, though she couldn't quite name why. Perhaps she worried about his innocence. Though she'd never been down to Puerto Isadore, she knew rural village life well, had seen their simple, old-fashioned, and sometimes backward ways of living. Acapulco ran faster and hotter than anything country villagers like Héctor could possibly comprehend, and she worried about his safety in his desperation to make quick money.

Emanuel drummed his fingers on his beer bottle, but Ana María caught a flicker of hesitation in his voice when he said, "Héctor? I don't know. Working, I think."

"Working," she said, her voice flat and more cynical than she'd intended. "He's fishing, right? So those guys are now running fishing charters at night, eh Emanuel? I doubt that. I truly doubt that." She took a swig of her beer and watched the last patrons leave the restaurant.

Diego and Emanuel glanced at each other, then focused their attention on the *futbol* match. The men made noticeable efforts to busy themselves with mundane nothingness and idle chat of World Cup players and scores, so that Ana María had no doubt that tonight Héctor was doing something unscrupulous and perhaps dangerous.

Even before Abejundio emerged with a mounded platter of

half-moon-shaped *molotes,* the delicious aroma of chorizo and hot grease had wafted from the kitchen.

"For Diego the Magnificent," the old cook said, as if Ana María and Emanuel were Diego's pet dogs rather than his human companions. Abejundio's face was the color and texture of a coconut hull, though slicked with sweat. He set the food before them and pulled a bottle of tequila from beneath the bar. He grabbed four short cups and filled them each halfway.

"*Salud,*" old Abejundio said, raising his cup to Diego.

Before long Ana María felt as drunk as she'd suspected the men to be. They toasted one another, the cliffs of La Quebrada, Diego, and his fellow divers. They drank to the Mexican *futbol* team and to players the men admired. Then Ana María said, "To Emanuel's guest, Héctor. He should be with us here!"

"Who kicked that one?" Abejundio said, his black eyes glistening. The way he turned his head toward the television reminded Ana María of the ancient tortoise she'd observed in the zoo on a school trip years ago, its neck thick in straining tendons and weathered skin.

"Was that Cuauhtémoc Blanco?" Even as Abejundio said this, Blanco's name flashed across the screen. "That guy," he said, shaking his head in adoration. "I love that one. That's the third World Cup he's scored in, you know that? No one else has done that!" he shouted. "At least no Mexican."

"To Blanco, then," Emanuel said, grabbing the tequila bottle for another round, but its contents were spent.

Old Abejundio took the empty bottle and tossed it into the trash bin. He lifted a hand in departure—*No más, no más*—and stumbled off into the kitchen.

"So you're intrigued by my guest, Héctor, yes, Ana María? Héctor, Héctor, Héctor," Emanuel said. "You want to go find him? I know exactly where he is. Mischief," Emanuel said, dragging the back of his hand across his lips. "He's out getting into mischief."

Ana María listened to Emanuel but gazed at Diego who seemed uninterested in anything about Héctor, until Emanuel said, "He's out making some sort of run for his new bosses. That's what your Héctor's up to tonight."

"Not my Héctor, Emanuel," Ana María said. "I don't know this guy. I just worry about him, you know? A *naco* such as he is."

Of course, Emanuel had kept this information of Héctor's whereabouts tonight to himself when she'd questioned him earlier in the evening, but the beers and tequila had loosened that news from him. Héctor was out doing a run. What did that entail?

"He's working for Santiago and Ignacio tonight, eh?" Diego said. "He told you this?"

Emanuel didn't seem to catch the concern in Diego's voice, a slight change in pitch, or notice his sudden interest in Emanuel and Ana María's conversation. Ana María eyed Diego, watched his expression with curiosity when Emanuel answered, "Well, he tells me things he might not tell others, you know? I'm his host. I hook him up with shit like a bed and a job. He should tell me whatever the hell I ask him, shouldn't he?"

Ana María considered this, and sucked the last warm drops of beer from the bottom of her bottle.

"Let's go check on him," Emanuel said, rising to his feet.

"Check on him? Where?" Diego said, looking in no rush to go anywhere.

"The dock. The boat, that boat he fishes," he said to them both. Then, to Ana María, "You know, what's it called, that boat?"

"How would I know the name of the boat he fishes?" Ana María said, suddenly needing fresh air.

"The *Gabriela*," Diego said, to Ana María's surprise. Diego didn't really know Héctor, did he?

Emanuel seemed a bit surprised, too. "Damn, you have a good memory. I didn't think you even knew the name of the boat."

"Oh, sure. Why wouldn't I know that? You recall, I introduced him to those guys he works for," Diego said. "Did he tell you what he was doing for Ignacio and Santiago?"

Emanuel's typical reserve in such matters had given way to bravado in his drunkenness. He shrugged. "Sure, he tells me. He's out picking up a cooler. That's it. Just picking up a cooler."

"A cooler?" Diego said, shifting on his stool. Something in his creased forehead, the way he cocked his head, hinted that Héctor's new duties didn't surprise him.

"Yes, and I have a feeling the cooler's not hauling fish," Emanuel said, with a smug lift of his eyebrows. He was like the cock strutting among small, skittering hens in a thorny hedgerow, feeling a sense of dominance and great importance because of some knowledge he possessed. This wasn't his typical way, and Ana María knew the tequila and countless beers were to blame.

Ana María hated Emanuel in that moment, hated his indifference, his sarcasm, that this naïve old friend of his could be up to bad dealings, and Emanuel didn't seem to care.

"So he didn't tell you what he's transporting," Diego said. "He gave you no clue as to the contents of that cooler?"

"He didn't know," Emanuel said, his eyes nearly closed.

"He didn't know, or did he just tell you he didn't know?" Ana María said.

Diego watched Emanuel with great focus now.

"Let's walk down to the boat. Wait for his return and see what he's up to, no? Pop the cooler open, and take a look inside for yourself," Emanuel said, swaying, or maybe he wasn't swaying. Maybe Ana María was the one swaying. She steadied herself with a hand on the bar.

"Let's go," she said, her worries about Héctor now matched by her curiosity concerning the cooler.

Diego stood, a somber look darkening his eyes. "I'm done. Diving tomorrow and all that, like I said. I'll have a mother of a hangover as it is, and if I stay out any longer I'll likely smash my head on the rocks tomorrow. I'm taking off."

"Ah, that's shit. Total goat shit. You could dive those cliffs blindfolded, backward, and drunk with two monkeys on your back," Emanuel said.

"Well, that's true, I could do all that even if those monkeys were drunk, too, but I'm out of here," he said, then slipped through the door after a slight bow to them both.

"Screw him," Emanuel said, pulling Ana María toward him and kissing her surprisingly gently on the lips. "You want to walk with me?"

"Yes. Let's go see my Héctor," she said, teasing him.

"Ah, your Héctor. Your Héctor. Héctor, Héctor, Héctor," he said, taking her hand, pulling her toward the door with a slight stumble.

The night air she'd been craving knocked Ana María a bit off-kilter, and she focused on Emanuel's words—he was talking so much—to keep her head in the conversation and to hold the world steady, because walking made her dizzy. Or perhaps standing after so much sitting on a stool was the thing that made the world spin. She held tight to Emanuel's hand as they headed toward the dock and the *Gabriela,* determined to check on Héctor, to discover what he was up to on this dark and wobbly night.

Chapter 23

Héctor

The wooden steps, weathered and worn, supported Héctor's weight well enough, but even so, they were narrow and in spots slick with some invisible slime Héctor imagined would be the green of some primal ooze in the light of day. He worked his way in darkness toward the top of the cliff, focusing with great effort on each footfall, knowing he could not afford a misstep and a tumble to the rocks and foam below. Even before he reached the top and saw the container he was to transport, Héctor wondered how he could get the thing, surely cumbersome and likely heavy, down the rickety ladder while getting himself down intact. And what would happen if the cooler tipped or tumbled from his grasp, spilling its content of only God knew what? And what, he finally allowed himself to consider, would spill from the cooler? He hadn't been able to ponder that question for fear his spine would go weak and he'd back out of the deal, like some grimy-faced pauper about to steal a chicken egg only to be deterred by an unfamiliar cur napping near the nest. Would the reward be worth the risk? Or would the perilous effort prove foolhardy and irreparably life altering?

He heaved himself up over the cliff's edge, landing hard on the rocky soil, unsure which way to look until a bright light blinded him from somewhere off to his right.

"Who are you?" a gravelly voice called from beyond the light.

"I'm Héctor. I was sent here. By my bosses. By Santiago and Ignacio," he said, uncertain how much he should say.

"You're alone?" the voice asked.

"Yes, yes," Héctor said, rising to his feet, careful neither to step backward off the cliff nor forward toward the man.

"All right, then," the voice said, at once killing the bright light and switching on a small-beamed flashlight. "Let's do this."

Héctor walked forward, unable to see the man until they were but a meter apart, and even then the man used care not to illuminate his face so that his features were dulled and indeterminate under the moonless sky. He stood beside a pickup truck, its tailgate down. The man turned the flashlight toward the truck, its glow landing on a large, dark-colored cooler that spread the width of the truck's bed. The man brought the light to his brow and snapped it into place there so his hands were free as the headlamp lighted what they needed to see.

"Grab that side," he said.

Héctor grabbed the handle closer to him, and with effort they hauled the cooler to the cliff's edge and set it there. The man returned to the truck and came back with a long length of rope, one end trailing behind him toward the truck. He fastened the other end through the cooler's handles.

"You have a light?" the man said.

Héctor pulled the flashlight from his pocket and flicked it on without a word, careful to shine it toward the cooler and not at his companion.

His gut knew what he'd find if he opened the cooler. He envisioned bundles, neatly wrapped in waterproof packaging. He wondered which would be heavier, bricks of cocaine or of marijuana, but he knew determining the container's contents simply by heft would be impossible. His mind couldn't linger on such thoughts.

"We're going to lower this. It'll take both of us. When we get it to the rocks, you go down behind it and hold it steady. I'll come after you, and we'll work the cooler into your boat. Then you take off, and I'll call Santiago and let him know you're on your way. He'll be at the dock waiting for you."

Héctor nodded, then said, "Okay," realizing the man likely couldn't see him in the darkness as he busied himself with the rope. Héctor understood the man's implied message: He was to go straight back to the dock without a stop, detour, or delay, and surely without opening the cooler.

The wind had kicked up, and Héctor shivered as his sweat cooled in the breeze. The gusts blowing across the cliff's edge from the water chilled him, though the night remained balmy. They worked the cooler over the side of the cliff, then lowered the rope hand over hand, Héctor standing behind his nameless cohort in much the way he and the boys of his youth had played tug-of-war on the beach with a length of rope left behind or lost by some fisherman. Only on this moonless night the teams were Héctor and a stranger against this mysterious container. Héctor guessed the distance from where they stood to the rocks below to be about eighteen meters, and he wondered if the rope was long enough. The lid of the cooler had been taped shut, but perhaps the tape wouldn't hold fast, the way the container banged against the rock face as they lowered it. If the lid popped off and the contents spilled into the sea below, certainly the man would be furious. He'd taken great care to meet Héctor under cover of darkness, great care to seal the cooler and to get it, with Héctor's help, to Ignacio and Santiago. Héctor wondered if a sharp, steely blade were just out of sight, tucked into the man's waistband, for quick access in case he needed to gut Héctor on the spot.

"There," the man said. "It's to the rocks. Go down and hold it steady. I'll tie the end off at the truck."

The man turned away, disappearing into the darkness, save for the thin beam preceding him, fading into nothingness where his truck waited. Héctor eased himself over the edge and down the wooden slats toward the surf and stones. To his surprise the cooler had landed on a boulder and tilted slightly backward so that one side rested against the rock face, bridging a short span of seawater. The weight of the container, along with the way it had wedged between the rock and the wall, held it firmly in place for now, but getting it from where it sat into the boat would be another matter. The rocks were slippery and with the increasing wind the sea had gotten choppy.

Héctor had tied the boat to the bottom step, and even in the wind and splashing, foaming surf, he could hear the boat knocking against the rocks. He feared the *Gabriela* would suffer damage, but what was he to do? He'd followed the directions he'd been given.

The stranger joined Héctor, holding tight to the cooler's handle for support. "We're going to have to get this onto the bow," he shouted above the wind.

Leaving the *Gabriela* secured to the ladder, Héctor pulled the boat as close to them as he could get it, leaving about a meter and a half between the cooler and where it had to go. With one foot on the bow and the other balanced on slime-coated rock, he grabbed the handle of the cooler.

"Okay," Héctor said, wondering how the two of them could possibly accomplish this task.

Either its contents had shifted or the container had wedged deeper into the gap between the rocks than Héctor had anticipated, and when he and the man heaved the cooler toward the boat it didn't budge. The resistance caught Héctor unprepared, and he lost his footing, scraping the length of his shin against rock and smashing his knee. Now soaked in seawater from his hips down, he grunted in pain.

"Look at my feet," the stranger yelled, aiming his headlamp downward. "See. You have to wedge your shoes into the rocks at an angle."

Héctor worked his way back up the rock, further scraping his knees and elbows, pulling himself by the cooler's handle and fearing his weight would lodge it deeper into the crevice where it remained. He found a foothold for each of his shoes, then nodded blindly into the beam of the man's headlight, now trained on Héctor's face.

This time the cooler gave way just a bit. Each man adjusted his purchase among the rocks and hoisted the container again. Centimeter by centimeter they worked the cooler toward the lip of the boat.

When the bulk of the cooler rested on the bow, the stranger shouted, "Go on. I'll untie you when you get it settled."

Héctor flopped across the starboard side, surprised by the exhaustion that overcame him. As the stranger's headlamp closed the distance to the wooden slat where the bowline remained tied, Héctor pulled the cooler the rest of the way onto the *Gabriela*. Without another word, the stranger untied the boat and tossed the rope at Héctor, where it landed like a long, wet snake across the top of the cooler and the bow, its end dangling overboard.

Just a boat-length off the rocky shore the depth of the water dropped fast. Héctor cranked the engine and eased away from the cliff side. When he looked back, no sign of the stranger remained, only the wind and darkness endured, and if the solid evidence of the evening's activity didn't sit before him, he could almost imagine the events of the previous hour to be a wild fantasy, whipped up on the sea wind from the distant and strange place where daydreams formed. But the shadowy proceedings on land had been real, and Héctor carried with him now the mysterious results.

A list began forming in Héctor's mind of what the contents of the cooler could be. Drugs? What kind of drugs? A body? Oh, God, not a body. A body wouldn't fit in such a space. But even as he considered the unlikelihood that he was transporting a corpse a part of him knew well that the body of a child or the dismembered body of an adult could indeed fit into the container speeding across the water with him now. And what would he tell the authorities if he were stopped?

The truth, of course. He would tell the truth. He had no knowledge of what he transported. But who would possibly believe that? His heart began to thump in his chest the way it had raced during his crossing to *el norte* when he'd been sealed by blowtorch in the undercarriage of a truck, certain he'd made a fatal mistake. He slowed the boat, idling in the darkness, and prayed God would guide him. He listened for the voice of God in the gusts that rocked the boat, but all he perceived was the lonesome howling of the wind and the cool, wet sea spray on his face. He shivered in his uncertainty and fear.

Héctor knew what he must do. He would throw the cooler overboard. That would be the smartest action. If he were caught with it and the contents were illegal, which, of course, they were, he would be imprisoned. And if he were jailed, he'd be guaranteed never to find Alejandra, and, perhaps, never again to see Lilia and Fernando, never to meet his unborn child Lilia carried.

He stood and grabbed hold of the cooler. He could work it up to the side of the boat and heave it over the transom into the white-capped sea. But what would Santiago do when Héctor returned to the dock empty-handed? Santiago would understand, wouldn't he? Héctor could say the cooler had toppled from the *Gabriela* when he'd been blindsided by a rogue wave. What could Santiago do to him? Maybe Héctor had enough pesos to get to the border and conduct whatever business he needed to conduct to find Alejandra. Continuing to work this way for ill-gotten pay was foolish. This risk he now took hauling mysterious cargo could change his life and the lives of his loved ones in irreparable ways, just as his choice to cross to the Estados Unidos had fractured everything for them.

If he'd never gone to America, if he'd not chosen to cross, Lilia would never have left Puerto Isadore. She'd have had no reason to follow him, to seek her own coyote in an effort to join him. She'd never have met that woman who took their daughter.

An overwhelming urge to cry struck him, and he swayed in the bobbing boat, the wind blowing tears from his cheeks. Paralyzed in indecision and panic, he steadied himself with one hand firm upon the cooler's handle waiting for a plan to develop.

As he rocked on the waves, contemplating his next move, a pinprick of light permeated the black expanse from which he'd just traveled. The light belonged to a vessel coming in from the sea. The approaching boat startled Héctor, snapping him from his uncertainty into a very real understanding that he must leave this spot at once. Perhaps the approaching boat held the authorities. They would see the cooler floating if he pitched it into the sea, and they would fish it from the water and open it. They would track him down, suspecting he'd tossed it, and they'd arrest him.

He cranked the engine and gunned the *Gabriela* toward the distant shore of Acapulco, to where Santiago awaited his arrival. He had not heard the voice of God as he'd hoped, but his choice had been made by circumstances beyond his control. And perhaps, Héctor told himself, in such situations, when we feel most helpless, God makes our decisions for us.

Chapter 24

Karolina

Karolina had finished her paperwork for the evening. She'd been thinking of the priest from Oaxaca when the day-shift nurse, Cristina, came through the front office.

"How's that little Francisco doing?" Karolina said. "The pitiful boy who arrived this morning from the dump?"

"He's holding steady. I cleaned up his scrapes and scabs and dewormed him, and he has a bottle full of warm milk in his belly. So I guess he's better than he's ever been in his life," Cristina said.

Karolina shook her head. "Despite his mama dying this morning."

"Yes, I suppose so. Despite that," Cristina said, grabbing her bag to leave for the day.

"Hey," Karolina said. "How long have you worked here?"

"I'm in my sixth year."

"Do you recall a few years ago a little girl arriving, the lone survivor of a car crash?"

The nurse twisted her mouth to one side, mulling the question.

Karolina continued, "She arrived with false papers, papers for a little boy about the same age. She would have been a baby then. Her papers said her name was Ernesto?"

The nurse nodded, slowly at first and then faster as the memory came to her. "Yes, yes. I remember that child. We brought her in and until we changed her diaper we thought she was a boy. She was dressed like a boy, you know? Very well cared for and clean, unlike most of our arrivals. Even swaddled in a blue blanket. And then with those papers, why wouldn't we think she was a boy?"

"You're kidding? Really? You remember her?" So rare was good news here, Karolina laughed at this discovery.

"Yes, I remember that day well because we'd needed rain, and a rain shower came through, and I guess the roads were bad, slick or something. We actually got two kids from two accidents that evening. That little girl called Ernesto, and also a three-year-old boy who stayed with us just one night before we located a family member. But the girl stayed here for a while, a pretty child. Yes, yes. I remember her. We named her . . . What did we call her? Esther! Yes, little Esther. Because you know, of course, who could call such a pretty orphan girl Ernesto?"

"Where'd she go?" Karolina said.

"My recollection could be off, but as I recall she left us to go to one of the other orphanages. Or maybe she was adopted, I just can't be sure," Cristina said. "Why?"

Karolina relayed the details of the priest's phone call.

"So Esther's real parents are alive and well?"

"Yes, apparently so," Karolina said. "I'm always hesitant to believe such calls, but this priest sounded legitimate."

The nurse shrugged. "The surprises, both good and bad, never end in this place, do they?" she said, her smile weak and her eyes tired. "I hope you can reunite them, that they're good people."

"I wonder where she is," Karolina said.

"You can check the files, now that you have a name and more

information. My memory is fuzzy. I hope she's at another center. Not already adopted out somewhere."

"Thanks," Karolina said, rubbing her temples, as Cristina wasted no more time heading out the door.

The small, cluttered front office needed cleaning, and Karolina's trash bin overflowed with paper. She'd tidy the space before leaving tonight so that when she came in tomorrow morning, her day would at least begin with a fresh start, no matter what sad stories arrived on her doorstep. She began stacking the jumble of loose papers on her desk and decided she would call the priest in Oaxaca tomorrow.

Chapter 25

Rosa

Rosa had been sweeping Lilia's yard when a young boy she recognized as the grandson of the widow lady down the lane ran through the gate.

"Señora," he shouted to Rosa. "Señora Lilia has a phone call. Down at *la farmacia*. Armando sent me. He said the call is from Señor Héctor."

Rosa thanked the boy and told him she'd be right down. She leaned the broom beside the front door and hollered inside.

"Call for you at Armando's, Lilia. Stay put. I'll take it," and before Lilia could respond, Rosa followed the barefoot messenger boy down the lane.

At Armando's Rosa pushed past a couple of young mothers chatting in front of the canned soups. One lady had a baby on her hip and the other had a little girl, maybe seven years old, tickling the feet of the baby and making him giggle while their mothers exchanged gossip.

"Rosa," Armando said, holding the receiver out to her. "I guess you're here on Lilia's behalf?"

Rosa barely nodded. Armando always pushed his nose into the business of others, like an old goat determined to be where he should not.

"*Hola,* Héctor," she said into the receiver. "This is Rosa."

"Rosa?" Héctor said, the worry evident in his voice. "Is Lilia okay?"

"She's in bed, Héctor. This baby doesn't want to wait the full term, but I'm doing my best to keep it in place as long as I can."

"Is Lilia sick?" he said, his words rushed, high pitched in his concern.

"Not so much, just tired, and she's had a few complications. But she's in my care. She's flat on her back, and for now, I think, we've postponed things."

For several seconds Héctor didn't speak, and Rosa thought they'd been disconnected. Then, "Thank you," he said.

"But Héctor, I have important news for you! We've been waiting on your call. The priest came to see us last night. He's found an orphanage that knows of Alejandra!"

"What? Tell me!"

"Yes, yes. The orphanage in Matamoros called him back. An employee there recalls a baby fitting Alejandra's description arriving about the time she went missing. She had the Ernesto papers, Héctor. This child was Alejandra!"

"Go on," he said, nearly yelling into the phone.

"So you must get there. You must go to this place and see these people. The priest says you should get there immediately to ask the questions, to follow her trail. The woman who called said Alejandra is no longer at their orphanage. They changed her name to Esther. That's really all we know. She told the priest that perhaps the child was acquired by a larger, evangelical Christian orphanage in a little town on the eastern outskirts of Monterrey, inland and away from the border. It's where they sometimes send children. Or perhaps she's been adopted. But without proof that you and Lilia are her real parents they'll tell us nothing else."

"Why? Why would one orphanage send her to another one like that?" he said.

"The priest said this happens sometimes. The woman in Matamoros told him that her orphanage suffers terrible over-crowding, that it's in an area of great need. They only house newborns through four-year-old children."

"Did the priest call the other orphanage? Oh, God, Rosa, I cannot believe this, after all this time! She's alive! My baby girl is alive."

Rosa at once feared she'd been too optimistic with Héctor. "She is likely alive, yes. We know she survived the car crash, and we know the authorities brought her to the orphanage. We know she's left that orphanage. But beyond that the path gets weedy, Héctor. The priest says you must go there. See these people face-to-face to ask about her, to find her. They refuse to share any more information over the phone. You have to go there to prove you are the father and not some fraud trying to gain information about a child."

"Yes, of course," he said, lowering his voice as if now mulling what this news meant for him in the coming days.

"Have you earned money? Has the fishing boat paid you enough to get you up north?"

"Yes," he said. "Tell Lilia the fishing pays a fair wage, but that now I also make deliveries of sorts for the boat captains, and these deliveries . . ." His voice trailed off.

"Yes?" Rosa said, watching the two young mothers and their children leave the store, the bell on the doorknob jangling in their wake.

"These deliveries are much more profitable. I've made a couple deliveries now, and each pays far more than a fishing charter."

Rosa wanted to ask details, but she suspected the answers would only leave her with more questions. "And these deliver-ies? What? Are you delivering fish?"

"I don't ask," he said. "I just pick up boxes and transport them to my bosses."

"You don't ask? Surely you can't expect that to add up, Héctor? You don't know what you're transporting?"

"No, Rosa, and in truth, the job flows best that way. I don't ask. I do as I'm told, and I receive payment. Don't worry Lilia with these details, Rosa. Just let her know I'm making money. Good money. And I have enough to leave this place, to pursue Alejandra."

"Okay, Héctor," she said, though she didn't believe him. "Be safe. I'll tell Lilia you'll head north toward Matamoros, toward Casa de Esperanza, House of Hope, that's the name of the orphanage, and that you'll contact us when you get there."

"Okay, Rosa. I'll take the bus in the morning. And Rosa?" he said.

"Yes?"

"Please keep my unborn baby well. I don't think Lilia could handle more loss. Neither of us should have to endure losing another child, especially," he added, "if this promising news doesn't bear fruit, you understand?"

"I'll do all I can, just as I always do for all my babies, Héctor. God's in charge here, as He always is."

She imagined Héctor nodding on the other end of the line, standing at a pay phone somewhere in Acapulco, fancy people in shiny jewelry all about him and expensive cars passing on the street.

"Give Lilia my love, Rosa. Tell her to stay strong, to keep that baby safe inside her. How much longer does the baby need?"

"A couple more weeks at the least, a month would be better, and five weeks would bring the child close to full term. But Héctor, she won't last five weeks. This baby may not wait a week. You must understand this."

"I understand," he said.

"Go with God," she said, before replacing the receiver. She

stared at the wall above the phone where a tiny dark spider wrestled with a struggling brown moth in a cobweb. When she turned to leave she bumped into Armando as he dusted the shelving closest to the phone.

"Everything well with Héctor?" he asked, pushing his wire-frame glasses up to the bridge of his nose.

"All's well," she said, then walked out the door, even as Armando called behind her, "Hello to Lilia! Come back soon, Rosa!"

Chapter 26

Héctor

The *Gabriela* had stayed docked all day because of heavy rainstorms and choppy seas. But now, as Héctor and Emanuel sat on two plastic chairs in front of Emanuel's apartment, the sinking sun torched the retreating clouds a glorious orange, and the night looked to be clear. The beauty of the sky along with the news from Rosa that Alejandra's trail had been detected filled Héctor with a warmth and lightness of spirit he had not known in months. He breathed deeply and sipped a beer, watching a yellow bird flit among the fronds and purplish-red berries on a scraggly palm tree above him. Emanuel smoked a cigarette and listened to the end of the first half of Mexico's World Cup match against Uruguay on a boom box at their feet, but neither spoke, each reveling in the end of an easy workday and the passing of the torrent that had flooded the streets earlier.

"So I may be leaving tomorrow, Emanuel," Héctor said, not taking his eyes from the little bird in the tree.

"Oh?" Emanuel said, exhaling.

"I got word from home today that Alejandra has been located. I need to head north, to get my daughter."

"Fantastic!" Emanuel said, flicking his cigarette butt into an oil-slicked puddle. "That's great news, Héctor. Where is she?"

"That's what I have to figure out. She was in Matamoros, at an orphanage there. This much we know. From there she was taken somewhere else, but the orphanage won't relinquish details unless I go there. To prove I'm her papa."

After a moment Emanuel said, "You know, Ana María and I were going to spy on you one night. At the dock." He watched his spent cigarette float in the puddle.

"What? Why?"

"No worries. We never got there. She was too drunk so I just walked her home. We were hoping to see what you've been up to. With your mysterious job," he said, glancing at Héctor.

"You'd have seen nothing exciting. You know as much as I do about my so-called mysterious job," Héctor said.

Emanuel cleared his throat and spit. "Héctor," he said, his tone different now, somber.

"Yeah?"

"I should . . ." Emanuel began, turning his gaze from the puddle to look Héctor in the eyes. "I'm sorry about everything. About what you and Lilia have endured." He sat up taller, straightening his back as if at once uneasy in his chair. "Your daughter, you know? Everything. I'm sorry, man. No one should go through what your family's suffered. I'm just really sorry all this has happened."

Héctor nodded, uncertain how to respond, unaccustomed to Emanuel speaking like this. He couldn't say "No problem" or "It's all okay," because things were not okay. Not yet, anyway. Instead he shrugged and said, "Until you have a child of your own, a wife of your own . . ." He paused, shaking his head, searching for the right words. Héctor loved Lilia, had always loved Lilia, and their children, too, with a depth Emanuel could never comprehend. "You can't imagine, Emanuel. But at least I have some direction now." He didn't know what else to add.

As they spoke a shiny blue truck approached from down the hill.

"Diego," Emanuel said, pointing toward the street.

Diego parked in front of Emanuel's apartment and stepped from the truck. In his dark jeans, boots, white shirt with silver snaps, and cowboy hat, he looked like "the Magnificent" should, indeed, be part of his name.

"Boring match so far. We need to score," he said.

"Half's just started," Emanuel said. "Our guys need to step up."

"Rafael Márquez is the man! He and my cousin are good friends, you know? He'll come through for us."

Héctor glanced at Emanuel to see if he were as awed as Héctor by Diego's connection to a member of the national *futbol* team.

Emanuel shrugged. "I hope so," he said.

"Come ride around with me, Héctor. Check out my truck, eh? You got anywhere else you've got to be?" Diego said.

Héctor had hardly seen Diego since the day they'd met. Because he was saving every peso he made, Héctor didn't go out drinking at night with Emanuel and Diego, and so he had never ridden in Diego's fancy new truck.

"No, I got nowhere to be for a while," he said. Then lowering his voice, "I'm making a delivery for Santiago tonight." He never spoke to anyone about his work for Santiago and Ignacio, but Diego had arranged their introduction, so speaking to him about work didn't concern Héctor.

"Come on, then," Diego said.

Héctor slipped into the truck's cab, where Diego had the station playing the World Cup match turned up loud. The truck smelled as Héctor imagined it would, of fresh, rich leather and a hint of pineapple from the small, fruit-shaped air freshener hanging from the rearview mirror. Along with it dangled a silver crucifix on a thin leather string and a framed photo of a young boy and girl dressed in Sunday clothes.

"My niece and nephew," Diego said, when he saw Héctor eyeing the photograph. "Their first Communion photo."

"They live here?" Héctor said.

"No, they're my sister's kids. They live in Mexico City. My brother-in-law's in politics, you know? He's a big shot. Always has to be near the action."

Héctor couldn't imagine someone being a bigger big shot than Diego, as beloved as he and the divers were here in Acapulco.

Before they'd traveled a minute, Diego lowered the volume a bit and said, "So how's your job with my friends? You like your work?"

"I do," Héctor said. "They're nice guys. They pay me as promised, you know? It's been good, and I thank you, Diego, for hooking me up."

Diego lit a joint and sucked in the pungent smoke for what seemed to Héctor an impossibly long time before offering it to Héctor. Though he wasn't much of a marijuana smoker, he'd been feeling particularly carefree this night, and besides, one day he could tell people he'd smoked a joint with Diego the Magnificent de La Quebrada.

Héctor pulled on the joint, the sweet taste of the bud smoke filling his lungs until he erupted in an embarrassing fit of coughing.

"Hey, it's good shit, this, you know? Take it easy, Héctor," Diego said, laughing. "So tell me about your job. You like it. That's good. My friends say you do fine work, that you're loyal and don't ask questions, and you always deliver as scheduled."

Héctor nodded, studying the passing cars and houses, but the edges of the world had softened, and he wondered for a moment if the rain had somehow melted everything just a little bit. He wanted to ask Diego if he noticed the melting, but instead he nodded. Then he realized Diego had stopped speaking, and now it was Héctor's turn to talk. What had Diego just said?

"I like my job," Héctor said. "I have another delivery tonight, out to sea and back. For Santiago. And Ignacio," he said.

"You like the money you're earning from them? It's good, right?" Diego said, turning onto a street unfamiliar to Héctor. They were traveling east, away from the bay and the sinking sun, farther into the hills. In the distance, above the trees, a thin smear of smoke rose into the clear but darkening twilight sky.

"The money is what I'd hoped for. After tonight, though, I've got to move on, Diego. The people in Matamoros believe they've located my little girl. I still think of her as a baby, you know? But she isn't. She's a little girl now. Walking and talking and shit," he said, and for some reason this was funny, the idea of a walking, talking little baby, and he began to laugh.

"That's good, Héctor," Diego said, drumming fingers along the steering wheel to the beat of the music on the radio. "Hey, congratulations. I know you're very happy about this. I can see you're tickled about this news." Diego started to laugh, too, which somehow made Héctor laugh harder.

Amusement could be contagious; Héctor had forgotten that. So long he'd gone without lightness, without easy thoughts, and now tears of holy laughter streaked his cheeks.

When he slowed for a breath, he said, "I'm grateful to you for landing me a job, an income. It's the only way I could get to the north and hunt for Alejandra."

"Do you have enough money?" Diego said.

"I think so, yes. What I have now has to be enough. I have to go, to get there. The longer I wait the colder her path may become."

"Héctor, do you know what you've been transporting in those boxes on your runs from the cliffs?" Diego's tone remained light, and he continued to smile, but his words, the subject of Héctor's late-night shifts, had been something Héctor had made up his mind he must not consider. This he'd decided after his first run, the night he almost tossed the cooler into the sea.

"No. I don't ask," Héctor said. "That's not my concern."

Diego had turned down another road, narrower still, that split a ramshackle neighborhood of shanties, corrugated-tin structures barely fit for feral pigs. Héctor wondered how the occupants could have possibly stayed dry in the rains that had pounded them relentlessly all day.

"That's true, Héctor. That is not your concern, and that is why my boys, Ignacio and Santiago, have sung your praises. So," he said, slowing to a stop in front of a small clearing between two shacks where five boys kicked a ball in the last light of day, "I have another job for you, a little more serious, but a good bit more money. It involves making runs for some other guys I know. They're looking for someone like you, a deliveryman, of sorts." He was studying Héctor now. Héctor could feel Diego's eyes on him, but he watched the boys playing *futbol*. He imagined that if Diego lowered the volume on his radio he could hear the boys' shouts, their carefree boyhood joy. What was Diego offering him? What was he saying?

"That's kind of you, Diego. Very generous, I'm sure. But I have to go, you know? To Matamoros. To my daughter."

"What are those guys paying you, Héctor? Like eight hundred pesos a delivery?"

Héctor nodded.

"My friends, my other friends, they can triple that," Diego said, easing his truck back onto the road.

They wound their way deeper into the hills, Diego's pace

slower now, the road bumpy and puddled, where the shacks were fewer but even shabbier. They were nearing the darkening coil of smoke that hung low in the still air over the green hills.

Neither spoke for a minute, and Héctor considered that if Diego's other friends could triple Santiago and Ignacio's pay, he'd make in one delivery what he'd made after three trips for his current bosses, and though he'd been working for them for a few weeks now, tonight would be only his third delivery. His thoughts weren't clicking at a normal pace, but he considered how much more money he would have made these past weeks if he'd been working for these other people. Instead of twenty-four hundred pesos, which he would have in his pocket by tomorrow, not counting the additional money from the fishing charters, he'd have . . . What would he have? He tried to do the math. Three times eight hundred times three.

Diego rounded a slight bend, and in front of them a gray car smoldered on the rutty roadside, flames licking its trunk and hood. As they neared the car, to Héctor's horror he saw movement behind the windshield.

"Holy Mother of Christ," he said, glancing from the car to Diego. Diego's gaze remained on the car.

Diego stopped a distance from the car but close enough that Héctor made out a man sitting in the driver's seat, his forehead bloodied. The unmistakable stench of gasoline hung in the air.

"Holy Jesus," he said. "Holy Jesus!" He had to help this man. Héctor sprang from Diego's truck, but then froze beside his open door. What could he do? He had to smash the window.

Heat from the car rose in visible currents, mixing with the blackening smoke. Héctor waved his arms and called to the man inside, almost hidden now behind wicked flames leaping from beneath the hood. The man appeared unresponsive at first, his head against his chest as the blaze grew around him. Héctor searched wildly for anything to smash the window, knowing he had to get to him before the inferno engulfed the car.

He searched for a stick or a pipe, anything to slam against the window. Litter lay about the roadside: juice cans, broken beer bottles and plastic soda bottles, and paper scraps, but nothing helpful. He looked to Diego, but Diego remained in his truck, shaking his head as if already resigned that Héctor's cause was futile.

Héctor ran toward the nearest shack where a skeletal cow stood tied to a post. Frantic, he searched the sparse yard for anything to break the glass. He saw nothing but a child's plastic toy truck and a single bike tire, bent with broken spokes. He grabbed a blackened pot from a cookstove beside the shack, flinging its top to the ground, and ran back to the car.

The flames licked higher now, the smoke thickening, and Héctor ran to the car's front, raising the pot above his head, wildly looking for the best place to break the glass. Crusty, days-old beans oozed from the pot down Héctor's upraised hand and wrists. The man, who'd seemed unresponsive at first, now shook violently and shrieked for help with such fierce and absolute terror that Héctor knew no one, save for demons and those who'd burned in the pit of hell, had ever matched.

"I'm here! I'll help you!" Héctor screamed, heaving the pot against the passenger-side window, hoping not to shower the man with shards.

The window webbed into a thousand cracks with the brunt of the pot, and Héctor's second blow smashed the glass into the car. The sudden rush of air fed the flames like a bellows, the heat blasting to an unbearable inferno. Héctor ripped off his outer shirt and wrapped it around his hands so he could reach in and unlock the door, but as he stepped closer, to his horror he saw that the man's wrists were chained to the steering wheel where they jerked with such force the bones would surely snap, and the full evil before Héctor paralyzed him, rendering him useless, incapable of anything. He met the man's crazed, animalistic eyes for the briefest moment before they rolled back into his head, his singed hair and scorched clothing now smoking and melting like something from only the vilest regions of the netherworld. The man convulsed with such intensity, Héctor could not breathe, and he stumbled backward, though he could not look away, the man's screeching and the fumes of burning hair demanding Héctor bear witness to the horror.

Then the car exploded with such force that for an instant in his terror and confusion Héctor believed someone had kicked him to the ground, perhaps the demonic monster who had perpetrated this vile and grisly act. He sat in the street dazed, watching the blaze and the sickening black column of smoke that now drifted in no hurry into the hills.

Héctor was certain of the man's death, the funk of burning flesh, hair, and rubber permeating everything about him, and with bile rising in his throat, he stepped into the weary cow's yard and vomited into the mud.

"Let's go," Diego called through his open window, his demeanor serious, commanding.

Héctor wiped his mouth with the back of his hand and noticed angry blisters rising there, his mind a tumble of thoughts and images he was incapable of processing into a coherent comment. His shirt? Where had he dropped it? He looked around and saw the blue bundle, smoking beside the cow. He left it there and slipped into the seat beside Diego, where he noticed the black soot coating his arms, chest, and jeans.

They were going down now, out of the hills back toward the bay, and at once Héctor wondered if Diego had somehow known the burning car would be there, if witnessing that horror was somehow Diego's intention. Otherwise, what had their intended destination been?

As they passed by the lot where the boys had been playing ball, now empty and in dark shadow, Diego turned up the radio as the second half of the World Cup match had resumed.

Héctor wondered what the man had done to bring about such torture and whom he had crossed. He suspected the victim to be about his age, certainly no older than twenty-three or twenty-four, though that was impossible to know. He prayed that when he'd looked into the man's eyes, he'd conveyed his sympathy, rather than reflecting back the complete wickedness he'd witnessed, and that the man died knowing the last face he'd seen had shown compassion for him. Héctor leaned his head out the open window and sucked in the passing night air, trying to escape the smell of himself and hoping to keep at bay the sour vomit lingering in his throat.

After a moment, Diego said, "If you stick around here a little longer, you can earn enough money not only to retrieve your daughter but to give her the things a little girl such as she deserves, you know? I don't have children, but I imagine a good papa wants to give his girl dollies and pretty dresses, the finer things that the poor bastards living in rat squats like that can't even dream of." He jutted his chin toward a hut where a withered *abuela* scraped something from a skillet into the dirt, where a black rooster and two yellow hens pecked at it.

When Héctor didn't speak Diego said, "I'd like to know what you think is in the coolers you haul on the *Gabriela* at night, Héctor."

Héctor turned toward him, a sickening stench still lingering in his nose and the strangeness from the marijuana tingeing his thoughts so that nothing about him felt balanced or normal. The world lay off-kilter, and he struggled to form words.

"I don't . . ." he began, shaking his head. "I don't know. Marijuana, I guess, maybe cocaine. I assume drugs," he said so slowly he believed something might be permanently wrong with him.

Diego shook his head. "And how do you feel about that? Are you bothered by that thought?"

Though something had shifted deep inside Héctor, he was certain Diego's tone had changed. Diego was working his way toward something with these questions, but an unfamiliar hum in Héctor's brain couldn't let him understand exactly where Diego's end of this conversation was headed, and so he spoke with honesty and brevity.

"Like I said, my job isn't to think about that. No, I can't think about that. If I did I'd compromise my goal, my determination to get my child."

Neither spoke for a while as they descended the hill toward the tranquil sea, now invisible before them.

In the morning the sun would rise and illuminate the sparkling bay that graced thousands of postcards in the shops he'd passed each morning since he'd arrived in Acapulco just a few weeks ago, but now the Pacific lay before him like spilled ink.

"I'm glad to know you take your work seriously, Héctor. You're a good man," Diego said.

They passed a boarded-up hotel, graffiti lacing its every surface so that Héctor could only guess what the façade had looked like in its prime. He wondered at the many fancy guests who had likely stayed there before this city's crime and dangerous reputation choked out much of Acapulco's business except for those along the luxury high-rise hotel strip, and even their seemingly peaceful existence remained so because of the police who patrolled the area with vigilance in their new-model trucks with long-range semiautomatic weapons. He wondered how many of the occupants of the closed hotel had gone to the cliffs of La Quebrada to see Diego the Magnificent plunge into the foamy sea and surface with his wide smile intact and a thumbs-up to the electrified crowd.

Sunrise here had become Héctor's favorite time of day, not just for the empty streets and the morning's coolness but because he felt safest, and the air smelled better in the predawn stillness than it would the rest of the day. In the evenings, like now, the air thickened with the stench of barrel fires and pollution that faithfully rose into the hills and settled there, lingering long after midnight, permeating the poorest neighborhoods with the effluence of all of Acapulco's contamination.

He wondered if he would ever escape the stench from tonight. Somehow the smell felt like a tattoo, an invisible but real tattoo of odor instead of ink, one that would reside permanently in his nose and taint all other smells for the rest of his existence. He shook his head to clear the thought.

Diego slowed to a stop. They were in front of Emanuel's apartment, but Emanuel no longer sat in the plastic chair under the palm tree, and Héctor suspected he'd gone into town to drink with Ana María as he did most evenings.

Héctor opened the door and stepped from the truck, feeling that courtesy dictated he should thank Diego for the ride, but why? No hint of gratitude rose within him, but rather a cold wretchedness he could not name.

"Think about the opportunity I'm offering, okay, Héctor? Stick around a few more weeks. I know people who can fill your pockets, man."

Héctor nodded and turned onto the short walkway lined with conch shells that led to the apartment.

As he neared the entrance he realized Diego had not pulled away, and he glanced back toward the street where Diego remained. Their eyes met, and Diego put the truck in gear but didn't leave. He seemed to have something yet to say, though Héctor couldn't guess what that could be. The entire evening's encounter with Diego felt dreamlike and fuzzy, as if somehow wrapped in soft, suffocating gauze.

"Hey, Héctor," he called.

"Yeah?"

"You're nothing like that man in the car."

"What?" Héctor said, taking a step toward Diego.

"You're honest. Loyal. You're a good man," he said, before easing off down the street toward the bright lights glittering bayside below them.

Chapter 27

Lilia

"You had no mama," Rosa said to Lilia, laying a cool cloth that smelled of lavender and mint across Lilia's brow, trying to cool the fever she'd developed that afternoon.

New, strange worries had been bubbling up in Lilia ever since the priest had delivered the news from the orphanage woman in Matamoros, and this afternoon Lilia had been thinking about her own motherless upbringing, though deeply grateful for her grandmother who raised her. She'd been trying to explain to Rosa how Alejandra had been motherless now since infancy, and how worrisome that was to Lilia.

"Yet look at you now," Rosa continued. "You're a wife and a mother, and you do just fine."

"Ah, yes, look at me," Lilia said, her voice cracking. "I'm a mess. When I look in the mirror I can't believe the person looking back at me, and I wonder how this could have happened. Where's that fresh-faced girl who married Héctor? He used to love my long hair, you know?"

Rosa nodded. "Don't be so vain, Lilia," she said, though not unpleasantly. She had become tenderer to Lilia since she'd confined her to bed. Not so long ago Rosa had been Héctor's harshest critic, and Lilia's, too. She'd been so angry at Héctor for crossing into *el norte,* and even angrier at Lilia for following him and taking Alejandra. Perhaps she was still their harshest critic, but she'd become less vocal about her disapproval.

"When I crossed, the man at the border house made me cut my hair. Did I ever tell you that, Rosa?"

"No," Rosa whispered. Fernando had fallen asleep on a mat on the floor, and she pointed to him, so that Lilia might lower her voice to let the child sleep.

"With a knife. I chopped my hair with a knife, then dyed it an ugly reddish color I would've never chosen on my own. But a murderous stranger, my temporary guardian, with a much sharper knife than the one he'd given me, stood watch over me. He said I had to do it, to be less conspicuous to the immigration officers."

"How so?" Rosa said.

"Because not anyone could have such long hair as mine. It was a specific, recognizable characteristic. He said I needed to match the false identification I'd receive, and that with the chopped, dyed hair, I could better pull off various looks."

"Ah," Rosa said, brushing a loose strand of hair from Lilia's face with such tenderness. Lilia reached up and grabbed Rosa's cool fingers and pressed them against her hot cheek.

"I know it was only hair, but when I think back on that day, it represents something larger, not just a change in my appearance but something deeper, a shift in my whole world." Lilia paused, searching for the right words. Rosa eyed her, listening, waiting.

"Until then my life had existed in two parts: life with my grandmother and then my life after she'd passed," Lilia said. "But those were the thoughts of an innocent girl. Now I know that the two parts of my life occurred on either side of that day, the day I chopped my hair at the border, the day I swam the river, the last day I held my Alejandra before handing her to that woman who never returned her to me."

Rosa nodded and took a sip of water from the mug she'd clamped between her knees.

"Rosa, I want to be excited about this news the priest brought us," she said.

"Of course you do. This is what you've hoped for for years now," Rosa said.

"I've often thought Alejandra could be dead, but I told myself if that were true, then at least only I would continue to suffer, but she wouldn't have to suffer. I told myself I could take that. I mean, that's the fate of mothers, isn't it, Rosa? My mother died so that I could live. Like Jesus Christ. He died so that we could live. I'm not saying my mother and certainly not I am like Jesus, but good mothers possess that Christ-like trait, Rosa."

She wasn't certain her words were conveying what she needed Rosa to hear, though Rosa's eyes were comforting.

"But if I knew Alejandra has been living out there somewhere," Lilia continued, "I'd worry more than if she were dead, because maybe my child needed my help. I worry she's suffered evil, that she'll never know that she was conceived in love and loved fiercely by her mama, that she'll never know that our separation has been crushing for me. Perhaps my girl will grow into a bitter woman, angry about all the trials and pain she's endured without the solace of a mama who she believes abandoned her."

Fernando cried out in his sleep then rolled onto his side, the soft, deep breathing of his slumber resuming.

"I don't think I can bear more loss, Rosa. If I lose this baby and if Héctor can't track down Alejandra, I'm not sure I can figure out how to put my feet one in front of the other anymore, and I am ashamed to tell you this because you could do it. You're far stronger than I."

Rosa shook her head. "Lilia," she began, but Lilia interrupted her.

"No, Rosa. Let me say this."

Rosa exhaled. "Go on."

"I've longed that my daughter know my love for her. I've ached, imagining the suffering she may have endured since I lost her, a crushing weight that I hold in my chest like a rough, cold millstone, because I can't take the hurt away from her, I can't unburden her."

"Lilia, all mothers feel that way at times," Rosa said. "I'm sure you've felt that way about Fernando, too. We can't shield our children from pain, even if we carry them in a sack against our breasts. Still the bee can sting, the thorn can prick."

Lilia shook her head. Rosa wasn't understanding what Lilia needed her to hear. "If Alejandra had been able to see my face and know my heart all these years," Lilia said, "even if her life's physical suffering has been harsh, somehow she could have witnessed my discomfort, my sorrow for her suffering, and in that sharing between us of suffering and grief, Alejandra's pain would be lessened. Rosa, if my little girl lives out there in this world and bears heavy burdens and wears the ragged scars of life without a mother's love, my love, as a salve, that, to me, is the worst kind of agony a mother can know."

Lilia clasped Rosa's hand between her own hot, dry palms. She needed Rosa to grasp her words, her concerns. Rosa squeezed Lilia's fingers, but she didn't speak, letting Lilia continue.

"I worry Héctor will find Alejandra, but that her suffering has been immeasurable, her scars too deep for me to knead out, Rosa. Do you understand? How can we pick up the pieces and be a family, a mother and daughter, if I've failed her in irreparable ways, ways that will define her, ways that have broken her?"

"Enough of this talk, Lilia. You do this to yourself, you always have. Don't waste your energy and emotions on things that can't be helped. You cannot conjure good from evil. No

amount of wrangling out the endless possibilities of bad scenarios will diminish the likelihood that bad has occurred to
Alejandra. Instead, focus on your new, unborn baby and on
your hope that Alejandra will be returned to you. That's where
your mind should be. Only there, and also on little Fernando,
the living, breathing, rambunctious boy who danced so long in
puddles today he's exhausted himself."

Rosa stood. "You rest while he rests. I'm going to the market
to get a few things for our dinner and then stop at my house
and check on my José. My man needs a little loving to keep his
head right, you know," she said with a smile. "I'll be back in a
while. Do you need help to relieve yourself before I go?"

"No. I'll rest now," Lilia said, rolling onto her side as Rosa
left the house. She listened to Fernando's soft, sweet breathing
and tried to match it with her own. She willed herself to dream
of her two daughters, laughing in the surf, the three of them
holding hands, splashing at the edge of a calm sea, perhaps
waiting for Héctor and Fernando to return from a fishing trip.
How strange to think with such uncertainty on these two girls'
existence, as if they were strangers who may or may not cross
her path sometime in the future, yet she loved them with such
ferocity their existence simply had to be. She prayed God would
not let her thoughts drift to the dark places, and that, indeed,
her girls would live and thrive and know love and goodness.

Chapter 28

Héctor

The ocean, dark now except for a spot in the distance where the moon glowed between fat clouds like melted silver, stretched before Héctor, the surface smooth and concealing what lay below. He wished memory could be like the sea, leveling everything into an infinite plain that spread so far and distant that even the most tragic of events would be thinned and washed to the horizon, remaining no more indelibly in one's mind than the simple mundane events that composed the majority of a man's existence.

He'd left the dock earlier than necessary, anxious to leave the land and get out onto the water, and so now the *Gabriela* with Héctor at the helm receded from the lights of Acapulco at a more leisurely pace than usual.

The scents of the burning car tainted Héctor's being, though he'd showered and even swum in the sea earlier that evening, hoping to cleanse himself of all the nastiness that lingered.

This run to the cliff side would be his last, and for many reasons, he would wait no longer after tonight to leave Acapulco. Twice before he'd done this and each time had been the same. His contact and he would meet, speak little, lower the cooler to the boat, and Héctor would leave. Then, God willing, if God were involved in such undertakings, Héctor would meet Ignacio or Santiago back at the dock. The men would waste no time loading the cooler into a pickup truck. Héctor would receive eight hundred pesos, and within twenty minutes of his arrival he'd be back in Emanuel's apartment, grateful for the money and that the night had been uneventful.

When he reached the cliff, he secured the boat and climbed the ladder up the rocky bluff. As usual, his contact emerged from the darkness, and the two spoke no words as they went about their now-familiar proceedings. Only this time, after they hauled the cooler to the cliff's edge, the man said, "I have two for you tonight."

Héctor wondered why the amount had doubled this week, and he wondered if his bosses knew this or if the double order would surprise them. They had not mentioned an increase.

"Okay," Héctor said, following the man back to his truck for the second cooler, careful not to scrape his throbbing, blistered knuckles on the cooler's handle.

When they'd returned to the cliff's edge and were preparing the ropes to lower the cooler to the boat, the man said, "Been a very good few days here."

Héctor nodded, unsure what to say to this. He considered telling the man that this would be their last meeting, that after today he'd be long gone, headed north, but he thought better of it and instead busied himself in silent work.

When he'd secured the coolers in the boat, he untied his bowline and eased away from the rocks, glad to be done with this bit of business.

With the dark cliff shrinking in the distance behind him, Héctor revved the engine and turned the boat toward Acapulco. The night air felt cool and velvety on his skin, and he realized how much he'd come to love being on the water. When he could make out the distant shore of the bay twinkling a mile or so ahead, he slowed the boat and cut the engine, though he wasn't sure why he'd done so. For several seconds the momentum of the boat brought the lapping sound of water against the bow, but then all was still and calm, and Héctor wished he could freeze this moment, the best part of this horrific day.

He heard a whale purge somewhere off to his left and he studied the surface as best he could, hoping to see its silhouette rise. He heard the whale blow three more times, then it was gone, leaving Héctor in silent contemplation.

He'd been wrangling all evening with the conflicting desires to block out the proceedings of his ride with Diego but also to make sense of it. He'd been able to do neither. He told himself that after tonight, he'd be gone from this place and on the path to his little girl, and that was all that mattered now. He could do nothing to parse out the events of the day. As he sat there replaying his conversation with Diego, he considered Diego's questions about the contents of the coolers Héctor hauled on these runs, and he wondered if Diego knew the answer, if he weren't just testing Héctor. He stood and turned in a slow circle, his view the oily darkness of midnight. For a few moments the moon peeped from between the clouds, but even then the moon was just a quarter moon and not too bright.

No one would ever know, he told himself. He fingered the flashlight in his hip pocket. Diego had called him honest and trustworthy, but if he lifted the cooler's lid, if he peeked inside, wouldn't he be disloyal? Dishonest? He'd buoyed himself the past two weeks not to care or consider the contents of the coolers, but something about today sabotaged his steadfastness, and as he bobbed on the gently rocking sea, his curiosity mounted with each passing minute.

What did his knowing matter? He had every right to know. He'd been the one taking the risks, working under cover of darkness, meeting the quiet stranger late nights on a cliff's edge. Nothing had gone wrong, but that was just dumb luck, or God's will.

He slipped the flashlight from his pocket and illuminated the closest cooler. It was not unlike the coolers they used on their fishing charters, but these had been painted black, and the ones for fish were white. If he were careful, he could peel back the tape, lift the lid, verify what he already suspected, then seal it just as it had been. He'd deliver as planned at the dock, and this time tomorrow he'd be on his way to northern Mexico. But he had to hurry. Santiago or Ignacio—he never knew which one would be at the dock—would be expecting him soon.

He worked a fingernail under the edge of a corner of tape and tugged. The adhesive was sealed tight to the plastic surface and very sticky, but Héctor suspected he could secure it back in place without difficulty. Slowly he worked free one strip and then another, glad for no wind that could tangle the loose bands dangling from the side of the cooler now. When he'd freed one side he worked the front and then the other side, and he realized that, despite the milder than normal temperature, sweat beaded on his brow.

As he labored Héctor noticed for the first time the tiny pits pricked into the four sides of the cooler. He'd not studied the cooler this closely before now, and the holes were all but invisible along the black surface.

When he'd freed all the tape, he inhaled sharply and blew a deep breath. "Okay," he said aloud, looking around again in every direction to be certain no boat had approached without his knowing. Nothing had changed, and for all he saw the *Gabriela* was the only vessel on the entire sea this peaceful, dark night.

He lifted the lid and turned the beam of his flashlight into the cooler. At first he thought he'd been the victim of a strange and puzzling joke. Green, yellow, and red, the bold colors of a child's crayon drawing. Downy, textured softness, as if a feather blanket lay over the cooler's more important cargo, cloaking whatever lay hidden beneath it.

But the eyes! So many eyes, dark as obsidian beads but full of life, full of fright. A cooler of birds. What the hell was this about? He moved closer, wary of touching them, and shone the light close over the dense mass of living, trembling, fettered parrots. He ran a hand through his hair trying to make sense of this. Laughter almost rose in his throat, as he considered the many suspicions that had played through his mind about his freight.

"Goddamned birds?" He said it aloud, shaking his head. "I've been hauling goddamned birds."

Leaving the cooler's lid open, he sat but continued to stare at the birds. How many were in there? He guessed at least forty or fifty, maybe more. And how could they possibly survive very long like that, especially the ones on the bottom. He tried to imagine how the man on the cliff had captured them, surely with illegal methods, otherwise he'd not be running them to shore in stupid coolers at midnight. He considered the birds flying free, an entire flock. They'd land in a mango tree or some other fruit- or berry-bearing bush, expecting a meal, and then, what? Would their captors spring a giant net over the bunch, then bundle them like dead fish in these coolers? No wonder the man had told Héctor to go straight to the dock with no stops. He wondered what one of these birds brought in? How many pesos did Ignacio and Santiago pocket for these parrots?

With sickening remorse he recalled that first night, when he'd almost tossed the cooler into the sea, and he uttered a silent prayer of thanks to God for stopping him.

But then he looked at them again, studying them in the white beam of his flashlight. What magnificent creatures they were! And how horrific this transport had to be for them!

He was taken back to his crossing, how terrifying that had been for him and his fellow *pollos,* their fates uncertain and the potential for death significant. How helpless he'd felt, packed into the sealed undercarriage of that delivery truck, much like these birds were stacked in this cooler. He stood again and gently slipped his fingers beneath a parrot, careful not to break its feathers. Each bird had been wrapped tight in a sheer netting. The heft of the bird surprised him. He would let them all go. He could unwrap each one and set them free right there from the bow of the *Gabriela.* But just as he had that thought he knew he could not do so, for as he'd told Diego earlier, he could not compromise his plan to earn money and get to Alejandra.

Alejandra. Héctor sighed and lowered the parrot back into the cooler, a heaviness in his chest for his part in this illegal trade. The birds had been plucked from where nature, where God had intended them to be, and he wondered at their future, the future of the ones that would survive. Would they be kept in a clean cage, adorning the courtyard or fancy house of some rich family in Mexico City, or America, or even that faraway and cold country of Canada? Just as he could not possibly know what had happened to Alejandra when she'd been plucked from him, so he could not know the fate of these birds.

Héctor needed to hurry, to be on his way to the dock so that the parrots' chance of survival might increase and he could have this unpleasantness behind him. The longer he sat here, the longer the birds would be bound and stacked and perhaps the greater the likelihood of their suffocating.

But he had to do something. The foulness of these dealings would linger with him long after he'd delivered the parrots to

Santiago and Ignacio. Héctor imagined the silent pleading of the birds' eyes haunting his dreams for years to come, reminding him of his inability to save them.

He reached again into the cooler, moving several of the birds aside, choosing a parrot squashed somewhere in the middle of the bunch. While holding his flashlight in his teeth and the bird in the crook of his arm, he began removing the binding from its trembling body. The blue of its wingtips reminded Héctor of fishing offshore, of the place where the emerald and pale blues of shallower water gave way to a blue as dark as midnight. Mindful of the powerful creamy-yellow beak just centimeters from his bare fingers, Héctor used the blade of his pocketknife to free the last bits of mesh from the bird's upper parts near its head, then he set the parrot on the bow and stepped back from it.

The parrot hopped to its feet and studied Héctor with glossy black eyes rimmed in delicate red feathers. It shook its wings twice with a strange shudder, then extended them wide, revealing a few brilliant red feathers Héctor had not previously noticed under the outstretched wings.

Something about this, two of God's struggling and curious creatures sizing each other up, appealed to Héctor, and he could have watched the bird perched there for a long while. But with a sudden flap the parrot took flight and in an instant vanished in darkness. He listened, longing to hear the beating of its wings lifting the bird to freedom, to safety, but the breeze swallowed the sound, and only Héctor's imaginings of fluttering wings lingered.

Héctor closed the cooler, hoping, somehow, that the remaining birds felt some relief with one less parrot crammed among them.

He carefully replaced the tape, thankful it maintained its

stickiness. When he'd secured the last strip he noticed beside his boot a lone feather. In the flashlight's beam the tip of the brilliant green feather looked as if it had been dipped in yellow paint. Héctor considered this a gift from the one parrot he'd freed, and he slipped the colorful quill into his breast pocket. Then he started the engine and gunned the *Gabriela* toward the distant lights.

When he neared the bay, he slowed and eased the boat toward the dock. Santiago emerged from the shadows and stood under the single, flickering security light at the end of the pier. No one else could be seen around the marina, and the men worked quickly.

"What's this?" Santiago said when he noticed the second cooler.

"I received two tonight," Héctor said, not meeting Santiago's eyes, busying himself with the rope with which he'd secured the coolers to the boat out of habit, though the tranquil seas this night had not warranted that precaution.

"Excellent. Excellent!" Santiago said. "I was beginning to worry about you. As calm as this evening is I'd expected you back sooner, but I guess the delay was this double load, eh?"

"Yes. Tonight took a little longer with two coolers to lower to the boat and secure," Héctor said.

"Sure, I get it now. Here," Santiago said, peeling Héctor's payment from a roll of bills. "Good work, Héctor."

"I need to tell you, Santiago, I'm leaving tomorrow," he said, folding the pesos and slipping them into his back pocket. He expected an emotional response from Santiago, some sense of disappointment or even anger about Héctor's departure.

Instead Santiago shrugged and nodded. "Tomorrow? You sure?"

Héctor didn't want to talk anymore. He didn't want to be

here a moment longer, but he willed himself to stay put, to finish the conversation without angering his boss.

"Yes, I have to get going. To my daughter. I have to get up north."

"Okay," Santiago said. "We knew you were only passing through, you told us that. It's why we wanted you, you know? Just a guy passing through on his way to someplace else. Usually you guys are the best workers, anyway, hungry to make a buck."

He extended a hand to Héctor and the two shook. "Safe travels, then," Santiago said, lighting a cigarette that had been tucked behind his ear. "So, hey. I need to get going," he said, already halfway to his truck. "I'd offer you a ride, but I got to get this load out of here."

Héctor nodded. "Yeah, sure. Thank Ignacio for me," he called with careful indifference, as if he had no sense of the time sensitivity of Santiago's delivery. He watched Santiago's lights recede. Héctor looked back at the *Gabriela,* thankful for his time with her, then began the last walk he'd take up the hill toward Emanuel's apartment to sleep for a few hours. At dawn he'd make his way to the bus station, and for only the second time in his life, he would head to northern Mexico.

Chapter 29

Rosa

She saw him approaching from down the lane long before he saw her rocking in the dappled shade of the ficus tree in the courtyard. She knew his reason for coming, and she stood and went inside to tell Lilia she'd be back shortly.

"Go with you, Roro, go with you!" Fernando shouted.

"No, no, child," Rosa said, handing the boy a sugar cube from her apron pocket. "Stay here and take care of your mama. I'll be right back."

Rosa met the messenger boy before he'd reached the yard, and together they walked the direction from which he'd come, back to Armando's shop and Rosa's waiting phone call. A black hen with a clutch of tiny yellow biddies pecked among the small, weedy bed of pink flowers growing alongside Armando's shop.

"Just hatched this morning," the barefoot boy said, grinning, revealing brown, decaying top teeth. Rosa slipped him a few coins and thanked him for calling on her, then she went inside and made her way to Armando's phone.

"*Hola,* Héctor?"

"Yes, Rosa. Hello! How is everyone there? How is my family? I sure wish I could speak to Lilia. Tell me about her," he said. He seemed rushed.

Armando, for once not eavesdropping but occupied with

customers at the cash register, couldn't hear her speak, and so Rosa could be more candid with Héctor now than she'd been during the last call, when Armando had jammed himself so close to Rosa she could smell the old goat.

"Héctor, Lilia has had some bleeding, but for now I think it's stopped. She is flat on her back and being an obedient patient, which, as you know, is not always her way. That girl can be hard-headed. She's had a low fever the past few days, but I'm not sure the source of it, and I've been keeping her hydrated and still."

"Is she okay?" he asked, just like a man. You could tell them everything about a situation, yet they still needed a woman to explain the meaning of things.

"She is. For now. This baby isn't breech like Fernando was, so that's good. I believe this one's a girl, and her head is way down already. We'll see, Héctor. That's all I can say."

"And my boy?" he said, raising his voice over loud noises suddenly blasting near him, nearly drowning him out.

"He's perfect, that one. Fernando is just fine," she said.

"That's good, Rosa. Thank you for taking care of them," he said.

"Tell me about you, Héctor. Are you still in Acapulco?"

"No. I left a couple of days ago. By bus. I'll get to Matamoros tomorrow. These buses," he said. "So many stops and delays. So much waiting. Two flat tires already since I left Acapulco."

"Two flat tires?" she asked. "On the same bus?"

"No. The first one was on the drive from Acapulco to Mexico City," he said.

"Mexico City! You went there! Did you see the capital? What was that like? I'm sure Lilia will want to know."

"No, Rosa. I saw only a bus station. You forget, I've been there before, when I went to *el norte,* or maybe you didn't know. But I have visited that place before. It's very dirty and nothing like Puerto Isadore."

"Hmm," she said, nodding and thinking about this. How could the capital city be anything but beautiful?

"So from there, I took another bus that stopped in Teotihuacán. Then another bus, one that had a flat tire, carried me from there to León, and then to Zacatecas, and that is where I am now."

"I'll tell Lilia all this if I can keep straight in my head these towns. She longs to know your progress, Héctor."

"I'll sleep here tonight, and tomorrow I'll board a bus to Real de Catorce, and then on to Matamoros. I'll call you after I've visited the orphanage, okay Rosa? Tell Lilia I love her, and kiss my boy for me. Tell him Papa will see him soon, and I will bring him a gift."

"Yeah, sure, sure, Héctor. Of course. *Vaya con dios,*" she said before placing the receiver back in its cradle on the wall.

Armando was at the far corner of the shop, showing a teenage boy a magazine that Rosa suspected, based on their hushed voices and rapt attention, held photos of nude women. She rolled her eyes, thankful for Armando's distraction, and slipped through the door before he had a chance to annoy her.

When she stepped outside she noticed one of the little chicks cheeping beside a flowering cactus, its blossoms as yellow as the bird's down. The hatchling seemed to have gotten himself separated from his mama and brothers and sisters. Rosa bent down and scooped him up, searching for the rest of the brood. Then she thought of a different plan and lowered the chick into her apron. Fernando would enjoy him, and it was time he learned how to be gentle with tiny, living beings. Soon enough he would be a big brother.

Chapter 30

Héctor

The bus ride from Zacatecas to Real de Catorce would take several hours, and Héctor grabbed an abandoned newspaper from a bench to read along the way. A man with a boy, maybe ten years old, and a girl, maybe twelve, sat together on the floor along a back wall of the bus station. Something about their appearance, their demeanor, intrigued Héctor, and he had a feeling they were traveling to the border. They'd kept to themselves since they'd arrived, about an hour after Héctor had arrived the previous evening. Their clothes were filthy, and their eyes remained downcast. They sat close together, sharing an orange the man peeled. Perhaps they were Hondurans, poor and scared, working their way to *el norte.*

Héctor had seen others from Central America during his trip north several years ago. He didn't mind them or begrudge them the opportunities *el norte* could afford them, but he'd heard others spew mean-spirited words of disgust for such travelers passing through Mexico, as if their presence sullied Mexico.

When the time came to board the bus to Real de Catorce, Héctor worked his way to an available seat near the back. He opened the newspaper and had begun to read a story about one of the Mexican World Cup team's assistant coaches, a name unfamiliar to him, when he glanced up and saw the three from the back wall of the bus station making their way down the aisle toward him. The man took the seat in front of Héctor and directed the children to take the open seats across the aisle from Héctor. The man passed a cloth sack to the girl, but motioned toward the boy.

"Tell him he can use it as a pillow," the man said to the girl. She took the sack then turned to the boy, and using hand signals explained the purpose of the sack. The mute boy nodded and wedged the sack between his grimy window and the seat, then nestled into it to rest.

Soon the bus rumbled to life and lurched onto the highway, and Héctor hoped this one had good tires full of air and without leaks. He watched the scenery passing by his window and took in the countryside, from scorched plains of creosote bush, mesquite, and tar bush to stark mountains, the site of which left Héctor lonely and heavyhearted.

When he'd traveled to *el norte,* he had not come this way exactly, or maybe he had. But he didn't recognize anything outside his window. He would pay attention because one day, when Alejandra was older, he would tell her about this journey and how her papa had traveled a great distance to find his girl and bring her home with him to her mama and brother and soon-to-be-born baby sister or brother.

After a while he felt the girl's eyes on him. Both the boy and the man traveling with her had fallen asleep, but the girl seemed alert and interested in everything around her. When their eyes met, she said, "Are you from here?"

She was a shy-eyed girl who looked at Héctor from an angle, as if turning her face directly toward him would be too bold or disrespectful.

"Yes," he said, detecting an accent in her Spanish that told him she was, indeed, not from these parts. "Well, not from here"—he pointed out the window—"but from south of here. And you? Where are you traveling from?"

The girl glanced up at the man with whom she traveled to be sure he wasn't listening, and when she'd ascertained that he still slept, she leaned in toward Héctor and said, "Honduras. We're going to *la línea* to cross to *el norte*, but my uncle, he tells us we must be careful, that our journey is a secret. He says people here are both good and bad just like they are everywhere, but that because we aren't from here we can't know for certain which is which, you know? Who is the good and who is the bad. You aren't bad, are you?"

Héctor thought about that. "No, not too bad, anyway." He smiled at her. She was a pretty child with curious eyes and deep dimples.

The girl nodded, pleased with Héctor's answer. "Have you been to *el norte*?" she asked.

Héctor considered how terrifying crossing as a girl her age might be. "I have," he said.

She seemed to think about this, likely wondering why he was back in Mexico. Héctor suspected she'd heard stories of Norteamérica's greatness, stories that had lured her and her uncle and her brother to the north.

She looked out her window and Héctor out his, and neither spoke for several minutes. He could not know what these Hondurans were leaving behind, and he wondered if the girl's uncle would look back on this journey in a few years' time and think the effort worth the risk, the price these children might have to pay. The girl's skin was clear of acne, but dirty from the grime of her travels. She'd barely started to develop into a young woman yet, but some men, evil men like the coyote Lilia had enlisted, would prey upon such innocence in the vilest of ways. He wanted to tap the sleeping uncle on the shoulder and tell him to turn back to his country, that he couldn't know the risks he was taking with these children. But just as he thought these things, he recalled his own fire and determination to get to *el norte*. No amount of warning would have deterred him.

"My sister was killed," the girl said, looking at Héctor again with the same curious expression, her head turned slightly to the side.

Héctor had not expected this, and when he didn't respond immediately, she said, "She and her boyfriend. A gang member shot them, and my parents had to fetch their bodies from the mountains. That's where the shooters left them."

Héctor wished he could offer the girl a piece of gum or a candy, though she didn't seem overly burdened in her sadness. "I'm sorry," he said.

"The gangs in my neighborhood are terrible. Our house sits on the corner, and every day we can hear gunshots nearby, and at least once a week someone is killed on one of the corners near our house. My brother," she said, glancing at the sleeping boy beside her, "he's deaf. He's at the age the gangs like to recruit new members, so my mama and papa are sending us to *el norte*, to get my brother and me away from the gangs."

"So your parents remain in your country?" Héctor said.

"Yes, they have to stay because to pay a coyote to take us all costs a lot of money, you know? And I have two more little brothers and a baby sister, and so my parents are staying behind with them."

"I see," Héctor said, wondering where this girl and her brother would end up and if they had family already in America or if they would stay in the home of a friend. He'd heard of gangs, of course, but in Puerto Isadore, they'd not been a problem. The reasons people left his village for *el norte* were for better-paying jobs, for opportunities and education for their children.

After a moment he said, "Why'd the gang kill your sister and her boyfriend?"

The girl shrugged. "We think the gang killed them because my sister's friend is the girlfriend of a boy in another gang, but that girl doesn't have a home, not really, and so my sister and her boyfriend let the girl sleep on the floor in their house. The girl's boyfriend was very angry about this."

Héctor studied her face, trying to make sense of her tale. "Angry that your sister and her boyfriend helped her?"

"No, angry that the girl had been in the house of a rival gang member."

Héctor wondered about the fate of the girl, the one who'd angered her murderous boyfriend, but he decided not to ask about that.

"How old was your sister?" he asked.

The girl looked beyond Héctor now, out the window at a small pasture of cattle. "She was fifteen. Her name was Linda."

At this the girl turned, leaning against her brother as if to rest, and spoke no more.

Héctor shifted toward his window and thought of Alejandra. He prayed God would give him the ability to protect her from all the evil in this world. As a younger man, Héctor's thoughts had only skirted the edge of contemplating evil. His youthful naïveté and hunger to experience the world had kept such considerations at bay. Now he often considered the horrors happening every day everywhere, tragedies unfathomable to him as a younger man. He looked across the aisle where the girl and her brother seemed to slumber, somehow, in peace. He prayed for their safe crossing, and that their uncle was better equipped to protect them than Lilia and he had been at protecting Alejandra.

Chapter 31

Karolina

The fan turning and stirring the warm air in the corner of the front office squeaked every time it reached the end of its oscillation to the left, and Karolina swore, not for the first time, to replace it or oil it before the week's end. She was pouring the last bit of water from her mug into the clay pot on her desk where a short, fat cactus stood guard over stacks of papers, when the buzzer at the front door sounded. She was glad to see the visitor wasn't a beggar or a starving young mother wanting to give up her child. Instead, a thin man in a red T-shirt and work pants and boots waited at the door. He held his hat in his hands, and dipped his chin to her as she approached the glass. He seemed clear-eyed and deferential with no tattoos or other visible signs of gang membership.

"May I help you?" she said.

"Yes, I think so. I believe, I mean I am sure, at least for a while you may have . . . I think you've had my daughter here." He looked her in the eyes and stood still as if his boots were nailed to the mat beneath them, but his hands fidgeted mightily with his hat.

"Come in, please," Karolina said, motioning toward the chair across from her cluttered desk.

The man nodded and followed her gaze to the chair. When

he'd sat, Karolina said, "Okay, tell me what you need me to know."

The man cleared his throat as if he were nervous or perhaps preparing to divulge a long, detailed story of great importance. Karolina had had such visitors before, men who suspected a former girlfriend had given up a baby she'd not mentioned to him.

"My priest called you. From Puerto Isadore, in Oaxaca. Do you recall?" The man spoke softly but in earnest. "He told you I would come when I saved enough money. He told you about my daughter, Alejandra, and that her papers said her name was Ernesto." The pitch of his words increased as he spoke, the urgency of his message spurring him to rush the words, but his sense of politeness and decorum weighed them and slowed them down.

The man's sincerity and the desperation in his eyes drew Karolina to him, to his story. "Ah, yes," she said. "The baby from the car accident. Of course, yes. I didn't know when or if you'd get here. But yes, I did speak with your priest."

The man's face hinted at a smile, but his worry tamped it to a mere grimace.

"So, yes, as I told your priest, I recall this child. Because of regulations I would need some proof of your relationship to the child before we can discuss much else."

He looked at her as a schoolboy might look, confused but trying to understand.

"For the child's protection. For privacy reasons," she said.

"What can I offer as proof besides my story, besides details of her life with her mama and me in Puerto Isadore?" He looked as if he might cry.

"Unfortunately such details, while important, aren't as fool-proof as science. I'll need to do a DNA test. Do you know what this is?" She didn't want to insult the poor man, but she knew from experience that such unworldly villagers knew little about modern medicine and science.

"No. What is this thing, this test? I'll answer whatever questions you ask me."

"It's not a test like you would have in school but rather a blood test. We do blood work on all children who stay here. We do it for this very situation."

He stared at her, searching her face for a scrap he could comprehend.

Karolina took a breath and forced herself to smile, to ease the man's discomfort. "May I get you a cup of water or coffee?"

The man shook his head. "No. Please, just tell me what I need to do."

"We'll take a small sample of your blood. It's quick and not too painful," she said, standing to refill her cup with coffee from the coffeepot on the table at the far wall. "We use a needle to get the blood, then we send the small vial of your blood off to a science lab, a medical laboratory. The people in the lab can tell by comparing your blood with anyone else's blood if you and that other person are related." She paused and sipped from her cup.

"So when we have proof that you and this child are father and daughter, we can proceed with our talks, with the location of her whereabouts."

The man was pushing up the short sleeve of his T-shirt, nodding, as if he thought she'd take blood from his shoulder. "From my arm? Yes, get your needle. I'm ready."

Karolina had to smile, moved by the man's innocence and determination. "Hold on. I don't take the blood. Our nurse will stick you. You don't want me anywhere near you with a needle."

He nodded and let his sleeve drop.

"She'll draw it from the inner part of your arm, at your elbow joint. Can you read and write?"

"Yes, of course," he said, and Karolina thought she detected something prickly in his tone, as if her question had offended him.

"Then I'll get you some papers to complete, giving us permission to draw blood and to submit the DNA test. After that the nurse will see you. We'll have to mail the sample off, and we likely won't hear anything for up to a week." She turned to go to the back office to find the necessary forms.

"A week? Can I do nothing for a week?" He'd grabbed his hat from his lap and had begun fidgeting with it again.

"Well," she said. "You can wait here at an inn in Matamoros. We have several nearby. Or I suppose you could go back home to . . . was it Oaxaca? And we could call you with the results."

"No, no," he said. "I can't possibly travel all the way back home. Not yet. When the blood results come in, proving that my daughter was here with you, I'd just have to come right back to get her next week, and the journey is not so easy. I'll wait."

Karolina nodded and left the man worrying his hat as if it were a living thing in need of attention. She found the consent forms easily enough. Finding an available nurse would be more difficult.

When Karolina returned to the front office the man stood at the barred window, his back to her, peering through the glass. The front office was accessible to the street, but the bulk of the facility lay hidden behind her office protected by a tall fence, rimmed with barbed wire. A security guard kept watch there, manning the gate. Stealing one of Karolina's babies would be no easy task, though that had rarely been as issue. Most people visiting this place, aside from clergy, nuns, caregivers, and a few administrators, came to deposit babies, not to claim them.

When the man heard her return to the office he said, "Do you like living here?"

Karolina said, "I don't live here at the orphanage if that's what you mean," as she handed him several sheets of paper, a pen, and a wooden clipboard.

He took the papers and sat down. "I mean in Matamoros. It's just so different than my village. Mexico is so big, you know?" He'd begun rifling through the papers, and she wondered how well he could read.

"Let me know if you have any questions. I mean, about the paperwork. As far as Matamoros," she said, "living here is not so bad. I've been here a few years. I come from Mexico City, and I'm glad for the change. So much smog and pollution there. Have you been there?"

"Yes, a couple of times," he said. "The sky was like something burned, and I couldn't figure that out. How can clouds burn? But that's what they looked like. Very different from storm clouds. Not gray but actually brown, like chocolate."

Karolina sipped her coffee, now much cooler than she'd prefer it. Perhaps this man before her was better traveled than she'd suspected. Most people coming to this office were poor locals. She didn't recall anyone else ever arriving from somewhere as remote and distant as Puerto Isadore down in Oaxaca. Only recently she'd read in one of the American newspapers that often made its way across the border from Brownsville that Oaxaca and Chiapas were the poorest parts of Mexico. If this man's blood work proved his paternity, she would question him about Oaxaca and how his child came to be separated from him. But for now, she would not concern herself with what-ifs. In her line of work, what-ifs could wear a woman down in an instant. She hadn't energy or time for that.

But then he added, "Both times I visited Mexico City briefly on my way north. The second time was this week on my way here when the bus passed through there. My first time was a few years ago as I traveled to the border. I guess I can't say I know your hometown very well." He smiled as he said this, then returned his focus to the papers in his lap.

He seemed a gentle, genuine man. She wondered if that trip he'd mentioned to *el norte* had something to do with his losing his child. Such nastiness was not unheard of. When he'd completed the forms, Karolina led him back to the nurse's office where he offered his arm without a flinch. Karolina then sketched out directions to the nearest, cheapest inn that would be this man's home until the DNA results came back.

When he'd gone, Karolina went to her files to look up the child Alejandra/Ernesto/Esther, whom the man claimed was his daughter. Karolina hoped he was the girl's father, indeed, and that she could locate his child easily. Reuniting them, if all the pieces fit together, would be a sweet reward for her work among these orphaned and abandoned babies. She'd not bothered to actually look into the child's whereabouts after the priest's call, thinking she'd deal with that if the supposed parent from Oaxaca ever actually showed up to claim parental rights. Having a village priest make a phone call was far different than following through and showing up, submitting your DNA for proof. Karolina never expected anyone to surface in this case. Yet he had, and what a simple, kind man he seemed to be.

"Ah, there you are!" she said aloud, after fifteen minutes of digging through a thick file. Ernesto, she read, had arrived the twenty-fourth of January, in healthy condition, the lone survivor of a car crash. Karolina continued reading through the notes, scrawled by hand the week of the child's admittance. As she read, her faith in the priest's story and the nurse's memory grew exponentially. What each of them had said matched what the file stated.

Karolina reached for her cold coffee and turned the page to read the last two sentences in Alejandra's file.

"Oh, no," she said. "No, no, no. This can't be." She closed the file and rubbed the bridge of her nose, dreading the poor man's return, hoping his DNA didn't match this child's after all.

Chapter 32

Héctor

Héctor found a room at a small motel several blocks from Casa de Esperanza. The woman at the orphanage, Karolina was her name, had said the rooms were affordable, but perhaps that word meant different things to different people, and Héctor worried his money would run out if he were not prudent. He needed to have enough left at the end of the week to purchase bus fare back to Puerto Isadore. He certainly couldn't hitchhike or travel any other less safe way, especially if, somehow, his little girl were by his side.

The walk to the motel had taken less than ten minutes, but the heat bore down with an intensity Héctor had not known in Puerto Isadore. His shirt dripped with sweat by the time he'd arrived in the lobby.

The clerk, a squat man with a shaved head and thick glasses, watched a soap opera on a tiny television set on the far side of the desk. He eyed Héctor with a hint of suspicion, and asked him to pay in full for the five nights Héctor requested. The clerk assured him rooms would be available if Héctor decided he needed to stay longer. Héctor lifted his shirt and counted out the bills from a money pouch he'd strapped to his waist. The man passed him a key and motioned to a narrow hallway to his right.

"Far end of that hall. Toilets and showers at the near end of the hall," he said, before turning his attention to the grainy image of a beautiful woman speaking in a hushed but urgent and breathy sort of way on the television.

Héctor found his room right where the clerk said it would be, grateful the key worked. He imagined such clerks, intent on television programs, could on occasion mix up keys. In his travel bag, Héctor carried an extra shirt, one pair of socks, one pair of underwear, and one pair of pants, along with a toothbrush and toothpaste and a photo of Lilia and Fernando.

Karolina had warned him of bandits and thugs who populated the streets of Matamoros. "They're bad, and they prey on visitors such as yourself. Walk around like you know where you're going. Don't ever look lost, even if you are. The criminals will more likely leave you alone if you look confident."

Héctor sat on his motel bed, staring out the barred window, listening to traffic and wondering how one could look not lost if one were, indeed, lost, and how one could look confident, even when he wasn't sure about anything in his life.

He pulled his boots off and lay back on the bed, studying his surroundings. The floor was orange tiles, the walls comprised brown plywood, and the threadbare bedspread a pink floral. A lamp with no bulb sat on the bedside table, along with a Bible and a book about northern Mexico. Two framed works of art hung on the wall opposite the bed. The top frame held a painting of a black horse in a green field of orange flowers with snow-capped mountains in the background. The bottom frame held a picture of Jesus with a bright red heart flaming in His chest as Jesus looked skyward.

Héctor peeled back the tape holding a square of gauze to his inner arm. A dot of dried blood marred the white bandage, but otherwise no sign of his having been stuck remained with him.

He folded the sticky tape around the bandage and dropped it to the bedside table, wondering how someone in a laboratory could look at his blood and Alejandra's blood and tell that he was her father. The thought took his eyes to the inflamed crimson heart in Jesus's chest. He wondered if the Virgin Mary knew Jesus's blood when she saw the stains on the shroud, or if she questioned and doubted.

Karolina had told him that the orphanage took blood samples from all children admitted to their care, so that if Alejandra had lived there, her sample would be on file. He wondered, but had not asked Karolina, what "on file" meant. The blood would dry up. Nothing would be left of the sample if it were kept years, would it? He considered the spot of blood on the gauze. Even that bit, barely an hour old, had started to turn from red to a rusty color.

How accurate were DNA tests? Most of Héctor's mind felt excitement about the news Karolina would have for him in a week, but no small part worried and wondered about a multitude of potential mistakes. What if the child named Ernesto wasn't Alejandra? Maybe Alejandra was only one of a thousand infants who'd used smugglers' papers naming them Ernesto. Perhaps the girl Ernesto that the orphanage had had was a different girl, someone else's child. Perhaps Alejandra had never been at this orphanage. He would never understand the scientific processes regarding blood work and DNA, but he knew he must trust the orphanage's methods. He had no alternative plan.

Would he know Alejandra when he saw her? When their eyes met would she recall something in him, something lingering in her small brain that told her he mattered in her history, in her very blood and being? Or would he and she look at each other the way two minnows passing in a stream might blandly acknowledge each other as nothing more than two bodies, no more or less meaningful to each other's existence than any other minnow might be. How often he'd considered these questions, but never had he felt closer to discovering the answers.

A week? Héctor had never been anyplace a week without working. How could he possibly occupy the next five or seven or more days and nights? He picked up the book about northern Mexico and flipped through it. When he came to a section about Matamoros he stopped and studied the pictures, reading their captions. He considered for the first time how very close he was to *la línea*. For so many years dreams and images of Norteamérica possessed him, haunted him, and taunted him, begging him like some enchantress from a fairy tale to come to her. Now, since his return to Mexico and the loss of Alejandra, the voice of that magical place had been all but silenced for him. He could never dream of leaving Mexico again, not as long as Alejandra's whereabouts remained a mystery.

Beneath a photo of a fancy municipal building was the sentence "The Matamoros-Brownsville metropolitan area comprises the fourth largest metropolitan area on the Mexico–U.S. border."

Héctor wondered what the other large metropolitan areas along the border were, though he doubted he'd ever get to any of them. He read about the special fiesta days here and wished this were February instead of August so that he might attend the Sombrero Festival. He'd not heard of this festival before, but such a fiesta sounded joyful and light. As a boy he'd always anticipated fiesta days in Puerto Isadore, when the entire village burst with music, dancing, laughter, costumes, banners, and parades to honor Isadore, their patron saint. He and the other children understood from the earliest age that such celebrations mattered, and the more celebratory the community became, the more their fishing and their livelihood would be blessed by their patron saint. Somewhere over the years Héctor had lost his enthusiasm for the fiesta days, and he knew his lackluster attitude bordered on sin.

Despite Karolina's warnings, the book on northern Mexico told many wonderful and impressive facts about Matamoros, and if he and Alejandra were reunited he would share with her the fascinating bits of information he'd learned while awaiting their reunion. He would teach her their country's national anthem and say to her, "My darling Alejandra, did you know that our anthem was played for the first time in public at the Opera Theatre in Matamoros?" His beautiful girl would say, "No, Papa! Tell me more of the things you learned while you waited to save me and return me home from Matamoros to Mama and Fernando and the baby!"

"So," he said, jutting the book toward the opposite wall and the red-breasted Jesus, "this is how I'll spend my week."

He would read this book and he would explore this place so that one day he could share all he'd learned with his children. He could not possibly know if he'd ever pass this way again, though he doubted so. He'd use his mind when he had no physical work to occupy this time of waiting. He'd wander the streets and take in all this new scenery, careful to look like he belonged here, whatever that meant, so as not to be robbed by the street thugs of which Karolina had cautioned him.

His thoughts returned to the man he'd watched burn in the car in Acapulco. Perhaps he had been lost earlier that day and had become prey to a thug, and that had been his only crime. Héctor sighed, realizing he was thirsty, and looked about the room for a cup, though none was to be found.

Some events in life were destined to remain mysteries, but resigning oneself to that acknowledgment proved difficult. He'd never know why a man had been chained and burned in the hills of Acapulco, but Héctor knew the vision would haunt him all his days. He'd never understand why a gang would find necessary or take pleasure in killing teenagers in Honduras. He'd never comprehend why walking around the city of Matamoros, a place rich with history and in such proximity to the great Estados Unidos, must be dangerous and filled with ruffians intent on robbing, or worse. He'd likely never discover answers to many, many questions that plagued him, and his prayer, among a long list of prayers, was that God would release him from his intrigue and worry about such inequities.

But even as he pondered these things, he knew that every man had his price, every man harbored some potent desire or insurmountable weakness so powerful that no explanation or teaching or begging could sway him. How could anyone stack in boxes living birds, bright and beautiful creatures from God, like bundles of sticks for the cook fire? Though he'd not packed the parrots into the boxes with his own hands, he'd delivered them. He'd played a part in the process that surely would lead to the demise of many of those lovely birds, gorgeous beings whose only fault had been to fly into hidden nets set for them in fruiting trees that supplied their sustenance.

Any man could possess a trace of evil, he decided, but he hoped a man's acknowledgment of his wrongdoings and feelings of guilt over his evil acts could lead to his redemption. What if a man perpetrated one evil as a result of a worse evil done to him? Was committing a sinful act excusable if the deed was done for a higher cause, a greater good?

He'd beseech God to let those parrots live and thrive wherever they arrived, and he hoped God would understand why he had participated in such corruption as their illegal trafficking. Finding Alejandra trumped everything. Yes, Héctor, too, had his price.

Chapter 33

Lilia

The familiar sound of a goat pulling a trash cart woke Lilia from her sleep, and she rose on one elbow to watch the goat, a large brown-and-white male, through the frame of her window. The damp cloth Rosa had draped across her brow earlier that afternoon had slipped from her head to her pillow, and she tossed it to the table beside the bed. The old man guiding the trash cart whistled a tune vaguely recognizable to Lilia as he passed, though otherwise he could have been asleep, his eyes closed and the loose reins resting in his lap. A trace of the stench from the cart, the goat, and maybe even the old man caught on the breeze and wafted to Lilia, and she was glad her nausea had subsided. She watched them until they were beyond her field of vision, and still she watched until she could no longer hear the man's tune or the clip clip clip of the goat's dainty hooves and the rickety cart's wheels grinding down the bumpy lane.

Never had she longed to go someplace, anyplace, as she did now. She would happily climb into the cart beside the old garbage man, enduring the scent of goat flatulence and rotting cabbages, if only to leave this bed, this house, and feel the breeze and the sunshine on her face. At her request Rosa had put a calendar beside Lilia's bed, and many times a day Lilia would lift the calendar and count the days until her due date. Lilia knew well that she'd likely deliver before the full term, but each day she ticked off the calendar meant one more day the baby had developed and strengthened in her womb.

She had not had a fever for several days now, and Rosa had told her if she could keep the baby inside for just three more days, it should have a decent chance of survival. While "decent chance of survival" was far less appealing than "fat, healthy, and thriving," Lilia had tried to adjust her outlook and hopes to realistic expectations.

Rosa and Fernando were in the front courtyard visiting with the widow from down the lane. The woman had stopped by that morning to say she'd return later in the afternoon with pork stew for their dinner, and Lilia could hear the faint sounds of the women's chatter.

Rosa had been insistent that Lilia call her when she needed to rise to relieve herself, and she'd put a pot beside Lilia's bed for that purpose. Lilia was sick of the pot and sick of this room. With her fever gone she felt more clearheaded, and though the pressure in her pelvis was mighty, she felt more like herself than she had in weeks. She eased herself to a sitting position, lowering her feet to the floor, an incredible urge to urinate overtaking her as she shifted. She stood and lifted her arms above her head in a wonderful, liberating stretch, and decided she would make her way to the latrine behind the house. A few steps there and back would be refreshing for her and therefore for the baby.

She padded lightly across the floor, careful not to alert Rosa that she'd arisen. When she'd taken a few steps into the yard she lifted her swollen face to the sunshine, envisioning herself as some bloated creature emerging from a strange darkness. Never had warmth and light felt so life affirming. Lying about all day made her feel less than human, like a subterranean being destined to slog beneath the soil.

She heard Rosa bidding the widow woman goodbye, and

Lilia knew she must linger no more and make her way to the toilet before Rosa caught her and scolded her. As she reached the latrine and pulled open the rusty tin door, warm water trickled down the insides of her legs. Feeling foolish for her inability to hold her urine, she eased the door shut behind her and emptied her bladder with great pleasure and relief. When she finished, she rose and slipped out the door, careful not to let it bang, then made her way toward the house. As she crossed the threshold, a surprise gush of water wet her legs anew, and the fear she'd suppressed at the latrine hit her square: The sac in which her baby floated had broken. This child would wait no longer in her dark, damp womb. Like her mama, this baby girl longed for sunlight.

Chapter 34

Héctor

MATAMOROS

Day 1

My dear Alejandra, I arrived at this inn in Matamoros this afternoon, nothing like the fancy inns of Acapulco—but clean and dry—with bed, water, and a toilet. Innkeeper is not talkative. Watches television. He has hands that have never labored in fields. He gave me this paper and loaned me this pen. Today I bled into a tiny needle that pulled my blood into a small glass vial. I've never thought of blood as I do now. Blood contains more than a man's eyes can see, my Alejandra. Magic, power, and ties so deep run through our veins. I, a grown man, your papa, weep over such mysteries, meanings. I will never understand the invisible markers of such crucial bonds, but I know in my heart they exist for the scientists just like the signs along the road to Matamoros from Puerto Isadore, telling the bus drivers which highways connect to which other highways. I feel those blood ties as sure as I feel the pounding of them in my chest. And they will reunite us, my angel. And I tick away the days of waiting with documenting them here, for you to read when you are a grown-up girl and far smarter than your papa will ever be.

Day 2

I dreamed of your mama. Cannot recall the dream, except
that she had the long hair and face she had when we were in
school. I miss her so, but not the way I miss you. I wonder if
you look like her. I hope. Today I will walk about this city and
see the interesting places pictured in a book that sits beside the
bed here. I'll remember every detail to describe on this page,
Alejandra, so you will know what your papa knew, what I felt,
on the final few days of my suffering without you. When I get
you back, I will never let you go again. God knows this, as I have
told Him so every day for over three years.

Day 2 evening

This place is very different from our village, Alejandra! So many
cars and people and businesses. And the noises are strange and
various. At home we hear natural sounds—cocks crowing, doves
cooing, the barks and snarls of dogs, the brays of donkeys, and
endless tweets and chirps and twitters from a thousand birds.
We hear the fruit seller peddling his melons and oranges and
strings of garlic, and if we listen we hear the sounds of seabirds
in a great fiesta as the boats come in at the pier, and sometimes
if the wind is active we hear the surf along the bay down the hill,
Alejandra. And you will know all these sounds as well as you
know your own voice. But in this city the strange sounds keep
me awake. Somewhere nearby is the Gulf of Mexico. But I have
not seen the ocean, only signs pointing the way. I did see the Río
Bravo, which the gringos call the Rio Grande, and I thought of
the fateful day your mama swam that river and lost you, not in
the river but to a woman she entrusted with your care. If I were a
blackbird I could fly just a few meters and land in a cottonwood

tree in America. The book here says that is the name of the
tree that grows along the riverbanks. Ah, but if I were such a
bird I would not care if the limb on which I sat were rooted in
Mexican or American soil. Unlike people, Alejandra, birds have
no interest in such man-made lines and definitions of place. I
saw a university building today. Perhaps one day you will go to
university, Alejandra. I also learned that this city of Matamoros
was not always called Matamoros. A long time past it was called
Villa del Refugio, in honor of a patron saint, Our Lady of the
Refuge of the Estuaries. I do not understand this changing of
names, Alejandra. Perhaps when you are grown and educated
at university you will explain to your old papa how a place
known as one thing can then be called another thing. In 1826,
the governor changed the name of the city to Matamoros, in
honor of some war hero, Señor Matamoros. I have such dreams
for you, my girl, that one day you will leave a mark on the world
that a governor will change the name of his very town in honor
of you. Perhaps one day we will travel to the city of Alejandra!

Day 3

Today I saw a man dying in the street. The terrible, disturbing
image keeps rolling through my brain like the endless swells on
the sea, and I can only write of the scene here knowing you will
not read these words until you are a much bigger girl, Alejandra.
I have seen too much of death lately, the death of strangers,
but I will not tell about all that now. People tended to the man
I saw today, but I am certain he was dead or close to passing
over to the spirit world. I moved on and did not linger. I saw
a monument to the former name of this city today, but the
monument said the former name was San Juan de los Esteros
Hermosos. I do not understand this unless the name has been

changed more than once. Because yesterday I read that this place was once called Villa del Refugio. If a place is known by a name why do officials change the name? I wonder what travelers acquainted with the first place think when they try to return and no place answers to the name they used to know. I am glad people do not do this with their own names, Alejandra! How confusing life would be if I got home and your mama told me she is no longer Lilia but that she is Rebeca. I would wonder what mischief she had been up to.

Day 4

This waiting wears a blister in my soul the way cutting agave in the hot field thickens the skin of my thumb and palm. Maybe one day the blister inside my soul will callous over to something hard and tough, but my prayer is I will have you in my arms soon, and the blister will heal into nothing but a memory on this page. I will call your mama today, though I will likely only speak to Rosa, as your mama is flat on her back. She will be having your baby brother or sister soon, Alejandra. By the time you read these words that baby will likely be older than you are now. That notion seems strange to me as I sit in this room, the ink wet on this paper and the noises of the city street screeching and beeping and dinging and shouting through the barred window as if all the cars and people were inside this inn. Perhaps I will have long forgotten the details of this place by then, but I will never forget the wait, the agony of these years without you. The not knowing was the hardest, Alejandra.

Day 5

How does one stop the worry? I tried phoning our village, Alejandra, but I couldn't connect with anyone. Armando didn't answer. I worry about you, about your mama, your unborn sister or brother, and about Fernando, though currently he is the least of my worries. Your brother, a sturdy little fellow, always smiles and takes great pleasure in chasing little downy chicks for endless laughter, as if each time he sees a hatchling is his first time. Tomorrow I will go see Karolina at the orphanage, Alejandra. Tomorrow makes six days. I know that my blood is your blood, but what I don't know, what I can hardly allow myself to think, to write here, what I don't know is if the child whose blood Karolina has in her files—I cannot know—if that child is you. This thought makes everything inside me turn to wet sand. Oh, my Alejandra. This has to be you!

Day 6, morning

The noise here begins early, and I cannot sleep, knowing today is the day I have sought for more than three years. I have washed my face and brushed my teeth. I have eaten a banana I bought yesterday at the produce stand in the market along a street not so far from where I stay. I drank a cup of water. And I am waiting for the sun to rise. Waiting waiting waiting!

I have stayed away from the orphanage the five days, never getting closer to the front door than a slow amble down the opposite side of the street. Six days is a day short of a full week, and the orphanage woman said DNA tests take a week. But my results may have arrived. Perhaps the results await opening among a stack of parcels just delivered. I hope my checking with her on the sixth day won't seem rude or uncooperative on my part. Each day on my walks, Alejandra, I stare at the tall fence shielding from my eyes whatever lies beyond the boards and metal of the orphanage fence. Today I will go to the door.

Chapter 35

Karolina

The results had been back since yesterday, but because she had no way of contacting the man, Héctor, other than going to the inn she'd suggested to him, she'd chosen to wait for him to resurface, seeking his DNA results. She'd hoped, somehow, he'd fade away and she'd not have to look him in the eye, not have to have the conversation they were on the brink of having.

Cristina had been with Karolina in the front office when Héctor arrived, but Cristina had slipped out, retreating to her nursing duties in the back, leaving Karolina alone with him.

He sat expectantly, eyes wide, his nervous energy and anticipation permeating the room like heat waves from blacktop, almost visible, uncomfortable.

"So, yes, Héctor," she began. "The results have come back. You timed your return here just right." She offered a weak smile, trying to make anything about what she had to say to him pleasant.

He inched forward in his chair. "Yes?"

"The child we had here, Esther, or, rather, excuse me, Alejandra, as you know her. She and you share significant genetic markers."

He stared at her with an unwavering expression, and she realized he didn't understand. "She's your daughter. The child we had here is your daughter."

She anticipated an emotional reply, but his guttural reaction and the volume of tears pouring freely from his closed eyes brought an unexpected heaviness to Karolina's heart. With his head bowed, the deluge fell into his lap, and he could not speak. He was powerless to do anything more than let the news wash over him. Karolina, moved by this man's close proximity to her and his intense physical response, was uncertain if this were joyful weeping or desperate sobbing that significant, disappointing news would follow, as if he had detected as much in her tone or delivery.

Karolina knew she must continue, though looking at him now unsettled her, as if she were peering into the private opening of a long-sealed tomb. "I have more to tell you, of course. I'm not sure how to proceed, as this has never quite happened." She paused, not only to give him time to comprehend this information but also to choose her wording with care. "I mean, one time we had a similar case as yours, a case in which a woman arrived, adamant she was a child's long-absent mother."

Héctor's sobbing slowed and calmed, but still his nose dripped and he hiccuped, unable to steady his breath.

She continued, "We did the DNA testing on that woman, just as we did on you, and the report came back that the two shared no DNA. The woman, upon hearing the undeniable truth, admitted she'd been a childhood friend of the girl's dead father and she'd hoped to raise the girl as her own."

Karolina realized she was talking too much. Héctor had raised his head, opened his tear-filled, confused eyes, and now studied her with the expression of a dog who has just been kicked by a child who only moments before had tossed him a bone streaked with juicy bits of meat.

"Your daughter was here. She's no longer here. She's safe. She's well cared for, please rest assured about that. But she's been adopted."

"Adopted?" He seemed not to understand the word.

"Yes. She's gone to live with a couple who've become her parents. They've had her for more than two years."

"How? I don't understand. What . . . what do you mean?" He ground his fists into his temples as if to crush the bewilderment budding in his brain.

"Mr. Santos, please. I can imagine the difficulty of this news," Karolina said, struggling for soothing words.

"Alejandra has real parents. I am her parent! My wife is her mama. She has a brother and will soon have another brother or a sister. Where is she? I want my daughter," he said, his confusion giving way to anger.

"Can you share with me the circumstances under which your daughter ended up here in our care?" Karolina needed to know as much as he could tell her before she shared much more about Alejandra with him.

He rubbed his eyes, nodding. "I was in America, working. My wife came to join me. She had a coyote who didn't cross with babies, so he directed her to give Alejandra to a woman, another coyote. My wife crossed and waited on the other side, but the woman never came. We have not seen our daughter again."

Karolina nodded, scribbling notes on a pad of paper.

"We found out later, years later, just recently, that the woman died in a car crash near here and that a baby was in the car with her. The baby survived. We suspected the baby had to be our Alejandra, and so our village priest phoned a few places, and you know the rest. Now I am here, and I want to take my daughter back home with me to Puerto Isadore, to her mama. Her mama misses her so much. You can't . . . We just . . ." He faltered. "Please," he added, feeling inadequate in his anguish and with a sudden shortness of breath.

"Your daughter has been adopted by a wonderful couple," Karolina said, at once regretting her words, as if she were implying the child's birth parents were less than satisfactory, but the right words tripped over her tongue and would not come out.

Héctor stood, his anger mounting. "Where is she? Where are these people?"

"They are in Colorado, in the United States."

"In America? My baby is in America?" he said, easing back down into the chair as if his legs might fail him. "Americans have my baby?"

"Alejandra was adopted by an American couple. But they are also Mexican. He is a respectable man, a doctor of letters, and he teaches at a university there. His wife is an artist, her work is sold for large sums of money in America, according to my files. But they are also Mexican. They are from our country, but they are United States citizens, too. They have dual citizenship. Your daughter is their only child," she said, thumbing through the folder in her lap as if she were reading, though she'd memorized its contents already.

"Will they give her back to me?" he said, his demeanor changing and his tone shifting so drastically she feared he might faint. She knew he felt weak and powerless at the thought of the adoptive Americans.

Karolina opened her mouth to speak but at once realized she had no answer to offer.

"Do they know," he said, "that Alejandra has a real father and a real mother who love her very much?"

Karolina shook her head. "No. I . . . I wanted to speak to you first. Now that we have spoken, I can contact them if you wish."

"Yes, I wish so, of course. This is my child, and I want her back with her family. Her real family. Do they have a telephone? Can you call them?"

Karolina suspected all Americans, certainly these well-to-do Mexican Americans, had a telephone.

"Surely if these are decent people they will bring her back to me, when they understand that Alejandra's real parents have been located they will bring her. Otherwise they are evil people. They are people who would steal a child," he said.

"Señor, please. They went through legal channels. This couple, I assure you, are very decent and good folks. Remember, no one could locate anyone related to this child. When this couple requested to adopt her, their offer seemed to be the very best option in the world for your daughter. They'd wanted children for many years and were unable to conceive one. They did missionary work in Mexico through their church in America, and that's how they met Esther. I mean, Alejandra. They were on a mission trip here, doing good things with their time and energy and financial resources. They wanted a Latina girl so that she would look like them. They could have adopted an American child, but Alejandra is the one they chose, the one they fell in love with. I promise they are providing everything this child needs to thrive."

"Call them. Call them now," Héctor said.

Karolina nodded. "Of course. As you wish." She'd known in her gut since the test results had come in that he would request this, that he would push her and demand the child be returned to him. She would have done the same if she were in his situation. She rose.

"Wait here," she said. "I'll see what I can do. I'm also going to contact legal counsel."

"What does that mean? Who is legal counsel?"

A wave of empathy and tremendous sadness for Héctor washed over Karolina.

"Someone knowledgeable about such situations," she said, before retreating to the privacy of the back office to make the calls she dreaded.

Chapter 36

Rosa

Lilia's first contraction hit before she made her way back to the bed. As soon as Rosa saw her she knew without Lilia saying a word.

"Lilia?" Rosa said, stepping toward her, helping Lilia ease onto the bed beside which she stood, one hand on the wall and the other pressed against her hardening belly.

Lilia, unable to speak, pointed to her skirt, drenched in fluid from her womb.

"Now that your bag of waters has opened we'll change our methods, Lilia," Rosa said. "No use trying to keep that little one in there anymore. This one is ready to see the world."

She'd brought her birthing stool to Lilia's house days ago. Rosa fetched it, a bowl, towels, and some cocoa beans for Lilia to chew to get the contractions going in case this one was false or in case the second one stalled in coming, but in a short span Lilia's contractions became regular and mighty.

Rosa placed her hand across Lilia's belly. It felt knotted as a tree root. She hummed a tune and in between verses prayed to Mary, the mother of Jesus, that the child had working lungs and a steady heartbeat. She called, too, upon Saint Raymond Nonnatus, the patron saint of expectant mothers, newborn babies, and midwives, and asked for his guidance, for him to be her heavenly advocate, to intercede here.

Lilia gripped the back of the birthing stool and grunted, calling out the indecipherable but familiar sounds of labor. Rosa moved behind her, massaging Lilia's back to relieve the pain of her contractions. Lilia cried out and squatted in her need to birth this baby, and Rosa shifted around to face her. In less than twenty minutes the crown of the baby's head, matted and slick with thick, curly hair, just as Alejandra had looked, peeked between Lilia's legs.

"This will be quick, Lilia. Usually the third child comes faster than the first and second, though Fernando didn't have to pass into the world the normal way," Rosa said, recalling the boy's perfect, round head at birth, so different from the more pointed heads of babies who'd labored through the birth canal.

Fernando sat in his little chair in the corner of Lilia's room. What a good child he'd become during Lilia's bed confinement. Rosa glanced at him, all the while holding a clean folded cloth to Lilia's bottom, dabbing at the fluids seeping out there around the tip of the baby's head.

"Your mama's going to be fine, little one," she said to Fernando. "She just has to work a bit to give you a new baby. She'll be able to rest after a while."

"I want to see my baby, Roro. I want to see my baby," he said, standing up from his chair and darting toward the women where together they labored at the stool.

"In a little while, my boy. Now I need you to do something for me, to bring good luck to this baby and to your mama. Can you do a job for me, my love?"

"What to do, Roro?" he said, his eyes wide.

"Slip into the courtyard, but you must be very quiet. Very quiet. I want you to listen for birdsong, to see if you can understand what they're saying, what message the birds send to your mama and to your baby. Listen closely to their tunes for me. Can you do that?" Rosa whispered, all the while keeping a hand on Lilia.

"I can do that," the boy said softly, nodding.

"That's good, Fernando," Rosa said. "Your mama needs to work. You go on, now. You have to be the big boy your papa expects you to be while he's away. Go spy on those birds for us, so you can tell us their meaning."

The boy grinned, then padded on silent toes toward the door.

"He's a good child," Rosa said to Lilia. "And very soon, God willing, he will have a baby to love and help you care for."

A hen darted into the room, and Rosa swatted her out.

"This one has a lot of hair like her sister did," Rosa said, carefully placing the folded blanket on the floor beneath Lilia.

Lilia did not speak but crouched, pushing and groaning, and Rosa hummed and dabbed around the top of the baby's head that had eased out almost to its ears before sinking back into its mama.

"No, this won't take long, Lilia. Take a good breath and get ready. One more good strong effort from you and the hard part of this will be over," Rosa said.

She massaged with oil the tight circle of Lilia's skin through which the little head would soon pass. She knew doing so would ease not only the birthing but also Lilia's healing afterward, and oftentimes she found doing so prevented the flesh from tearing.

She could not tell from the crown of the baby's head if the child was too small to survive or how its lungs would be or if it could suckle or any of those mysteries only time and God knew.

And then, out popped the little head, small but perfect. Lilia felt it and exhaled a huge sigh. Then with the last bit of strength in her quivering, thick thighs, Lilia pushed again.

"Yes, yes, here we go now," Rosa said, easing the rest of the little girl's body from her mother's and into the world. She placed the tiny child on the folded cloth, and at the same time scooped another clean rag from the pile beside her and placed it over the opening from which the child had just come. Lilia slumped, leaning hard against the back of the birthing stool.

"Here, Lilia," Rosa said, as the blue baby started to cry, her little body turning pink. "Let's get you to the bed while I tend to your beautiful daughter."

Lilia's breath came in heaves of exhaustion and tears rolled down her cheeks, but she did not speak. Instead she nodded with closed eyes and shuffled to the bed as Rosa walked beside her, cradling the newborn in her arms as the baby was still connected by umbilical cord to her mother.

Until now Rosa had not noticed Fernando back at her side, quietly watching his new sister.

"Look at this, eh, Fernando! What do you think of this girl?" Rosa said, smiling at him.

"What's on my baby, Roro?" he said, clamping one arm tight around Rosa's knee and pointing with his free hand at the slick gray mucus and blood-coated infant making soft bleating sounds not unlike those of a baby goat. "That's a dirty baby," Fernando said.

"Then go hug your mama while I get your baby cleaned up," Rosa said, shooing Fernando to the head of the bed and into Lilia's limp arms, weakly reaching for him. Rosa's skilled hands moved with efficiency and urgency. She needed to get the baby cleaned, dried, and warmed, and she needed to move fast, in preparation for the arrival of the placenta. She pulled open the front of Lilia's blouse and placed the infant on her mama's bare skin to warm her as blood continued to pulse through the cord, nurturing the newborn. When the blood flow ceased, Rosa tied off the cord and cut it. She grabbed the bowl from where she'd placed it on the floor.

"Here we go, Lilia. Let's finish this work now. The afterbirth's coming," she said, gently pumping her fingers across Lilia's abdomen to ensure the womb contracted and Lilia's bleeding slowed. Rosa caught the placenta neatly in the bowl, easing out the remainder of the umbilical cord.

"How is she, Rosa?" Lilia said, straining to raise her head and shoulders from the pillow to study the tiny, living, breathing pink bundle now squirming on her chest.

"She's small but whole. I'm guessing she is forty-three, maybe forty-four centimeters long. And," she said, lifting the infant in one hand to clean her a bit more before wrapping her in a soft blanket, "she feels over two kilos. Maybe two and a quarter. A respectable size for a baby this early."

Lilia stared at the child with that unmistakable expression of wonder, curiosity, love, and relief that Rosa had observed a hundred times in mothers within moments of their babies' births.

"I'll call her Elizabeth," Lilia said, sniffling. "Can you say your sister's name, Fernando? Can you say Elizabeth?"

Fernando stretched on the tips of his toes to see his sister. "Leed—ah—bet!" he said, grinning and proud that he could say his sister's name.

Rosa cupped Elizabeth in her palm. She had delivered smaller babies, but she'd also delivered bigger babies who hadn't survived. This girl's ankles were the size of Rosa's little finger, but her coloring wasn't bad, and, though raggedy and rapid, her breathing was continuing. Her lungs were functioning.

"I know what the birds sang, Roro," Fernando said.

"What, my love?"

"They said, 'We hope baby Leed-ah-bet doesn't cry.'"

"That's a good message, my son," Lilia said. "Let's call your sister Elizabeth Esperanza, Elizabeth Hope, in honor of the birds' song."

"Okay, Mama," he said, gently patting Lilia's arm with dirty fingers.

"We need to keep her warm," Rosa said, opening the blanket to replace the baby, skin to skin, across Lilia's chest. "And we'll need to get her suckling to be sure she can do it. These early ones struggle with that. Later, when you're ready, I'll sit out in the courtyard with her, Lilia. Sunshine will get that yellow from her skin."

Rosa tucked the edges of the cottony fabric of a larger blanket over them both, then went to work tidying the room from Elizabeth Esperanza's arrival.

Chapter 37

Héctor

Héctor sat at a small table in the back corner of a café sipping a Coca-Cola, waiting.

When he'd left the orphanage the previous afternoon, Karolina had managed to arrange a meeting between him and the people who had Alejandra, and she'd promised to have a man there who understood such complicated situations. She'd explained they would meet not in person but on the computer, and she'd assured him this way of discussing the matter was the next best scenario. Héctor couldn't understand, and he felt as if a thousand insects had hatched within his body and were scraping at his skin from the inside, their tiny legs scratching and poking, their antennae searching for a way out of him.

Héctor had paced the streets of Matamoros until dark then retreated to the confines of his room at the inn, but he had not slept, and this morning he hit the streets again wandering without direction, thinking too many thoughts to organize in his head. How could someone have his child and not return her? What kind of evil lurked here? And why was legal counsel necessary? Wasn't this situation as clear as still water?

And poor Alejandra. What must she think, living with strange people in a foreign place, a distant state in an unfamiliar country with a family that wasn't her own. How could her little mind make sense of these things? He wondered if at night Alejandra dreamed of the smell of Lilia and the sounds of their village, smells and sounds she had missed for more than three years: the clip-clopping of the goats that pulled trash carts, the voice of the orange and melon vendor peddling his fruit through his tattered white megaphone each afternoon, the cooing of the mourning doves each evening, the pat-pat-pat of Lilia slapping out tortillas, the scent of Lilia's incense lingering on the salty Pacific breeze, of her lavender oils, of the bright flowers she grew. Héctor had been to America, and, though he had planned to stay there many years more than he had, these were the sounds and smells from Puerto Isadore that he'd longed for late at night in the quiet stillness on the tree farm where he'd lived and worked before his deportation.

He gulped the last swig from his bottle of Coke. The time had come for him to make his way to Casa de Esperanza, to Karolina and the legal man. He'd do whatever they requested in order to prove his determination to get Alejandra back home. He'd played this day out in his mind too many times, yet somehow nothing was developing as he'd envisioned it. Once he'd located her, the getting-her-home part of the plan should have unfolded with no seams, no hitches.

When he reached the door of the orphanage he offered a quick prayer then pushed the button that sounded the buzzer. Karolina opened the door for him, only this time she led him through her office to a corridor and down a hallway he'd never entered.

"Señor Castillo is waiting on us," she said.

When he didn't respond, she added, "He's the attorney who'll help us through this. He represents Casa de Esperanza. To make sure we do everything properly, you see?"

Héctor had dealt with an attorney only once before, and that

had been during his and Lilia's retention by the police in South
Carolina. Everything had unfolded in quick and unexpected
ways then, though in hindsight he realized he should have been
more wary, more cautious. He and Lilia had stopped at the
scene of a friend's accident. That was all, but that was enough.
Because of his concern for his co-worker who'd wrecked a farm
truck, Héctor had let his guard down and a lawman had noticed
him there.

The American attorney the farmer had found for them
had been kind, a smart and gentle man. Yet that attorney had
proved useless in his ability to secure Héctor and Lilia's stay in
America.

Héctor wondered how the attorney here would be.

Karolina stopped in front of a doorway to Héctor's left and
motioned for him to enter the room before her. Inside, a gray-
haired man in a dress shirt and trousers stood to greet him.

"Eloy Castillo," he said, extending his hand to Héctor. Héctor
shook the man's hand, which, like the hand of the innkeeper,
was the smooth hand of one who knew no manual labor in hot,
dry fields.

"I'm Héctor," he said. "Héctor Santos."

"Here, sit, won't you?" Eloy Castillo said, motioning to one
of two chairs beside him.

Karolina began typing on her computer, though Héctor
could not begin to understand what she aimed to accomplish
there.

Eloy was speaking, but Héctor was too distracted, worried that neither this legal man nor Karolina understood the
urgency of this situation, and he had to bite the inside of his
cheek not to scream at these people with their computer and
fancy office and soft hands.

"The situation is delicate and, no doubt, shocking for you,"
Eloy was saying. "We want what's best for the child, of course."

Héctor nodded, wondering if anyone in this room harbored any doubts as to what would be best for Alejandra.

"I've looked over the paperwork, the documentation from her adoption, and everything looks in order in terms of the Hague Convention on Intercountry Adoption, particularly since the adoptive parents maintained dual citizenship."

What was he saying?

"In other words," Eloy continued, "this orphanage did everything within its power to locate the parents, to find you, of course, and they disclosed everything they knew to the adoptive parents."

Héctor eyed him, listening, trying to follow the man's line, to predict where he was headed with his words, but he didn't speak or respond in any way to affirm or deny what the man said.

"Maybe I should back up. The Hague Convention . . . are you familiar with this?"

"No," Héctor said.

"No worries," the lawyer said. "It's just something to protect children regarding international adoptions. We all recognize children need families, loving homes, happiness, etcetera. So guidelines, rules, were established to govern adoptions, to make sure the best interest of the children will always be considered. Do you understand?"

"Yes, I think so. My daughter's best interest is to be at home with her mama and me. With our family."

The legal man cleared his throat, and seemed to be on the cusp of getting stern with Héctor, but Karolina said, "Okay, now. Here we go," as her computer seemed to come to life and chirp and whir strange sounds. Eloy turned his attention there, toward Karolina's computer, away from Héctor.

Héctor, too, turned toward the computer. On the screen he saw a man, his hand up against the corner as if he were inside the screen looking out, as if he were in a television set moving about, adjusting it from the inside. And Héctor wondered if they were going to watch some legal program so that he might learn about international adoptions or this convention the legal man had mentioned. But then the strangest, most unexpected thing happened, and for a moment, Héctor thought he'd begun to lose his senses. Karolina spoke at the computer screen, to the image of the man, and the man responded! He'd heard her.

"Hello, sir. Thank you for agreeing to Skype with us."

"Yes, hello. Certainly," he said, sitting in a chair and looking serious in front of the screen.

"I'm Karolina, the one you spoke to on the phone. I'm here with Eloy Castillo, an attorney, and with Esther's . . . I mean with the child's birth father, Mr. S."

The man nodded a greeting to which Eloy said, "Hello."

"You mean Alejandra," Héctor said. "You're talking about my Alejandra?"

"Pardon?" Eloy said.

Before Héctor could speak, Karolina said, "The child was named Alejandra by her birth parents. I apologize, Mr. S. Her adoptive father knows the child only as Esther."

The image on the screen moved with jerks and every few seconds appeared as if someone had tossed a fistful of sand across the camera lens.

Karolina glanced at Eloy and Héctor and sat up straight. "I'll begin," she said, shuffling papers in her lap. "To be sure we're all equally informed and at the same spot with all this, I'll summarize the situation. I understand this is an emotional issue, a difficult one."

Neither the man behind the gritty-looking monitor nor Héctor spoke, but Eloy said, "Yes, certainly, yes."

"According to our documents, the child was adopted by Mr.

and Mrs. H. when she was seventeen months old. The child is now . . ." She looked over her papers for Alejandra's age.

"Esther is four," the man in the computer said. "And she's healthy and thriving and happy with her mother and me."

Héctor dug his nails into his palms. He wanted to punch the computer screen with his fist, to harm the man behind that glass, the man who possessed Alejandra but called her Esther, who dared to tell him, Héctor, Alejandra's father, her age.

Did that man just call himself and his wife Alejandra's parents? Héctor leaned closer to the desk that held the computer. He slid to the edge of his chair. Could the man see him?

"So the child has been in your custody for two and a half years. During that time, her birth parents have searched for her, according to Mr. S. here, her birth father. Her whereabouts were unknown to them, but they never stopped questioning or looking. A while back I received a call from their priest, which ultimately brought her birth father here to discuss this matter with me and to submit to a DNA test, which confirmed his paternity."

"Yes," Héctor said. Karolina was finally starting to sway this in his direction. No one would refute his rights to his child after hearing about the DNA test. He looked to the legal man for affirmation, but Eloy had his head down, scribbling notes furiously on a thick yellow pad.

"So I thought what we'd do is give each of you, Mr. S. and Mr. H., the opportunity to speak, after which we'll have Mr. Castillo weigh in with his legal thoughts on this issue in terms of Casa de Esperanza's role in all this. Does that sound okay with you all?" Karolina said, looking to each of them for approval.

They all nodded.

"Very well, then," she said. "Mr. S., will you begin?"

Héctor cleared his throat. Their curious regard for him

burned into his face, and heat rose under their collective gaze. For some reason the image of bundled parrots flashed in Héctor's mind, their black, terror-filled eyes staring up at him from the cooler on his last job on the *Gabriela*.

"You've stated what happened," he said to Karolina. "My wife, Lilia, and I love our daughter and we want her to come home to us."

"How did you lose your daughter?" the legal man said.

Héctor inhaled and let the air out with a long sigh. "I left my village for the border. I hired a coyote to help me make the journey. My wife and my baby, Alejandra, stayed behind. Our plan was for them to wait until I could find work and save enough to secure their safe crossing, to join me."

Eloy continued to scratch notes on his yellow paper, but Karolina, despite having heard these details previously, stared at Héctor with such compassion etched into her face that he had to look away before he continued. He focused on his hands, clasped in his lap.

"I found work in South Carolina on a tree farm, and my employers were fair and good to me. Before I had enough money saved to get my family there, an opportunity presented itself to Lilia in Puerto Isadore. Her grandmother died. She'd raised Lilia since birth, and at that point Lilia was ready to leave our village. I cannot know exactly what was in her head, you understand, because I was not there."

He lifted his eyes briefly to be sure they were following him.

"So," he continued, "Lilia and Alejandra traveled to the border with a bad man. An evil coyote named Carlos who did bad things to my wife. When they reached the border he made her hand Alejandra to a woman. This smuggler, she crossed with babies all the time, Carlos said. So Lilia handed Alejandra to this woman and then departed for the border with her coyote. Lilia was told the woman would meet her in Texas, in a place called Brownsville, in a safe house at the border. My Lilia swam the big river and got to the house, but the woman failed to show."

He had never told the whole, painful story aloud like this to strangers, and the recollection of it sickened him, and his chest ached as if his heart were bruised anew and his windpipe were shrinking. "Do you want to hear this?" he said to them all, still staring into his lap.

"Yes, please continue," Eloy said.

"I have little left to tell you. I drove to Texas and retrieved my wife. We looked as long as we could in Brownsville for this woman. What else would we do? We had no way of knowing if Alejandra remained in Mexico or if she'd crossed the border into America." He paused and took a long, slow breath before continuing. "One thing we knew for certain: Our money would run out. We had to return to South Carolina, to my job. Eventually we learned that Lilia's coyote, Carlos, had been killed in a car accident."

"And how did you verify that?" Eloy asked.

"Because Carlos was the uncle of a man Lilia knew in Puerto Isadore. Only recently were we able to track down that man, Emanuel, the one my wife knew from our village. He'd moved up to Acapulco. I found him and through him I pieced together the rest of the details, that a woman and a baby had been in the car with his uncle Carlos, that the woman died, and that the baby, a girl, had survived. You know the rest. That baby was my Alejandra. And now I'm here and ready to take her home to her mama, baby brother, and her baby brother or sister to be born in a few weeks."

Like the tides from two fast-moving rivers colliding in a violent confluence, so did Héctor's emotions of anger and despair, and he clasped his wet palms together in a tight grip to conceal their shaking. He could not look up for fear the man inside the computer would sense his powerlessness and consider him weak or effeminate.

"Thank you," Karolina said. "Mr. H., would you like to speak?"

"Yes, of course," the man said.

When Héctor felt certain the others' eyes were on the monitor, he lifted his face so he, too, could watch Mr. H. speak. What could he possibly say that mattered, that bore any weight whatsoever in this case?

"My wife and I each come from large families, and we have always dreamed of having children of our own. But for reasons only God knows, conceiving a baby of our own never happened. We've tried to guess why this is so. Maybe we should have tried when we were younger, but our schooling delayed us. I have a PhD in literature, and I teach Latin American studies at the university here, and Alicia, that's my wife, she's an accomplished artist and a teacher. Anyway . . . my goodness . . . I digress. I'm so nervous, please, pardon me," he said.

They watched the screen as Mr. H. pulled a handkerchief from a pocket and wiped his brow.

"It's just that . . ." His voice stalled and for a moment Héctor thought the sound on the computer had failed.

"I don't know what Alicia and I would do without Esther. She is the greatest joy in our lives, and a day doesn't pass we don't thank God for her. Every Saturday, you know, I let her choose what kind of breakfast we should have, American or Mexican. We want her to know her heritage, the culture from which she and Alicia and I come, but we want her to embrace her Americanism as well. She likes pancakes," Mr. H. added, with a strange, awkward laugh. He dabbed at his face again with the handkerchief. "Blueberry pancakes are her favorite food in all the world."

All eyes were on Mr. H. now, and Héctor studied him more closely than he had when his image first appeared on the screen, when Héctor had felt all eyes on himself.

The man wore a dress shirt and a jacket, very much in the style of a wealthy American. Behind him were bookshelves filled with books, and pieces of pottery and framed photos, though they were too far away for Héctor to make out the pictures.

Somewhere offscreen, a conversation began, muted but with feminine voices. Or maybe what Héctor heard was not the voice of a woman but that of a child. A girl child.

Mr. H. turned and spoke to whoever stood off camera, but his words were indecipherable to Héctor.

"Is that her?" Héctor said, his voice hardly above a whisper. "Is that Alejandra, there with you now?" he said more loudly, his voice quivering in a way he could not steady.

Mr. H. turned back toward the screen, visibly disturbed and indecisive, and opened his mouth to speak but stopped himself.

"Is she there?" Héctor repeated.

Neither Eloy nor Karolina spoke, as if the entire world had faded into nothingness save for the line connecting Héctor and Mr. H., as they looked into each other's faces from a thousand miles apart.

"Yes, she and my wife just arrived home from Esther's ballet class," Mr. H. said, wiping his left cheek as if a tear were there, though the screen went grainy at that moment, making such details impossible to see.

Oh, dear God in heaven she was there! Right there! Héctor leaned just a few centimeters from the computer's glass and said, "May I see her? Please, sir." He realized Mr. H. had the power, the choice, whether or not to grant his request, and a chill like he'd never known traced his spine.

Mr. H. stood and motioned toward someone offscreen, and

to Héctor's surprise spoke English. He'd not considered that this man, this Latino, could so fluidly switch languages.

What happened next occurred so quickly and without warning that even years later the memory of the impact stalled Héctor's breath in his windpipe, leaving him dizzy and downhearted for days.

A girl, a beautiful black-haired child, dressed in pink with pink ribbons in her hair, rushed forward, jumping into Mr. H.'s lap, and in English, shouted, "Hi, Daddy!" Followed by a string of English words Héctor could not understand. The man embraced the child as she wrapped her arms around his neck and kissed his face three times, unaware her actions were being watched by three people far, far away in a country she may not even recollect.

Mr. H. said to the child in Spanish, "Speak Spanish, my love," and to Héctor's amazement and anguish, the child, in the voice of heaven's sweetest angel, told Mr. H. in perfect Spanish with great joy about her dance class and an upcoming performance for which she would wear the costume of a flower.

The child could speak two languages, yet she was so small, so young!

"I get to be a pink flower, Papa! And I get to be in the front, and you and Mommy will come watch me. And Mommy says she will sit in the first row and clap for me. Will you, Papa? Will you sit in the first row to watch me dance in my pink flower costume?"

Mr. H., for a moment, seemed to forget all about the computer screen and Héctor and that he was being observed. "You know I will, sweetheart. I'm so proud of you! The buttons may burst from my shirt I am so proud!"

"You're a silly goose, Papa. That is so silly! Your buttons won't pop off your shirt," she squealed in a torrent of giggles, before slipping from Mr. H.'s lap and darting out of sight.

Mr. H. watched her go before returning his attention to the group assembled on the other side of the computer screen.

Unexpected emotions engulfed Héctor, rendering him ill. He stood and walked to the back of the small office and gripped the doorframe with shaking hands. He didn't trust himself to attempt speaking for fear he'd be unable to utter a sound, or that he'd vomit, or that he'd break down in such consuming and horrific wailing that those observing would declare him cracked in the head, insane.

"Alicia and I had been working to adopt for several years," Mr. H. continued, as if he were oblivious to the world snapping into a million jagged shards at that moment.

"We'd begun the process, doing all the legwork in as timely fashion as possible. We'd already completed our home study and passed that step when the priest at our church announced a mission trip to Matamoros. Alicia and I decided to go because, you know, of course, we love our home country and we adore children and helping those less fortunate. She and I volunteer with our church when our schedules allow, and this mission trip coincided with a break from the university, you see. We didn't go with the intention of adopting a child, I assure you. In our minds the process was unfolding through the usual channels. But then we saw Esther ... We fell in love with her," he said, as if that were that and no more explanation was needed.

Héctor's back remained to the computer. He wiped his dripping nose on his shirtsleeve and tried to keep his crying silent.

"When we left the orphanage, on the flight back home, we talked about her the entire journey, and we both knew we already loved her, that we would do all we could to be her parents, to love her and raise her knowing love and God and goodness. I assure you, she has brought far more to our lives in the time we have had her than we have brought to hers. She is our greatest blessing."

Mr. H. adored her, and as hard as that acknowledgment kicked him in his gut, Héctor knew the man's love for Alejandra, for Esther, was painfully genuine. And what ground his heart into his breastbone was his realization that Alejandra loved Mr. H., that she recognized Mr. H. and his wife as her papa and mama. What sickened him and brought bitterness rising in his throat was that the beautiful little girl he'd glimpsed on the computer had no recollection of him, no concept of the agony, the tears, the wretchedness of his very existence without her. Suddenly he realized his crying had become audible, and he clamped his palm to his mouth and clenched his teeth.

"Alicia's brother is a deputy in Mexico's lower house of Congress. We requested he write a letter on our behalf, and he graciously obliged. Because we'd long begun our Hague work and completed our home study, and because my brother-in-law's support carried significant weight, we were able to bring Esther home with us to Colorado six months later."

Héctor tried to piece together all Mr. H. said. If he'd adopted her at seventeen months, and he'd first met her six months prior to that, then he'd met her soon after Lilia and he had lost her.

He realized Eloy was speaking now, though he wasn't sure when he'd begun and Mr. H. had stopped.

"So you all see, nothing improper or illegal has occurred here, though this situation certainly is unfortunate for Mr. S. and his family, and in many ways for Mr. H.'s family. We must all remember, however, that the little girl at the center of this discussion is loved by many people, and she has not suffered in any way but rather has been very well cared for her entire life."

Héctor nodded, because yes, for the first time in over three years, he now knew this to be true.

"Let's cut to the reason we're gathered today," Eloy said. "Mr. S.'s family would like to regain custody of this child. Am I correct that this is your desire, Mr. S.?"

Héctor, still standing at the doorway, his back to them all, nodded weakly, but couldn't muster his voice.

"And you, Mr. H., wish to keep the child in your home in Colorado, in the United States, and raise her as your adoptive daughter, yes?"

"Yes, of course, I can't consider otherwise. Though please, if I may add something, sir?"

"Certainly," Eloy said.

"Mr. S., while you and I are in very different circumstances, elements of our situation are very similar. We both love this child and would do all in our power to protect her. I want you to know that Alicia and I promise to raise her knowing about you and her mother, and her village and your love for her. I beg of you to please reconsider fighting this adoption." He paused as if waiting for Héctor to speak. When Héctor didn't respond Mr. H. said, "Very well. I understand. But I want you to know, no matter what happens, I will be indebted to you and your wife for the rest of my life for this child, for your Alejandra. Because we love her, we must also love you. You and your wife are an undeniable part of who Esther, who Alejandra is and will be."

Héctor was overtaken by a sensation much like that of being tossed about in the surf when he'd lose his footing as a boy. He felt the same panic of lost control, of not knowing up from down, and he was slammed by a vivid memory of salty seawater deep in his throat, in his nose, and of a thousand foamy bubbles in his face.

"Okay," Karolina said, exhaling in what sounded like utter exhaustion. "Well, Mr. Castillo, do you have anything more to add?"

Eloy cleared his throat. "Mr. S. may indeed protest this adoption, and this little girl can possibly be repatriated back to Mexico, if Mr. S. can prove fraud. If any deceptions have occurred and they can be proved, the adoption can be nullified. If a gray area exists, he has the right to explore that. The courts would have to sort that out, of course."

They sat in silence a few moments, no one seeming to know how to proceed. Then Karolina said, "Mr. H., thank you for agreeing to meet with us. Why don't we break for now? Both these men, their families, have a lot to process, to think about." She spoke a bit more but Héctor no longer listened. His mind reeled as if a fish were caught on the spool of his thoughts racing away from him faster and faster until his thoughts were irrevocably lost in the unexplored depths of the sea.

"Let's break for lunch, okay?" Karolina said, her hand lightly on Héctor's shoulder. "How about we meet back here in two hours, after we've had time to fill our bellies and clear our heads. See you both here at, say, three o'clock?"

A few minutes later, Héctor found himself walking the streets of Matamoros with no thoughts of eating or any idea or any cares about where he might wander. He feared then that he, like the man he'd seen dying near this spot only a few days earlier, could expire among strangers in this unfamiliar town. The depth of his despair could slam him down to the pavement and he'd be forever powerless to lift himself up, crippled by his grief and the torment weighing on his soul.

Chapter 38

Lilia

With each of her deliveries, Lilia's milk had taken a couple of days to come in, and when it arrived she'd had no doubts about her ample supply. Her breasts swelled to hard melons, so thick with milk she ached to nurse, to relieve the pressure. She harbored no fears about her milk arriving on schedule with this baby. Still, Rosa forced her to drink potions concocted of ground fenugreek, alfalfa, and blessed thistle to stimulate her production of life-giving mother's milk.

Lilia grumbled about the nasty-tasting elixir, but Rosa insisted. "Lilia, I've seen this too many times," she said. "Elizabeth came early, and your body may not have been ready. Your milk could be delayed. The first days' milk will give her strength and resistance to infection."

Rosa could be tougher than an old iguana, but when the time came for her to tend to babies and their healing mothers, she knew more than anyone else in Puerto Isadore. She'd learned the art and science of midwifery from her mother and she from her mother before her.

Praise be to God, the Virgin Mother, all the saints, and to Rosa, too, for Elizabeth, at just eighteen hours old, suckled and cried and wet her diaper and did all she should do as a newborn. Lilia had not felt such lightness and relief in months. When the messenger boy arrived announcing a phone call at Armando's, Lilia told Rosa she would take it.

"Are you sure, Lilia?" Rosa said, pouring herself a cup of mescal. "You're bleeding and weak yet to make that walk."

"No, I want to tell him about Elizabeth, and I want to hear what news he has for us," Lilia said, already making her way toward the courtyard.

"Very well, you hardheaded old girl," Rosa called after her.

The messenger boy, able to walk at a far more rapid pace than Lilia, darted down the lane. "Tell him I'm coming," she called to him.

When she reached Armando's she leaned against the door a moment to catch her breath. When she entered, Armando was speaking into the receiver, "Ah, and here she is now, Héctor." He extended the phone to Lilia, who took it then turned her back to Armando.

"Hello, Héctor?"

"Lilia! I was expecting Rosa. You're out of bed? Is everything all right?"

"Oh, Héctor. Yes, you're a papa again, a papa of a tiny, beautiful baby girl. She's so lovely and dainty and, oh, Héctor, she's beautiful."

"And you? Are you okay, my love? This baby came so early. Are you both doing well?"

She recognized the genuine concern, the worry in his voice and the tone that conveyed his love for her and their family better than the words themselves.

"Yes, I'm well. I'm tired and I'm sore and all those things a new mother is supposed to be, but this is far better than Fernando's delivery when I couldn't walk for a week. You know how that doctor at the clinic split me like a pea pod then. Héctor, maybe saying so is bad, but yesterday was the happiest day, or one of the happiest days of my life, even happier than when Alejandra was born or when Fernando was born, because with this pregnancy I had such fears about this baby's well-being, about her survival because of my bleeding and fever and early labor, you know?"

"Yes, Lilia. Thank God. Thank God and Jesus and the Virgin Mother," he said.

"But you! Tell me your news," she said. "We've not heard from you this week. Have you arrived in Matamoros?"

"Yes," he said. "I tried to call you."

"Have you found the orphanage? Could the people there help you?"

He hesitated.

"Héctor, are you there?"

"Yes, Lilia," he said, and she almost thought she detected a hitch in his voice, as if he were drunk.

"Well, do you have news? Is Alejandra at the orphanage?"

"No," he said. "No, my love. She is not here, but—"

"Tell me what you've discovered," she said, leaning against the shop counter, her back aching and her legs shaky. She'd prayed that by now he'd have more news. She'd expected something. Anything.

"Lilia, I need you to answer something for me. This is important," he said, sober and serious.

"Yes, Héctor, of course. What?" The earnestness in his voice unsettled her further. What had he been doing since he'd left Acapulco?

"Tell me," he said, "what are your hopes for our new baby? My God, I don't even know her name," he said, half laughing, half weeping.

"It's Elizabeth. Do you like that? Elizabeth Esperanza. I hope that name suits you."

"Yes, Elizabeth's a lovely name," he said. "Now, Lilia, I want you to think, and I want you to answer me, please. What are your hopes for baby Elizabeth? Your hopes and dreams for her life, for her whole life."

Lilia and Héctor had discussed such thoughts of fancy many times late at night while newborn Alejandra and then newborn Fernando cooed or dozed beside them. She could only guess why Héctor would ask her such questions right at this moment. Héctor wanted to speak of Elizabeth because he'd missed her birth. Lilia understood that, but, oh, how she'd longed for news about Alejandra.

"I wish her always to have enough food and clean water to drink." She paused, wondering if this answer sufficed.

"Go on, Lilia."

His urgency and need to know these things disturbed her, and she pulled the stool at Armando's cash register over to her and sat.

"I . . . I wish her good health and that she will know love. To be loved and to love others. I wish her to be safe always." Lilia closed her eyes, understanding her answers somehow mattered to Héctor. Tiredness overwhelmed her, and thinking clearly suddenly became a struggle. She knew she should return to bed. If she could wish anything for baby Elizabeth what would she wish? What, besides the fulfillment of basic needs, did she dream of for her children? And the realization hit her then, that since their deportation from America, her dreams for them had been reduced to the fulfillment of basic needs. No longer had she harbored dreams of fanciful travels and university educations. Those were not her dreams to dream.

"Tell me more, Lilia. I need to know, please," he said, and she could discern the sounds of automobile traffic near him. She envisioned him standing in a big city with people all around him, and she wondered what smells he smelled and if anyone were listening to his end of the conversation just as Armando surely listened to her end of it here in this quiet shop.

"My dreams for her? For all our children? I hope our children will know God and rely on Him in lean times and times of plenty, and I hope they'll know many plentiful times and few lean times. I wish for them wisdom. Confidence. Strength. Years ago I dreamed of their education, that they would know far more than I ever knew. I suppose somewhere a grain of those grandiose dreams remains within me. I hope they know and appreciate beauty when they encounter it," Lilia said, tears welling in her eyes though she could not say why.

"Lilia," he said, "those are wonderful dreams. Without hope, without dreams, what's life?"

His affirmation bolstered her, and she continued, "I hope my children know that if they ever become separated from us, as Alejandra has been, that they'll grow knowing their mama and papa love them, that they were conceived in love, among our dreams, among our hopes."

She could hear Héctor's sniffling, but he did not speak for several seconds.

"Do you have anything more? Any other wishes? If God were to descend before you now to ask this question, to grant you these dreams for your children, would you have anything else to add, Lilia? Tell me."

Something terribly wrong had happened. Héctor sounded frantic in his desire to know her thoughts, her answers, many answers, to this question.

"I don't know, Héctor. I want my children to live a better life than I've had, for them not to suffer because of mistakes and poor judgments I've made. I want them to live a godly life, to respect nature and know how to survive in times of poor crops or bad fishing," she said, wiping her nose on the back of her hand. "I don't want my babies to know pain. Neither physical pain nor mental anguish, even though I know such suffering is part of life, for it makes us appreciate the lack of pain. I pray they never know suffering of the soul as we've known these past years. I want our children to have dreams of a future instead of dreading it. I . . . I don't know what to add to this. I want my children to be well always." She closed her eyes, weak and exhausted to her marrow.

"Good, Lilia. These are good wishes. I want these things, too. And if you knew that your children had a very good chance at having these things, would you be satisfied? Would you feel you had done your job as their mama, even if you were to die today, but you had secured such a future for your children, would your dreams have been fulfilled?"

Armando tapped Lilia on her shoulder and handed her a square handkerchief and pointed at her eyes. She nodded a thank-you and took the cloth, dabbing at her cheeks streaked with salty tears that rolled into her mouth as she spoke.

"Héctor, why? Why do you ask me these things?" She sensed the world beginning to crumble, but why? What had happened when only moments ago she'd felt such lightness. The realization struck her then that grief was an invincible beast, impossible to kill.

"Just answer me, please," he said, his voice rising. "Would you feel you had done your job as their mama if you'd secured these things for your children?"

"Yes, Héctor. My God, yes. I would feel at peace if I could ensure such blessings would befall our children."

The heat in Armando's shop had become suffocating. Her throat burned and her head throbbed. She needed to lie down. She needed to nurse Elizabeth.

"I love you, Lilia," he said, his tone calmer now. He sounded resolute, stronger than he had at the start of their talk, though she could not know why. "I thank God for our new daughter, that you and she are well. How is Fernando taking to being a big brother?"

"Fernando loves Elizabeth. He's a good boy," she said, feeling as if she were suddenly suspended from the rafters like a bat, disconnected from her body and looking down at her mouth moving far below her perch, speaking distant words to Héctor, words that sounded as if they'd traveled underwater to her ears.

"When are you coming home, Héctor?" Her determination to ask about Alejandra had slipped into vapor. She felt as if God Himself had pulled that thought from her heart and scattered it like a thousand seeds in a fallow field. She somehow knew not to ask him about Alejandra again, that he had nothing to tell her or that he would tell her in his own time.

"Tomorrow," he said. "I'll begin the journey home by bus tomorrow, Lilia. I have to go now. I love you, my Lilia."

"I know you do," her mouth said, far below where she floated among the dusty wooden beams of *la farmacia,* where spiders kept guard over their little gray eggs, far from the reach of anything that could harm them. "I love you, too, Héctor."

Chapter 39

Héctor

When the bus reached its stop nearest Puerto Isadore, Héctor climbed down its dusty steps, glad to bid farewell to its groans, jolts, and screeching brakes and finally to be nearing Lilia, Fernando, and baby Elizabeth. The walk westward to his village would take him forty minutes if he kept a respectable pace, and he'd get home to them by sundown. He set off on the last leg of this trek, slinging his bag of meager belongings over his shoulder. He'd barely slept in three days, and his limbs felt tight after being cramped and jostled over nearly the entire length of his country.

He passed a hand-painted wooden sign noting a narrow but worn and rocky path to a beach he'd never visited. He couldn't see the beach from where he passed because the path, which would have seemed nothing more than a burro or goat trail, curved and split a dense stand of cacti and scrub brush and disappeared in the thicket. He doubted many people other than those who lived in close proximity had ever visited such a remote beach. Nothing of importance stood in this area except for an occasional shack or patch of sugarcane or withering cornstalks.

At the outskirts of Puerto Isadore the burning stench of his village's incinerated waste drifted on the cooling air, and he wondered for the first time in his life if breathing that scorched garbage and refuse every evening since his birth could be toxic. Perhaps at this very moment something poisonous sprouted deep in his lungs or bones or blood. He realized now that human blood carried invisible, life-changing mysteries, and he prayed that the bodily secrets lurking and blossoming within his marrow or veins would be benign and surmountable in their effects. He wondered, too, about his children, about Alejandra. Would her life in *el norte* free her from the potentially toxic effects of his village's polluted night air, or had her brief time here been enough to infect her little body with impurities. Maybe the contaminants, invisible but noxious, had infiltrated her tiny vessels and organs, her pure heart and mushrooming brain, so that even though she'd left here at a young age, the damaging seeds had been planted. He shook his head and inhaled a deep, slow breath and told himself to abandon such ridiculous thoughts.

You're an exhausted lunatic. Enough. Enough, he told himself, kicking a clod of dirt with his boot. It exploded in a little cloud of dust and flushed two brown birds from the knee-high, scraggly weeds growing beside the road.

Every time his life had shattered, he'd arranged the shards anew, praying his altered existence would suffice, that what he had left of himself would be enough. Enough to support his family, enough to be pleasing to God and the saints, enough to love his children and his wife, enough to be as a man should be. He wondered how many times a life could shatter and still be a life of any use. Could the fragments become too splintered? Too different from the being of which they'd once been a part so that God would toss the hopeless remnants of that person aside? Perhaps Héctor's time of uselessness had come. And yet, he must walk. He must put one foot in front of the other along this dusty road until he got to his Lilia. And then what? What would he say to her? He stopped walking and looked to the vast sky.

"God, help me," he said aloud. "The closer I get to her, to my Lilia, the weaker I am becoming, and I don't . . . I just don't know how to do this."

As he stood there, unable to proceed, he was approached by a leathery, one-eyed farmer traveling home to his outlying shack and driving a donkey cart from which he sold produce several days a week in the village. Héctor bought two avocados and a mango from the man, who handed the fruit over with shaky hands and a toothless grin. He nodded farewell to Héctor and slowly resumed his journey down the road while Héctor continued on his path in the opposite direction, toward Puerto Isadore.

When Héctor reached Armando's shop, he stopped and bought two cans of guava juice and some chocolates, just as Armando was closing for the day. Parched from his travels, Héctor finished his juice in two long swallows. The other can and the sweets were for Lilia.

"You've been away, eh, Héctor? Glad to see you. So glad to see you. Did you have pleasant travels?"

"Good to be home," Héctor said.

"You have a new baby girl, I hear. Congratulations," Armando said, peering over the rim of his glasses.

Héctor eased away from the counter and Armando, toward the door. "Thank you, Armando," he mumbled, his mind on Lilia, but also always on Alejandra.

"I'm sure she's just lovely, just beautiful, like her mama. Lilia has always been pretty. You know, I remember her when she was a tiny girl herself, always so—"

The bell on the door jangled as Héctor headed home, leaving Armando in mid-sentence.

As he rounded the final turn before their courtyard, he regretted not buying anything for baby Elizabeth.

As good as Rosa had been to Lilia, Héctor was glad to see that she appeared not to be at his and Lilia's house but had likely returned to her own place. Lilia sat in a chair beneath her favorite shade tree with the tiny bundle of their new daughter in her lap. They both appeared to be sleeping, and so he crept close on soft feet to take in the soothing, welcome sight of them. How beautiful they were. How utterly peaceful and perfect and beautiful.

Fernando must have been napping or playing inside and when he saw Héctor he ran to him and wrapped his arms tight around Hector's leg. "Papa! Missed you, Papa," he said.

Héctor lifted the boy in the air, kissing each of his cheeks. He stood Fernando before him and bent down to the child's eye level. "What's in your papa's pocket?" Héctor whispered.

Wide-eyed, the boy shrugged his shoulders. Héctor tapped his heart, indicating his breast pocket. With cautious excitement Fernando dipped his stubby fingers into the fabric of Héctor's shirt and withdrew his prize for being a big, helpful boy.

"A feather," Fernando gasped, holding the bold colors up to the sunlight. "Did you see that bird, Papa, the one from that pretty feather?"

"Yes, sweet boy. The bird was a beautiful bird, and it gave me that feather for you."

Their talking woke Lilia, and she turned her head so lazily toward Héctor he thought she might drift right back to sleep. Then she seemed to realize his presence was not a dream but real, and her sleepy face brightened and split into a weary smile. She lifted her face to his when he bent to kiss her.

Any moment Lilia would give voice to the questions Héctor saw in her tired eyes. His answers would be difficult for her to hear, but Héctor knew, too, for the first time in three years, that today, finally, Lilia would have her answers. Héctor and Lilia had far more for which to thank God today than they'd had in years, and soon Lilia would come to know this as well as Héctor did. We'll be okay, he thought.

He kissed Elizabeth on the downy top of her head and whispered, "She's beautiful, Lilia. She's okay. We're all okay, and she's beautiful."

Acknowledgments

Special thanks to my agent, Marly Rusoff, and editor, Nan Talese, for believing in my manuscript then patiently and skillfully guiding me to make it even better.

Tremendous thanks also to Reverend Rob Brown, Dr. Gordon Sherard, and Jim Thompson for your expertise and your willingness to answer my many questions.

Many thanks to Brenda and Emerly for sharing your personal stories with me.

Thanks to Dorothy Josey, Tim Peeler, and Caleb Fort for reading early drafts and offering honest, invaluable feedback and unwavering encouragement.

Thank you to Karen Spears Zacharias for introducing me to several hundred Oregonians who cheered this book into being.

I'm indebted to and grateful for the Wildacres Residency Program and the Blumenthal Foundation for providing me a lovely space and rare solitude to write, write, write.

Heartfelt gratitude to Mayor Bill Barnet for his steadfast encouragement and insistence that this book needed to be written.

Thank you to Betsy Teter and the gem that is the Hub City Writers Project. I'm eternally grateful that you took a chance on me and published my first novel. The literary scene in the southeast—in fact, nationwide—is enhanced because of what you're doing in Spartanburg, South Carolina, and beyond.

To the LTDs: You are a positive force beyond measure and you inspire and bolster me in important and countless ways. My gratitude and love for each of you overfloweth.

To my family—the one I was born into, the one I married into, and the beautiful one Eliot and I have created—you are everything.

A NOTE ABOUT THE AUTHOR

Michel Stone is the author of the critically acclaimed
novel *The Iguana Tree* and has published more than
a dozen stories and essays in various journals and
magazines. She is a 2011 recipient of the South Carolina
Fiction Project Award and she is an Aspen Institute
Liberty Fellow. She lives in Spartanburg, South Carolina.

A NOTE ABOUT THE TYPE

This book was set in Legacy Serif. Ronald Arnholm
(b. 1939) designed the Legacy family after being inspired
by the 1470 edition of *Eusebius* set in the roman type of
Nicolas Jenson. This revival type maintains much of the
character of the original. Its serifs, stroke weights, and
varying curves give Legacy Serif its distinct appearance.
It was released by the International Typeface Corporation
in 1992.